Epilogue for Murder

Epilogue for Murder

ASBURY PARK PUBLIC LIBRARY
ASBURY PARK, NEW JERSEY

Larry Shriner

Walker and Company
New York

Copyright © 1994 by Larry Shriner

All rights reserved. No part of this book may be reproduced or transmitted in any form or by any means, electronic or mechanical, including photocopying, recording, or by any information storage and retrieval system, without permission in writing from the Publisher.

All the characters and events portrayed in this work are fictitious.

First published in the United States of America in 1994
by Walker Publishing Company, Inc.

Published simultaneously in Canada by Thomas Allen & Son
Canada, Limited, Markham, Ontario

Library of Congress Cataloging-in-Publication Data
Shriner, Larry.
Epilogue for murder / Larry Shriner.
p.   cm.
ISBN 0-8027-3182-1
1. Private investigators—Georgia—Atlanta—Fiction.
2. Atlanta (Ga.)—Fiction.   3. Florida—Fiction.   I. Title.
PS3569.H7415E64   1994
813'.54—dc20   93-33534
CIP

Printed in the United States of America
2 4 6 8 10 9 7 5 3 1

For Cindy and J. E.

Acknowledgments

Dr. Patsy Baynard of Florida Power Corporation kindly assisted me in the area of toxic waste disposal; Bob Thrasher of Thrasher's Police Supply in Tampa, Florida, shared his knowledge of firearms and ballistics. Their help was invaluable. Any errors are mine.

Epilogue for Murder

1

It was a bad day.

The reason was in black and white, page one, above the fold. Newspaper lingo for big news. The headline read, "Atlanta Novelist Walker Redgrave Dead of Self-inflicted Gunshot."

The story focused on the circumstances of the suicide in a roadside motel near a little town called Steinhatchee, on Florida's upper west coast. It detailed the writer's success, the many millions of books he'd sold in x number of languages, the money he'd made, the grieving widow he'd left behind. There was even a quote by me, taken from one of the books I'd written about Redgrave. It said something about his "enduring brilliance in the hard-boiled tradition of Chandler and Hammett."

Of course the reporter failed to mention the intrinsic quality of Redgrave's work, how he'd elevated his books above the level of mystery genre to that of quote serious literature, how he painstakingly researched his plots, how his characters came alive under his nurturing, real people with real emotions, real inconsistencies, real struggles between good and evil. No mention was made of his endless crafting of the language until it was distilled as uncompromisingly spare prose devoid of gimmickry and adornment.

The story was probably written, I figured, by some snot-nosed copy editor or swing-shift reporter who got stuck with the assignment because Redgrave had the audacity to kill himself after all the good newspapermen had gone home.

Walker Redgrave. He was my hero, one of them anyway. And, in a roundabout way, part of the reason I ended up in this business.

I leaned forward in my chair, eyed the half-full cup of cold coffee in front of me. I picked up my Thermos and poured a couple of inches of lukewarm coffee into the cup. Little pools of oily residue gathered on the surface. It smelled like creosote.

I took a sip. The liquid stuck in the back of my throat; I had to choke it down. The taste was incredibly bad, almost as sour as my mood. I put the cup down, shoved it out of reach, wiped my mouth with the back of my hand, and settled back into my chair.

Then the office door opened and in walked the grieving widow herself—Alexandra Redgrave.

I hadn't seen her in years, but she still had the same sleek silver hair falling just to her shoulders in a blunted, turned-in cut. She still possessed the same delicate features, the same controlled way of carrying herself.

She wore a simple dress of dark blue cotton, high at the neck, low at the hemline. Around her throat was a single strand of pearls. On her right wrist was a silver watch, on her left hand a simple gold wedding ring. She looked younger than her age, but haggard and unfocused. I could understand why.

Her eyes took in the room, completed the circuit—it didn't take long. She brought her gaze full circle, and said, "I was in your office once before, the one at the university."

We both remembered the contrast. "What goes up must come down," I said, glancing at my surroundings—office and waiting room above a barbecue restaurant on Peachtree Street in Buckhead. Desk with glass top. Squeaky swivel chair and three hard chairs for clients. A telephone that didn't ring very often. Shelves jammed with a haphazard clutter of books. Scarred door with gold-leaf lettering on the frosted window, which read "Bennett Cole, Investigations." Threadbare brown carpet. Dust motes. Everything old, a shabby homage to distant unreal heroes.

"Just trying to live the dream," I said to Alexandra Redgrave.

She sat across the desk from me in one of the straight-backed chairs, holding her purse demurely in her lap. She glanced at the newspaper lying on the desk. "So you've heard," she said.

"Yes, it was in all the early editions and on the radio." I looked across the desk at her. "How are you doing, Mrs. Redgrave?" It sounded hollow, and I didn't know what else to say.

"Not okay." She made an attempt at a smile, but it faltered and disassembled itself. "No, not okay at all."

"I'm sorry, it was a stupid question." What *does* one say to the widow? I thought. Pick a useless cliché? Fawn solicitously? Ask where to send the flowers?

I watched the thin light struggling through the one lousy, grimy window and tried to keep my foot away from my mouth.

After a while she said: "I'm not intending to be rude, Dr. Cole." I winced when she used the title. "I'm not thinking too clearly and I haven't slept since they . . . since yesterday."

More silence in the shadowy half light. "I need your help," she said.

"Mrs. Redgrave, you know I'll . . ."

She cut me off, her voice suddenly impatient. "Professional services, not sympathy. I'm here because I know Walker didn't kill himself. I want you to find out who did."

That broke the ice. Now there was something to talk about, something tangible to take us beyond the awkwardness.

I glanced at the story. "The paper said it was a clear case of suicide."

"That's what the police said. And I've heard all about the evidence. The story is accurate. He was found in a locked room. The gun was his. There was a note."

"So why do you think it wasn't suicide?"

She paused, seeming to look inward. A strand of silver hair fell across her forehead. Her voice thickened. "Because I know Walker. He was happy, probably more happy than he'd ever been. He was successful. He'd just been invited to be featured speaker at an international writers' conference in London. His last book was on the *New York Times* best-seller list for six months. We were planning a trip to Africa. He was a famous, wealthy, happy writer.

"And after thirty-five years," she said, "I think I'd know if he was sneaking around on me. In the note he said he was, you know. He asked my forgiveness."

I thought about all the good husbands and wives I'd come across who had been fooled by errant spouses, but I let her comment pass.

She tilted her fine chin down and began to cry. Tears ran down her cheeks, rivulets that cut creases through her makeup.

She shook her head, took a tissue out of her handbag, and dabbed at her cheeks. She put her hands on the desk, clutched around the tissue.

I reached across the desk and patted her hands. "One request, Mrs. Redgrave. Please don't call me Dr. Cole. I've kind of gotten to where that makes me feel a little awkward. The title isn't a big help these days. I'll take the job if you'll call me Bennett. Or at least Cole."

She looked up; her misty eyes blinked and she smiled a little. This time it held. She took another dab at her cheeks and eyes. "That does make me feel somewhat awkward. My upbringing requires the courtesy of a title, and precludes too quick a familiarity. But I'll try . . . Cole."

"See, the first time's the hardest." I opened a desk drawer and extracted notepad, tape recorder, and pencil. I slipped on my reading glasses and peered over the top of the lenses at Mrs. Redgrave.

"I would like to know," I said, "why you decided to come to me. We haven't talked since, what, 1979? I think I was writing an article on *Return from Nowhere*. That's when you came by my office; you were in Athens and delivered some of your husband's notes."

She tapped the newspaper with her finger and nodded. "Of course I saw your name mentioned in the article. My husband had always respected what you wrote about him. And I remembered you left the university to become a private detective and moved to Atlanta. Who else could help me? So I looked you up in the phone book. I—I just showed up hoping you weren't busy. I didn't even call. Was that all right?"

"That's fine," I said. I neglected to mention that I hadn't been very busy for months—and I could think of at least a dozen private detectives in Atlanta who could do a better job for her.

"It's an honor that he liked my work." I picked up the pencil. "Okay, let's get down to business. What do you know that wasn't in the newspaper?"

She didn't know much. "I can't say for sure how thorough the investigation was. Steinhatchee's in Taylor County, on the coast that curves into the Panhandle. It's pretty rural, and the police force there is quite small, I understand. I only talked to one deputy, the one who was in charge of the investigation. His name was Stubbs."

"What was your husband doing in Steinhatchee? It can't be very big. Is it a fishing town?"

"I have no idea. Walker never confided in me about his work. I know he was there doing research for his next book. But I don't know what kind of research, and I have no idea what his next book was going to be about."

I asked her how long he'd been in Steinhatchee. "Just a couple of days," she answered. "He drove up from Captiva. That's in south Florida, on the beach. We have a home there now, we spend—spent—a few months down there each winter."

"Anything else you can think of?" I asked. "Anything that would help me look into this?"

"I can't—I can't," she faltered, looking like a lost kitten. "Can you please go there and do—do whatever detectives do to find out the truth?"

Clouds had gathered outside, causing the room to drift

into shadows. I switched on the ceiling bulb. Mrs. Redgrave glanced at her watch. "I need to be leaving soon, and anyway I don't think I can talk any more about this. I'm very tired." As an afterthought, she added, "Don't worry about your fee, and spend whatever you have to. I'm not concerned about the money."

She glance around the office, her thoughts shifting. She got up and walked over to the bookcase, seeming to compose herself as she moved. She scanned the jumble of books, put her hand on one, and tilted it out a couple of inches. I could see the title—*Emerson's Forensics*—great bedtime reading if you're into autopsies.

She tilted it back, looked along the rows of books for another moment, and turned back to me. "That's quite a collection of books, Dr.—I mean Cole. Dostoyevsky, Lawrence, Faulkner, Flannery O'Connor. Not what one would expect, I guess." Her eyes showed life, for just a moment. "But then I don't suppose you're the typical private eye."

I found myself embarrassed by the symbols of my past life. "When I cleared out my university office a bunch of books ended up in boxes. I unpacked here and there they were. Besides, you never know when you need a quick quote from Auden to dazzle a prospective client."

I paused. "All my Walker Redgrave books are safe at home."

She came back to the chair and sat down. "Do you like being a real detective?" She nodded toward the bookshelves. "Do you miss the academic life?"

"To answer the last question, yes and no. I miss the easy hours, the summers off, the regular paycheck. Sometimes I even miss the research into all those arcane subjects we took so seriously. However, I don't miss the petty infighting, the incredible arrogance and egotism of the professors, the lazy students, the hopeless bureaucracy, the endless mediocre papers to grade. The—the stifling of creativity behind the ivory tower walls." I realized I was starting to preach, so I shifted direction.

"As for your first question, of course it isn't what I expected from reading all those novels." I smiled. "I don't mean to poke fun, but my work is far from romantic or exciting, just things like messy divorces, endless hours of watching dark houses, repossessing cars, the occasional insurance fraud or workman's comp case. After nine years, still no murders."

I regretted the last comment as soon as it was out of my mouth. The room grew heavy with gloomy irony.

"Well," she said. "That's about to change, isn't it?"

2

I CHECKED MY messages, updated all the files on my active cases, and tidied up—all of which took about three minutes—locked up the office, and got my car from the lot behind the restaurant. The wood fire at the back of the rib joint was sending blue smoke curling into the late afternoon sky. The smell of slowly cooking hog hung heavy in the air. Three years above the Dixie Pig had almost killed whatever taste I'd had for barbecue. Almost, but not quite.

I waved at Bennie, the guy who perpetually leaned against the side of the building by the wood pile. Bennie tended the fire, which involved a lot of leaning. He didn't look as if he was working, but the Dixie Pig was purported to have the best barbecue north of Macon. Bennie, it was said, had been leaning against that wall for more than thirty years.

The traffic was beginning to build up to the usual hideous rush-hour gridlock. I drove north on Peachtree, inching along in the slow crawl of traffic—glassy-eyed commuters headed home from downtown offices—made my way through Buckhead, and turned west onto Paces Ferry Road, a gracefully looping street that passes the governor's mansion and a lot of other prime residential real estate.

It is here that old-money Atlanta lives, comfortably sheltered from the crime and violence that, like a cancer, has invaded too much of the city. It is quiet, comfortable, secluded, and slightly unreal, as if an oasis of perfection had been plopped into a desert of chaotic growth and blight. There are lush lawns, stately pecan and flowering magnolia trees, English ivy running wild, stone and brick walls along the road that protect the big houses set back from it. The whoosh of a lawn sprinkler is a loud sound here, as if the city noises dare not creep into this genteel and protected world.

Redgrave had lived here for the last twenty years, after his books began to sell extraordinarily well. It was a long way up from the garage apartment he and Alexandra lived in when he was writing his first novels.

I drove past the governor's digs, and a little later came to Walker Redgrave's home, an imposing turn-of-the-century redbrick, columned house set well back from the road on manicured grounds. Mrs. Redgrave had said she would let Valerie Simmons, Walker Redgrave's secretary, know I was coming and to cooperate in any way she could.

I turned into the entrance to the estate and drove up the long gravel drive lined with pecan trees. Nothing had changed much since I was last here thirteen years ago. Except for one large difference—the master of the house was dead.

The drive opened into a paved circular turnaround in front of the house. There was a parking area off to the right, near a separate side entrance to Redgrave's office. Two cars were parked there, a fairly new gray Mercedes sedan and a dark blue Mercury Sable.

I parked my car and walked along a brick sidewalk bordered by thick shrubbery and trellised vines until I came to the side door. My knock was answered by a woman of middle age and imposing height. She blocked the entry protectively, then nodded when she recognized me. She looked as if she had been crying. "Dr. Cole, we met when you were here before, to interview Mr. Redgrave. I'm Valerie Simmons. Alexandra—Mrs. Redgrave—told me to expect you."

She stepped away from the door, turned, and motioned for me to follow her. We went down a short high-ceilinged hall with white moldings and dark green walls, and turned into a cluttered alcove furnished with a table, a couple of chairs, filing cabinet, copier, fax machine, telephone, and bookcase.

A computer, its screen crowded with text, sat on the table surrounded by haphazard stacks of papers.

Valerie Simmons sat in the chair behind the computer table. "You recall that Mr. Walker's study is down the hall, the next door on the right." She was stalling just a bit, as if reluctant to let me have the run of her boss's domain. "Mrs. Redgrave told me to let you in there alone." She was clearly not happy with the "alone" part.

"Thanks. I'll try not to disturb anything."

It was like walking into the twilight zone, memorabilia that had become memories, furniture that looked abandoned and forlorn. The room was dimly lit; the lone window was shrouded by heavy blue drapes. The walls were paneled in dark oak.

I switched on the lamp in the corner next to a brown leather easy chair. It cast a warm yellow glow, sending the room into a collage of light and shadow.

The study was an icon to Walker Redgrave's career. On the paneled wall behind the huge oak desk were more than two dozen framed photographs—a picture of Redgrave with President Carter, one of him beside an elderly William Faulkner. Pictures of Redgrave with Eudora Welty, with Senator Sam Nunn, on the deck of a yacht conversing with Nelson Rockefeller, at a restaurant table with Tom Wolfe. One that captured him with a sheepish grin as he held the plaque signifying his Pulitzer Prize. A smiling Redgrave at dinner with Isaac Bashevis Singer. Pictures of a full and successful life, pictures that captured life and held it even after death.

There would be no more pictures.

Another wall was crowded with plaques, framed certificates, and awards. In the wall opposite the desk was a fireplace, new logs placed decoratively on the andirons. Built-in bookcases occupied the space on either side and above the fireplace. The volumes were neatly arranged, most of them hardcover editions. The library was eclectic, everything from modern fiction to American and British classics.

There were books on topics as diverse as anthropology, politics, history, psychology, medicine, and theology. One shelf contained a number of books on forensic pathology, drugs, and firearms. Another contained the poetry of Robert Frost, Emily Dickinson, and Robert Service. On the mantel above the fireplace, away from everything else, were hardcover editions of every Walker Redgrave novel, arranged in chronological order and held at each side by heavy brass bookends in the shape of ducks' heads.

The desk was polished to a high luster; it was bare except for an antique inkwell and quill pen, a Mont Blanc fountain pen resting on a clean piece of white linen stationery, and a framed photograph of his wife.

A pair of gold wire-rimmed reading glasses lay on the end table beside the stuffed chair. Beside them was a book from the Atlanta Public Library. It was a coffee-table book, lots of pictures, titled *Our Vanishing Wetlands*. Redgrave, I remembered, shared with Ross Macdonald the passion for protecting the environment. I picked it up and glanced inside the back cover. It was a couple of days overdue.

A four-drawer oak file cabinet with brass trim stood against the wall opposite the desk. It held only a few neatly arranged files, mostly about publishing contracts, some communications with Redgrave's New York agent, details of conferences—nothing about work in progress.

But where in this museum did Redgrave actually write?

I opened a door that appeared to lead to a closet and peered in. The world changed dramatically. It wasn't a closet at all, but a light, airy room painted white, with three French doors looking out onto a brick patio and rolling grounds beyond, painted still life in the last vestiges of the evening light. Redgrave's word processor and printer sat on a teak writing table against a wall. A blue high-backed executive chair was positioned so as to afford access to the computer as well as a view beyond the room. A teak credenza against the wall opposite the doors held a tea service and coffee cups. A white metal file cabinet stood in one corner near a large ficus tree.

Other potted plants hung on either side of the French doors. There was no phone in here, just myriad stacks of papers neatly arranged on the shelves of the credenza and a yellow legal pad to the left of the computer.

I opened the top drawer and began sifting through Redgrave's files. The task was complicated by the fact that he had no discernible filing system. He—and no one else—probably had known just where to find whatever he wanted. And there were hundreds of folders and papers crammed into the drawers.

Patience, I told myself, you're working by the hour. Still, I dreaded reading through the personal papers of a dead man. God knows what I'd find.

Not much, I concluded after two painstaking hours. Redgrave had been a pack rat, all right; he'd probably kept just about every useless tidbit of information he'd ever come across. Many pages were typewritten; a great many others were written in Redgrave's neat script.

And there were folders containing plot outlines in various degrees of completion, the latest dated four years ago. There were a great number of descriptions of people, and notes on obscure and arcane subjects—everything from the ballistics of wound cavities to sociopathic character traits.

But nothing remotely having to do with Steinhatchee, or anywhere in north Florida for that matter. Nothing to indicate what he had been working on at the time of his death, nothing at all.

Even the computer yielded nothing of substance. I asked Valerie Simmons to show me how to access the computer files on the disk drive. Most of them had already been printed out and I'd come across them in the folders. The little bit that I hadn't seen was meaningless to me, connected to nothing that I was interested in.

I took a hodgepodge of papers I hadn't yet read into the alcove. Valerie Simmons was sitting at her computer, doing nothing. She looked like a cat staring at a television screen.

"Ms. Simmons?" I said. For a moment she continued to

stare, then shifted her gaze toward me, gradually coming back from wherever she had been. "Sorry," she said. "Were you standing there long? I don't seem to be doing such a good job of staying on task."

"Would it be possible for you to copy these?" I asked. "I want to read them but I don't want anything to happen to them."

The small consideration of not wanting to take the originals seemed to please her. "That's thoughtful," she said, almost to herself. She shifted into a more businesslike manner, taking the stack of papers from me. "It'll only take a few minutes. Would you like some coffee while you wait? It's not any trouble. Cream and sugar?"

"Just cream," I said. She left the room and returned a few moments later with a ceramic mug steaming with strongly aromatic coffee.

She handed the cup to me. I leaned against the desk and took a sip.

"The coffee's very good," I said. "I wanted to ask you a question if you have a minute."

"You can see I'm swamped," she said with irony. "Actually I can't seem to focus on anything at all." She seemed on the verge of fading away again, but caught herself. "Yes, what can I help you with?"

I told her how I had gone through just about every file and piece of paper in Redgrave's study, and planned on spending the evening reading the notes I was taking with me. "What seems odd is that there isn't anything that gives a clue about what he was working on at the time of his death, no obvious leads I can follow up on. Most of the dates are pretty old, and the undated stuff is just bits and pieces that don't seem to be related to anything current."

"Have you tried his office in Captiva?" she asked. "That's where he's been—he was working there most of the time the last few months. He had an office at his house there."

I remembered Mrs. Redgrave mentioning that her husband had driven up from Captiva to Steinhatchee. I asked her if there would be any problem getting into the house.

"Let me give you the name of the real estate agent," she said. She looked in her address file and jotted a name and telephone number on a piece of paper. "The day after Mr. Redgrave died Mrs. Redgrave told me to have it put on the market."

She retrieved the copies of Redgrave's notes and lovingly put the originals in a neat stack on her desk.

"I worked for Mr. Redgrave for more than twenty years," she said suddenly. "I respected him more than anyone on earth." She looked at me, her eyes pleading. "I know he didn't commit suicide. Please find out who killed him. I know that won't bring him back, but at least we can stop living with this awful—with the way things are now."

I told her I'd do my best. What else could I say? I left Valerie Simmons staring at her computer screen, not seeing anything.

3

I GOT UP before eight the next morning, showered, trimmed my beard, and made coffee. I poured a cup and padded to my study, where the phone was. I called Keith Hutchins.

Hutchins and I had known each other since the late 1970s, when we were both on the faculty at the University of Georgia. A few years ago Hutchins left Georgia to take a full professorship at the University of South Florida. He was the consummate academic, meaning he was completely out of touch with reality.

Hutchins came on the line almost immediately when I rang his university office.

"Cole, you old fart, still chasing gunsels and waving around your roscoe?"

"What'd you do, read a couple of old hard-boiled novels and now you're an expert on the vernacular?"

"I've reached the limit of my knowledge on the subject. I'm much too busy with important timely projects, such as my recently resurrected book on the Boer War."

"That's the nice thing about history," I said. "You go away and leave it for a while and it's still there when you get back."

"If I get back, old buddy. I've been thinking of running away, doing something meaningful for a living, like becoming a welder."

"You'd make more money, but you'd have to work a forty-hour week and maybe break a sweat somewhere besides the tennis court."

"You sure know how to shoot holes in a poor man's fantasy."

"Speaking of tennis, what are you doing in your office? It's before eleven." Hutchins' penchant for daily morning tennis matches was legendary.

"Light drizzle," he said. "Very depressing. I had to cancel, so I thought I'd do something terribly masochistic, like grading undergraduate term papers. By the way, where are you and why are you calling me? I know you're not one for getting in touch to hash over old times and rekindle the friendship."

"Do you still have your Cherokee?"

His voice got suspicious. "Why do you want to know?"

"I want to borrow it. It's not too clean, is it?"

"I don't hear from you in over a year, and you call up out of the blue and want to borrow my Jeep. You even want it to be dirty. Are you all right? Wait. Of course you're not all right. You haven't been all right since the day I met you. It's just that now you're more blatantly not all right."

"I prefer to think of myself as eccentric, Hutchins. It's more socially acceptable. Now, can I have the Jeep? I'll make you a deal. I'll let you borrow the Volvo I rented. It's very professional. I'll even put on a 'Save the Whales' bumper sticker."

"Crap," Hutchins said. "When do you need it? Do you want me to bring it over? Should I come right now?"

We made the arrangements for me to pick up the Jeep. As I was saying good-bye, I said, "Still got that slight academic lisp, Hutchins?"

"Cole, I've told you a thousand times I can't help—"

I hung up.

Next I called Mary Lamb, the real estate agent in charge of selling Redgrave's house. The receptionist who answered the phone said she was in, and a minute later a voice came on the line. "Hello?" She sounded hurried, as if the ringing phone had taken her away from a hot prospect.

"Ms. Lamb? My name is Bennett Cole. Valerie Simmons in Atlanta told me to give you a call."

"Yes, yes, she called me yesterday. You want to get into the Redgraves' house. That's no problem. When would you like to meet?"

"I'm driving down from Tampa," I said. "I'll be getting in I think around five or six."

I gave her the name of the motel where Valerie Simmons had made reservations for me. She said she'd meet me there around six.

But she couldn't hang up right away.

"Lord, what a waste, Mr. Redgrave killing himself. I sold them the house. It's a wonderful place, quiet and secluded, just like they wanted. After I met him I went and bought some of his books and read them. I never liked mysteries, but I liked his."

She paused. "I was in the middle of one of them when he died. Now I can't bring myself to finish it."

First Redgrave's wife, then his secretary, now the woman who simply sold him a house, three women feeling Redgrave's death deeply. Either Redgrave was very good at convincing women he was a wonderful man—or he truly was a wonderful man.

He'd seemed pretty okay to me, too.

I fed the cat, threw some clothes in a canvas overnight bag, and wrote a note to Shelly, my next-door neighbor, asking her to feed my cat if I was gone more than a couple of days. Shelly had a key, and she was used to my comings and goings. Besides, she liked my cat, though I wasn't sure how the cat felt about her.

I left by the side door and retrieved my car from the garage. I let it idle at the curb while I knocked on Shelly's door. When she didn't answer I stuck the note in the mail slot, got in the car, and headed to Hartsfield.

I slipped through downtown just as the gridlock was beginning to dissipate. They've been working on the midtown stretch of Interstate 75 for years now, and they still haven't gotten it right. The traffic jams are getting almost perpetual, and motorists spend most of their time—when they're not stopped on the roadway—dodging barricades and orange barrels.

I looked through the windshield at my adopted city. Atlanta is a morass of contradictions—Old South charm and New South gridlock. Stately homes and some of the worst slums in the nation. Genteel aristocracy and a crime rate that's among the highest in the country. The Fox Theater, built to show *Gone With the Wind*, stands just a few blocks from a stretch of Peachtree frequented by hookers and dope pushers.

I was at Hartsfield half an hour before my flight was scheduled to leave. I parked my car in the high-priced short-term parking garage—I had a paying client, I reminded myself—knocked down a cup of bitter coffee in a paper cup, and picked up a copy of the *Constitution*. Nothing about Redgrave; he was old news by now, remembered only by his friends, fans, and his grieving widow. And by one two-bit private dick with his heart where his brain ought to be.

I dutifully checked my .38, securely locked in its case, at the ticket counter. A grumpy-looking woman took the paperwork I filled out and looked at the gun like it was a snake. She looked at me as if I were some kind of terrorist freak. I handed her a separate box of ammo, gave her my best leering smile, and said, "You never know." She hurried off to help a family check their bags.

One cup of coffee later, my flight was called. I boarded the plane and settled into a seat that, like all airline coach seats, was uncomfortably small for me.

After we broke through the cloud cover a flight attendant with an emotionless professional smile brought me another paper cup of coffee. I leaned the seat back, got semicomfortable, and used the short flight to reflect on the case I'd been drawn into.

Walker Redgrave a suicide—or not? All the evidence so far indicated that he had killed himself. Even Mrs. Redgrave could give me nothing of substance to refute the findings; she had only her instincts and long association with Redgrave to go on. And a desperate emotional need to make the truth agree with what she wanted to believe.

A man is found with his own gun in a locked room. There's a bullet in his brain. The bullet came from his gun. The gun is lying beside him. His prints, and only his prints, are on the gun. There's a suicide note. It doesn't take a rocket scientist to come to the conclusion of suicide.

So why, in the face of all the evidence, was I flying to Tampa so I could end up in some godforsaken one-horse town called Steinhatchee to match wits with the local constables and somehow divine a new conclusion—a conclusion I wasn't at all confident I could come to?

I had no answer to that.

And if not suicide, what? Accident? Not if there was a suicide note. I took out my notebook and jotted down a reminder to ask for a copy of the note.

If not an accident, what was left? Natural causes? Not likely. A bullet to the brain isn't too natural.

That left only murder. And nothing, nothing at all, pointed to murder.

I knew I couldn't manufacture conclusions, or even guess at them very well. I could only do what I know how to do—turn over rocks and see what crawls out, see how ugly it is, smell it, follow it, and see where it leads me.

And if it led me back to a verdict of suicide, what then? I'd have to break the news to a grieving widow who wouldn't believe me even in the face of irrefutable evidence.

So why was I bird-dogging a case I'd taken against the odds? Sympathy for Alexandra Redgrave? No, I cared about her feelings, but I didn't know her well enough to have a real sense of deep emotional involvement.

Maybe it was nothing more than the romantic hope that somehow my hero Redgrave really didn't kill himself in that roadside motel room.

The attendant came around and granted me another of her dazzling smiles, the kind that go on and off in a heartbeat and are about as real as a politician's promise. She retrieved my tray and I dozed fitfully for a little while, just long enough for the undersized seat to make my oversized body stiff as a carp.

I was standing up in the aisle trying to stretch the cramps away when a tinny voice came over the address system, telling us we were beginning our approach to Tampa.

Forget introspection, I told myself as I buckled back into the seat. It just gets you in trouble. Just go out and turn over the rocks and take it from there.

4

I HAD THE Jeep pointed south on Interstate 75, steady at sixty-five, air conditioner on high, headed to Captiva in the afternoon heat. The three-and-a-half-hour drive from Tampa would put me at my destination just in time to check in to my motel and meet Mary Lamb.

I'd picked up the Jeep just after two, when Hutchins finished teaching his last class.

He had acted a little sullen when I met him in a faculty parking lot to exchange vehicles. But he brightened when he saw the rented Volvo I was leaving with him.

"Look, Cole," he said as he handed me the keys to the Cherokee, "just don't get shot in it and bleed all over the upholstery."

"Wouldn't dream of it," I said, flashing my best big-city private eye smile.

"What are you going to use it for?" he asked, his voice just the tiniest bit whiny.

"Case that's taking me in the woods," I said. "This thing'll blend in perfect. By the way, how come you don't have a gun rack?"

Hutchins closed his eyes and sighed.

I asked him if he knew anything about Florida history, particularly of the area where Redgrave had died.

"I don't know anything about Florida," he said. "Anything that happened in Florida is far too recent for my taste. But I know a fellow up at Gainesville who, for some bizarre reason, has devoted his life to the subject."

I collected the man's name, along with a promise from Hutchins that he would call and let him know I was coming. But first, I needed some time in Redgrave's Captiva office. I wanted as much information as I could gather before I went to Steinhatchee. I didn't think I'd get too much cooperation from the locals—small Southern towns are notorious that way.

I gunned the motor and squealed the tires leaving the parking lot. Through a rearview mirror I could see Hutchins angrily waving his fists at me. I figured he wouldn't take very good care of the Volvo, either.

I stopped just off campus and got out of the Jeep. I took out my pocketknife and scraped Hutchins' faculty parking sticker off the back window. Good investigative work involves attention to the smallest detail.

I motored along the coast as the Florida sun sank toward the Gulf of Mexico—iridescent shafts of color setting the evening sky ablaze with pinks and purples; the clouds luminescent, nearly translucent. It was a spectacular summer sunset, the kind Florida is justly famous for. I could almost imagine I was going to the beach for a long weekend. Almost.

By the time I reached Fort Myers the sun had broken through the last level of clouds just above the horizon, casting a light of sudden brightness, a playful and teasing bit of daylight just before darkness.

I turned off the interstate and drove through Fort Myers toward the coast. About fifteen miles out of town, I turned onto a long toll causeway that leads to the island communities of Sanibel and Captiva. I figured the three-dollar toll kept out the riffraff and curiosity seekers, letting the affluent island residents sleep better at night.

I made my way across the last bridge that separates the causeway leading to Sanibel from the island itself. Following Alexandra Redgrave's directions, I turned north at the Sanibel-Captiva Road, the main drag that runs the length of the long, narrow island. I took a left, a right, another left, and had become completely disoriented when I suddenly came to the street I was looking for, Middle Gulf Drive, a winding two-lane paralleling the Gulf of Mexico.

The evening sun blazed through the western clouds. I shut off the air conditioner and rolled down the window. I could feel the sea breeze, the air beginning to cool.

I drove along a stretch of road lined with modern condominiums, interspersed with private waterfront homes hidden from view by dense tropical foliage, until I came upon my lodgings for the night, a fairly new gulfside collection of cottages called the Ocean's Edge Resort. I pulled into the crushed-shell parking lot, eased into a space next to a red Mercedes convertible, and cut the engine. I sat for a moment in the sudden starlit silence, then grabbed my overnight bag and headed toward the registration desk.

Valerie Simmons had assured me I would be comfortable here. She was right. The weathered wood cottages overlooked sand dunes and sea oats, and beyond to the beach and water. There was a swimming pool for the sissies who didn't want to brave the waves and salt water. There was an open-air bar for those who wanted a few drinks to alter their perceptions of the beautiful natural setting. There were palm trees and tropical plants, the smell of salt air, and stars just beginning to come out in the twilight sky. A beautiful bit of South Florida tranquility, a long long way from death.

The woman at the desk obviously had two jobs—checking in cottage guests and developing her tan. She was close to perfecting the deep leathery look, taut skin baked to a mahogany tone. It contrasted smartly with her bottle-blond hair. She probably was in her midforties, but the tan only added about five years to her appearance.

When I mentioned my name she told me everything had been taken care of, handed me the key, and directed me to my cottage. It turned out to be a large one-bedroom efficiency with a good sea view, furnished in rattan and floral print.

I dropped off my bag, leaving the Colt locked inside—I didn't figure I'd have to shoot anyone at Redgrave's house. Then I went to the motel's bar, where I ordered a club soda and fiddled with the cute little umbrella the bartender stuck in it while I waited for Mary Lamb to arrive.

5

I WAS THE only person in the parking lot when she showed up, wheeling into the parking lot and coming to a screeching stop about three inches from where I stood. Dusty fragments of shell rose in a hazy cloud and drifted down around me.

She lowered the window of her Honda and I felt a quick draft of artificially cold air. "I'll bet you're Dr. Cole."

I confessed and she motioned me to get in. She crunched the car into first with a horrendous grinding of gears, snapped the clutch out, and chirped her tires on the road as she turned left in front of an oncoming car.

"I see you've really embraced the sedate pace of island life," I said as I snapped my seat belt in place.

"It's the best I can do," she grinned. "I'm a terrible driver. I've always been a terrible driver. Some people have learning disabilities. I have a driving disability."

She stamped on the accelerator, groped for second gear and found fourth instead, and let the car lug along with a clattering of valves. The driver of a car behind us laid on the horn. Mary seemed contentedly oblivious, staring straight ahead as the car slowly crept up toward the speed limit. The car following, a late-model Cadillac, whipped around us. The driver shook an angry fist at Mary as he passed. It didn't seem to rattle her. I didn't think she even noticed.

I risked a sideways glance at her. She was cute, maybe beyond cute. Her thick brown hair was cut in bangs just over her eyebrows, and pulled back in a ponytail held by a yellow cloth band. A spray of freckles dusted her cheeks and upturned little nose. She was wearing white slacks, a pale blue pullover with an alligator on the pocket, and beige sandals. I thought about asking her to the prom.

"It's about thirteen miles to Mr. Redgrave's home," she said. "The house is on Captiva, toward the end of the island."

"Captiva and Sanibel are different towns?" I asked.

"In more ways than one," she said. "Sanibel is where the action is. We've got a few bars and there's shops and banks. Captiva has—well, Captiva has really rich people."

"So what do the really rich people of Captiva do?"

"I don't know. Protect their privacy. Count their money. Stay for 'the season.' Turn up their noses at the poor clods in their $400,000 Sanibel condos."

"Old money never was very tolerant of new money," I said, "and it sounds like Captiva is overrun with old money."

The road continued through a mostly uninhabited area that Mary said was a wildlife preserve. A few miles later we crossed a short, curving bridge and passed a sign welcoming us to Captiva. It was a small sign, understated, as if the welcome were largely perfunctory.

Then we started passing the driveways. "They lead back to some awesome homes," Mary said. Who could tell? I thought. The houses were protected from view by lush tropical vegetation. The driveways, made of crushed shell, wound back into the private jungles. Here and there I got a glimpse of a cantilevered roof or a second-floor deck. By several of the drives were low wood signs with names written on them, names the owners had given their estates—Tranquility, Tidewaters. There was also an abundance of security alarm signs and No Trespassing warnings. Old money didn't exactly invite you in with open arms.

Suddenly Mary jammed on the brakes and turned abruptly into a driveway on the left, narrowly missing an overhanging banyan tree. She skittered down the curving drive until it opened up into an area behind a three-story house overlooking the beach. It was constructed of weathered wood and glass, with a steeply pitched tin roof styled after early Florida "cracker" farmhouses. There were porches surrounding both upper levels. The lower level contained two closed garages with wide steps that led up to double doors of white wood and leaded glass. The house looked old, was probably of fairly recent construction, and was undoubtedly very expensive. New made to look old, rich imitating poor—an odd juxtaposition. But the times are getting more odd every day. Just read the papers and look around.

I could see, beyond the house, a stretch of low dunes holding scattered patches of sea oats and a white sand beach that sloped gently down to the surf.

Mary stopped the car and cut the engine, and we were mercifully enveloped in a stillness that only privacy and secluded luxury can provide.

"The Redgraves bought the house about three years ago," Mary said. "I handled the sale. They said they wanted somewhere to come for peace and quiet. But I understand Mr. Redgrave found that he liked writing here, so they came down here more and more. He kind of became a local celebrity on the island. He wasn't snobby at all."

We got out of the Honda and went up the central steps. Mary produced a key to the front door, unlocked it, and pushed it inward. I was met with a distinct musty odor, as if the house had been shut up for some time. But I knew Redgrave had been there just four or five days ago. It doesn't take long for the ghosts to lock up and depart, I thought, taking with them the life that had been there.

We were in a wide foyer on the second level, facing a circular staircase. "Mr. Redgrave's study is on the third floor, in one corner," Mary said. "There are windows on two sides and he loved the view of the beach and the dunes."

We took the spiral staircase to the third level, to a wide hallway with several doors on each side. Framed Audubon prints dominated the white walls; several small tables held arrangements of silk flowers. At the far end of the hall

French doors looked out over a wide, wood-railed veranda.

Mary Lamb walked to the farthest door on the right side and opened it. She stood to the side and motioned me in.

I entered the room, feeling like an intruder, coming here to tread on sacred ground, to look into the hidden nooks and crannies of Redgrave's life. I hadn't felt this way in Atlanta; but it was here that Redgrave had been working, it was from here that he had made his way to Steinhatchee, to his death.

The room was much like the study in Atlanta—French doors opened onto the veranda. Windows with adjustable miniblinds took up most of two walls. A computer desk was set against one wall. A credenza, a book case, and low file cabinets, all in white wood, were positioned against an inside wall. A small floral print couch and matching chair and a gooseneck floor lamp completed the furnishings.

The room had more of a worked-in feel than the other office. Would I find something here, much the way the pathologist finds vital information from the dead during an autopsy? I'd only know if I looked.

I got to work. Mary Lamb had opened the veranda doors, letting in the sea breeze, and wandered out on the balcony.

More files. And more files. Again, much of it snippets of narration and description, a plethora of notes on ideas for scenes. Scraps of information collected on a host of arcane subjects. A carbon copy of the stuff in Atlanta—only with more recent dates.

There were only a few computer files, these containing general information on Florida—facts that appeared to come from an almanac. There were some statistics on Taylor and Dixie counties—number of people, principal industries, and commerce. And telephone numbers for the state attorney's office in Taylor County and a Steinhatchee fishing guide service.

Nothing else that connected Redgrave with Steinhatchee or the scene of his death. Did the man write down nothing and remember everything? Was he only there to fish? Or—the thought crept unbidden into my mind—did he fail to catch anything and decide he couldn't face life anymore?

The last thought disgusted me, and I pushed it away. Cole, you carry cynicism to new heights—or depths, I thought.

I was sick of the room, sick of having to violate a dead man's privacy, angry that all the prying and peering had yielded nothing of substance. I wanted a nice dinner, a swim in the Gulf.

I gathered up a few notes I wanted to spend more time with and told Mary I was ready to leave. I went downstairs to the car while she locked up. She came down in a minute and got in on her side, and begin to turn the car around.

She gave me a long glance. "I didn't know Mr. Redgrave very well, but I think he was happy here." She was serious now, the flippant chattering tone gone. "I loved this house so much. I was so excited to sell it to him. Now he's dead."

She paused, slowed the car, and looked toward the water. "I can't finish his book. And I don't think I can come back here again."

As we turned out of the driveway onto the main road, I glanced back for one more look at Redgrave's property. I saw something I hadn't noticed on the way. It was a small wooden sign tacked into two low posts stuck in the ground. In etched letters, the sign told the name of Redgrave's home: "Epilogue."

Later, sitting alone on the porch of my cottage, I decided I'd allow myself a small bit of introspection, here on the shore, listening to the waves, drinking strong coffee. A little introspection, but not enough to foul up a good investigation.

It all came down to this: If Walker Redgrave could kill himself, what did that say about my own mortality? What was my life worth if my hero could blow his brains out?

I knew that some part of me was beginning to believe, a priori, that he didn't kill himself. And I knew I would feel terribly angry and betrayed if he did.

I stood up. There was no moon, and a strikingly bright canopy of stars cast a flickering and surreal light.

"Death is but a three-pound trigger pull away," I muttered as if I were spouting Shakespeare.

I tossed the dregs of the coffee onto the sand. The cold liquid puddled and ran down toward the surf in thin, curving rivulets, reminding me of Alexandra Redgrave's tears.

I went to bed.

6

THE NEXT MORNING I took a quick swim in the sea. Then I called Henry Littlejohn, Hutchins's professor friend in Gainesville. He answered his office phone—amazing, I thought, academics are starting to keep actual office hours. When I told him what I wanted he said he could spare some time late that afternoon. We arranged to meet at his office on campus.

I dressed in faded jeans, lightweight pullover, and tennis shoes, checked out of the cottage, and stopped for coffee at a McDonald's in Fort Myers. I pointed the Jeep north on an interstate that cuts through some of a beautiful state's most boring terrain—scrub oaks, palmetto bushes, and billboards. I put the Jeep, and my brain, on cruise control for the four hours it took me to bypass Tampa, get off the highway, and head toward the coast.

Then, once again, thankfully, I came to the real Florida—a place beyond the interstates and fast food joints and condominiums. It is a world that feels ten degrees cooler, a place not dominated by billboards, a place where you can still get fresh coffee in a real cup, with real cream.

I did just that, in a little roadside cafe on U.S. 19 with a sign out front advertising chicken-fried steak, pork chops, and fresh collard greens as the specials of the day.

It got even better inside. They served sweetened tea, and the pies behind the counter looked fresh and home baked.

I ordered coffee and a piece of hot apple pie from a plump waitress with a flawless complexion and the tightest-fitting jeans I'd ever seen. She brought the coffee and pie, then sat down at a front table with three men engaged in an argument involving the various merits of John Deere and Ford farm equipment.

I sipped the coffee. I took a big bite of pie. Then I did something I hadn't done in more than ten years. I looked at a book I'd written.

I'd brought it with me from Atlanta. It was the first book I'd done on Walker Redgrave and his work, titled *Redgrave: Continuing the Hard-boiled Tradition*.

I flipped idly through the pages, having the disconnected feeling that the words might have been written by some stranger a long time ago. Probably true, I thought as I took a sip of coffee.

The coffee tasted good. I looked at the book, realizing I'd been so focused on Redgrave's death I hadn't thought at all about his life and his work. Yet for years I had carried on this vicarious relationship with the man through the study of his books.

I'd gotten interested in Walker Redgrave a couple of years after I completed my undergraduate degree at Chapel Hill. I had been offered a fellowship at Vanderbilt, and was coming out of a misspent time during which I thought I was an expert on Chaucer. I was fed up with the arrogance of professors who were of the mind that all important thought occurred before 1500. And I had no idea what to do with my life.

Then one night, desperate for something to ward off my frequent and incurable insomnia, I walked to a nearby convenience store and bought a mystery novel.

I didn't sleep until I'd finished the book.

The novel involved a private detective named Charlie Brandt. It was written by Walker Redgrave.

Reading the Redgrave mystery was like opening a Pandora's box. That book led me to other tales involving Redgrave's detective. And from there I worked my way back to Philip Marlowe, Raymond Chandler's lonely, brooding dick. I spent time with Sam Spade and the Continental Op. I read about the life of Dashiell Hammett. I hunted down the stories of forgotten writers from the old pulp days of detective fiction, and I learned about murder and motive and the human condition.

During my doctoral studies I even conned a professor into giving me a semester's credit for spending a couple of months in California, walking Marlowe's mean streets in L.A. and the Op's haunts in San Francisco.

Over time the fictional world grew bigger. There was Lew Archer, like Marlowe the lonely gumshoe, but with a penchant for cases involving weird family entanglements. Marlowe the lonely knight, Archer the amateur psychologist, Spade the man of action. Protagonist of writers who invented a completely new genre of American literature.

And there was Charlie Brandt. He was a detective in the classic hard-boiled tradition, beginning life a generation after the first wave of tough-guy detectives.

I focused all of my scholarly attention on Brandt. The other detective heroes were in the past, but Brandt was living from novel to novel; his character was developing and expanding. He offered the chance to work on Redgrave, a writer about whom very little had been written. And besides, I simply liked Brandt. A lot. Later on, I came to feel the same way about Walker Redgrave.

The plump waitress came by with the coffee pot. "Whatcha readin'?" she asked.

"Book I wrote," I said.

"That's nice," she said. She refilled my cup and went back to the front table.

I opened the book at random, to a chapter on Brandt's "moral fiber."

"Charlie Brandt is more than the traditional dick," I had written. "And, though he has been accused of being a clone of Philip Marlowe, he is more, much more."

"Brandt brings a new dimension of morality to the gritty morality play of the streets." What, I wondered, did that mean? I kept reading.

"Morality, as was traditionally defined, often involved a two-dimensional struggle between good men and evil men. But Brandt probes the depths of the intermingled forces of good and evil within the individual. His cases involved struggles not among people but within them."

I looked up, embarrassed at reading words I'd written so long ago. Especially these words. At the front table, a man in a baseball hat said, "Nothing runs like a Deere."

The waitress said, "Aw, Jake, did you make that up?"

I flipped back to the chapter on Redgrave's life, written while the author was still in the present tense.

"While Charlie Brandt's fee slowly went up from forty dollars a day to a hundred plus expenses, Redgrave prospered handsomely. The man who wrote his first books at night while teaching junior high school during the day now commands advances of several hundred thousand dollars.

"Yet he continues to breathe life into Brandt. The latest novel, *Easy Street Blues*, won the National Book Award, something no 'genre' mystery is supposed to do. Redgrave's work has stood the test of time. He started out writing paperback originals. Now he commands a place on the *New York Times* best-seller list. Charlie Brandt has brought Redgrave fame, esteem, and a worldwide audience, and that legacy lives on . . ."

I closed the book, harder than I intended, and put it on the table. It looked old and worn, pages dog-eared, dustcover torn. Meaningless words from a past life. A trite metaphor for the life of a two-bit gumshoe. A sad symbol for the death of a good man.

Charlie Brandt. He lived through twenty-two novels. He died from the same bullet to the brain that killed Walker Redgrave.

I had plenty of time to get to my meeting with Littlejohn. Just enough time for a little detour for a quick look at the so-called scene of the crime.

I got up, paid the plump waitress for the coffee, and walked out into the parking lot. The air felt ten degrees hotter. Across the street there was a huge billboard advertising used auto parts.

7

THERE WAS JUST a small highway sign, white letters against a green background, that read "Steinhatchee." An arrow pointed toward the coast.

Since I'd left the restaurant the afternoon clouds had gathered with increasing density; now, just as I made the turn, they began spilling their rain in torrents. The water hit the hot pavement and turned to steam, causing an eerie ground-fog effect. The wheels of the Jeep hissed on the road, and the wipers, turned to high, slapped at the rain pelting the windshield.

I'd passed through a few small towns with small-town names—Old Town, Cross City, places you passed through, places you forgot. Then there was nothing except an occasional run-down gas station or store. Traffic was light; most of the vacationers were wheeling along Interstate 75, stoked with McDonald's coffee and trying like mad to get somewhere else as quickly as possible.

I peered through the rain-diminished light at this unfamiliar territory. The two-lane road to Steinhatchee cut through the scrub land in long, looping curves, avoiding low-lying marshy areas and little streams. Scruffy oaks, pine trees, and palmetto bushes were the dominant vegetation. In a few pastures, cattle hunkered down in cool muddy ponds or rooted at the sparse grass. The rain, I thought, would be welcomed by the farmers.

According to my map, Steinhatchee was situated a few miles off the main highway, along the mouth of a river by the same name. It looked secure nestled between woods and water, a safe haven bounded by the gulf, the river, and the woods.

I came first to a little town called Jena, a depressing and dilapidated collection of a few rough wood houses and a couple of little country stores, the kind that sold everything from dry goods to overalls. I passed a bar that was doing a good business, judging by the congregation of whip-antennaed vehicles in the muddy parking lot.

Then I drove over a bridge that spanned the Steinhatchee River, and came into Steinhatchee itself.

The road turned into the main street of the little town, and I drove down along the river and paralleled the curve where the river meets the Gulf of Mexico. According to the map, the small harbor at the mouth of the river was called Deadman's Bay. I rejected any symbolism.

By now the rain had stopped, leaving a murderous afternoon sun and fierce vaporous humidity.

Compared to Jena, Steinhatchee was uptown. Along the main street were a couple of banks—one even had a drive-through—and a Shell station and garage, a couple of home-cooking restaurants, and a few frame or cinder-block houses.

And boats. A lot of boats—boats on trailers in yards, boats in lots next to stores, boats being pulled behind trucks and Jeeps. A couple of abandoned boats sat forlornly among weeds and grass. On the peeling side of one hull, someone had taken a spray can of red paint and written, "Fifty dollars, you haul away." Someone else had written over it, "Too much."

Along the shore of the river were the marinas and fishing camps, mostly ragtag affairs consisting of low block buildings behind which were jumbled assemblages of boats, trailers, and inscrutable piles of scrap. At several there were launching ramps, small docks, and gasoline pumps. And more boats.

I rounded a curve leading away from town and came to a building that looked to be somewhat better kept than the rest. In front of the frame facade of the storefront stood two gas pumps. The sign above the open door read "Smitty's." There were two repair bays, one empty, the other with a pickup truck raised on a rack.

I pulled in next to the pumps. Smaller, handpainted letters by the Smitty's door advertised "Bait, Boats, Motors, Hunting and Fishing Supplies, Permits, Ammo, and Cold Cold Beer."

I waited in the car and a man ambled slowly out of the store. On his overalls was a patch that read "Smitty." He was probably hurrying as much as he ever did. Without saying anything, he pulled the nozzle off its holder and jammed it into the Jeep as if he were force-feeding a baby. He set the pump to keep running and came around to the driver's side.

"Oil?" he said. He appeared to be in his late fifties, burned leathery by the sun. His hair looked sparse and wispy under a hat that advertised Red Man chewing tobacco.

"Just the gas," I said. He nodded, shuffled toward the front of the car, and began to clean the windshield. I got out and asked for directions to the rest room.

"Round the side," he said, pointing with his cloth. He went back to work on the windshield, methodically rubbing at the encrusted lovebugs, squished to death in the midst of their perpetual copulation.

From the side of the building I could see around back. There were three or four neatly arranged boat slips, each with a small skiff or johnboat tied up. In a larger slip floated a sinister-looking airboat.

I knew about airboats. They are not friends of man. They are powered by huge aircraft engines with backward-facing propellers. They slide across the water at bizarre speeds; they are frightfully loud, and they generally are driven by strange men, their lips peeled back in a hideous wind-induced grimace.

It's happened to me on lakes throughout Georgia. I'd be at a favorite fishing spot just after daybreak, drinking hot, steaming coffee and trying to entice a bass to munch on the latest hot lure.

Then, in the distance, there would be the sound of an approaching airboat. The noise would intensify until it was roughly equivalent to a low-flying P-51 Mustang.

Then the airboat itself would appear, skimming along the water at perhaps sixty miles an hour, headed in my direction. It would fly by me, missing my boat by maybe a foot. The driver would tip his beer can at me as he passed. And I'd be left with a shattered silence and a shaking boat.

An airboat is not a friend of man. It would be, I thought, a wonderful way of negotiating the swamps, wetlands, and bayous of the coast.

I went around the other side of the building. Behind a back window I could hear the low sounds of a country music station. A woman was singing along; I caught a few words about faded love and a lonesome heart. As I passed the window I caught a momentary glimpse of red hair and a pale face.

I came around to the front just as Smitty was removing the nozzle from the Jeep. "Fourteen seventy-seven," he said.

I gave him a twenty. He reached in his pocket and extracted a wad of bills and loose coins, counted out my change, and handed it to me.

"Can you tell me where I'll find the Hacienda Court?" I asked.

"Easy," he said. "Keep on goin' the way you're headed. The road'll curve out of town, that's the way up to Perry. The Hacienda is about a mile up, on the right."

I thanked him, started the Jeep, and pulled back onto the road.

I didn't have to drive far. There wasn't much along the road, just a couple of houses and a roadhouse called the Florida Bar, and more scruffy woods.

The sun was doing a job on the soaked road, and hordes of small frogs were hopping along on the steaming blacktop, headed wherever frogs go after a hard summer rain. The unlucky ones, caught by the tires of the Jeep, made little popping noises when they exploded. The windshield, heated by the sun on the outside and cooled by the interior air-conditioning, began to fog over.

I rounded a bend and the Hacienda Court came into view. It was nothing special, just like a thousand other roadside motels in a thousand little towns—endangered species being killed by the interstates and Holiday Inns of the world.

I pulled off the side of the road and stared at the motel. Just an office and seven units, with a small swimming pool in front and a neon sign of a silhouetted man leaning placidly against a tree, a sombrero tilted down over his face.

The architecture, if you could call it that, was vaguely Spanish, brown stucco walls and a terra-cotta roof. The place would have no amenities, I suspected, such as room service or even a room telephone.

No one was about, and only a couple of cars were parked in the lot. One had an Illinois plate; the other was from Florida. The building and grounds did look well kept, though; the pool looked clean and the grass was neatly clipped.

I counted down three doors from the office. Unit three, the room where Redgrave had splattered his brains around. Nothing special about the room, except that an exceptional man had died there.

I suddenly felt alone, in an unfamiliar place, separated from home and my familiar Atlanta surroundings by more than the distance of miles. I gunned the Jeep and threw gravel as the tires spun and caught the pavement. More frogs exploded.

I turned on the radio, hunted, and found the country station. The song about faded love was over; now Emmylou was singing an old gospel song. The clarity of her voice painted the words with that other-worldly quality of honest-to-God gospel music.

> *Farther along, we'll know more about it*
> *Farther along, we'll understand why*
> *Cheer up my brother, live in the sunshine*
> *We'll understand it, all by and by*

8

GAINESVILLE IS A college town, which made me feel right at home—almost. Life here revolves around the crowded campus of redbrick buildings. It is Florida's oldest, largest, and wealthiest university. It has a number of fine programs, and scores of endowed chairs and professorships are made possible by millions upon millions of old Florida money. The university team is called the Gators, and many students are known to do a dance called the Gator, which I will not describe here. At home games, corporate jets crowd the airport and a few sportive and well-heeled alumni land their helicopters near Florida Field.

The University of Florida is the most-hated nemesis of my Georgia Bulldogs. I was willing to risk venturing onto the Gainesville campus; I just wouldn't let on where I was from. The Florida plate on my Jeep would help; my accent was a liability.

I parked beside a fire hydrant by a grassy quadrangle near the middle of campus. Turlington Hall, a fairly new four-story brick building where the history department was located, stood about a hundred yards across a green expanse of lawn.

I walked across the grass, weaving my way through knots of students. They looked like the students at the University of Georgia, or all of the other campuses I'd visited during my academic life. Baggy sweats, dirty sneakers, old jeans, carefully unkempt hair, affected gazes of detachment. They were all young; some were talking, some looked at notes, a few were necking. I made it inside the lobby without being accosted.

There was a bank of elevators in the lobby. Beyond them was a stairwell. During my undergraduate days we wouldn't be caught dead taking an elevator—they used up too much energy. I headed up the stairs.

At the second-floor landing I stopped to look at a large bulletin board. It was a collage of college life: a flyer for an experimental play titled *The Young Dead Never Rise*, pitches for courses of study in Europe and South America. A notice for a lecture titled "Shifting Syntaxes of the Middle English Language During the Post-Norman Invasion Era" by a Professor Jules Sternberg. The Young Republicans were announcing their upcoming meeting, as were the Gay Coalition and the Computer Hackers Association. A cardboard pocket held applications for the American Express Card. Don't leave your parents' home without it, I thought. April needed a ride to Ohio; Otis was looking for his lost dog. Sabrina wanted to connect with a kindred spirit into "crystals, the right mantra, and a good time." People needed roommates, people needed help studying for exams, people needed help finding a job. People needed help. And I was one of them.

I went the rest of the way up the stairs to the fourth floor and walked down the hall to Henry Littlejohn's office.

I looked into the open door of a small office. Henry Littlejohn sat amid looming stacks of books, staring out the window into the twilight. If he was looking for an ivory tower he was going to be disappointed; all I could see was a slice of green lawn, a few students, and the loading dock at the back of the building across the way.

Littlejohn had obviously occupied his office for a long time. Books were everywhere; jumbled stacks of them rose awkwardly from just about every horizontal surface.

I made a small coughing noise, the international "I'm here" signal. Littlejohn turned from the window and eyed me from between two stacks of books on his desk.

"You must be Dr. Cole," he said. "If you can find a place, you're welcome to sit down."

He appeared to be in his forties, but it was hard to tell. He was clearly American Indian, with an ageless smooth complexion and deep black eyes. From the front his hair appeared closely trimmed. But I'd seen him looking out the window; he had a ponytail that nearly reached his waist, held closely by a number of cloth-covered rubber bands.

There was a chair in front of his desk. There was only one book on it. I picked the book up—it was a volume on the Seminole wars—and handed it to the professor. He took it and I sat down.

"You use the Dewey Decimal System, or have you converted to the Library of Congress?" I asked.

He laughed. "Yeah, right. But I know where everything is. Give me a subject."

I thought for a moment; the shift to academics came easier than was comforting. "Early history of St. Augustine, specifically about the development of the fort."

Littlejohn seemed to go into a trance. Then he opened his eyes, got up from his chair, and walked around the desk to a huge stack of books that tilted precariously on a credenza. He ran a finger down the stack, hesitated a couple of times, and finally stopped at a thick paperback. He pulled the book out of the stack—somehow without everything toppling—and handed it to me.

I looked at the title: *The Building of the Spanish Fortifications*, by E. L. Fleming, Ph.D. A hot seller, I was sure.

I handed the book back to Littlejohn. "I'm convinced," I said. "But what I really need is information on a couple of rural Florida counties, Dixie and Taylor specifically. Which stack is that in?"

"Don't need a book," Littlejohn said. "Keith said you were coming and told me a little about the nature of your inquiry, so I read up and checked some statistics." He pulled a yellow legal pad in front of him. "You ready?"

"All ears," I said.

Littlejohn looked at the legal pad, but I got the impression he didn't need notes. "Okay," he said, "we're talking about the Big Bend area, the coastline where peninsula Florida curves up into the Panhandle.

"Taylor County is not what you'd call crowded. Total population is about 19,000. Perry is the only incorporated municipality—population about 8,000. U.S. 19, the main road between Tampa Bay and Tallahassee, goes through Perry.

"Steinhatchee, a community of about 2,400, is situated along the southern border of the county, along the north side of the Steinhatchee River. There's a sheriff's substation in Steinhatchee.

"There are several beach communities—Keaton Beach, Fish Creek, Dekle Beach."

The professorial monologue was somehow comforting, as was the office cramped and cluttered with books. But, I cautioned myself, nostalgia can be highly selective. Things hadn't been comforting at Georgia, not in the end, not at all.

I realized my thoughts were drifting and shook them off. "Dixie County," Littlejohn was saying, "makes Taylor look like Jersey. Population is about 15,000. County seat is Floral City, that's a dot on U.S. 19. There's another incorporated municipality, Horseshoe Beach, right on the coast. It's actually fairly popular as a retirement area, so there are some nice homes on the inlets.

"Most of the land along the coast in that region is extremely marshy. No beaches, mostly mangrove swamps and wetlands. There are some scattered old houses, but it's almost impossible to get a building permit now because of the environmental restrictions and difficulty in obtaining fresh water and electricity. Four-wheel-drive vehicles can get into some areas, but airboats and 'bird dog' fishing boats are the preferred means of transportation.

"There is some logging industry, and several small lumber mills. A number of people make their living as commercial fishermen, mainly catching mullet and crabs.

"The nearest airport of any size is Gainesville Regional,

about 50 miles from Steinhatchee. The most accessible large international airport is in Tampa, about three or four hours away."

I sat and listened; here Henry Littlejohn was in charge. He hadn't given me any information I couldn't have gotten from an almanac. He and I both knew that, and he and I both knew I'd have to bide my time for the good stuff.

"But I'm not telling you anything you couldn't find out at the library," he said as if he'd read my mind. "That's not why you're here, is it? You're a detective, so I figure you want to know what really goes on in the marshes and the woods, right?"

"That would be a big help," I agreed.

"Come with me," he said. "I know a better place to talk."

9

THE TAVERN WAS cool, a respite from the suffocating heat outside. A few students were hanging out near a pool table and dart board. There was only one person at the bar, a student hunched over a paperback book.

During the short walk from Littlejohn's office, he had said, almost shyly, "Keith told me a little about you. He said you were, ah, quite the scholar up in Athens."

I turned my head toward him as he walked. "Keith thinks I'm crazy, but Keith thinks anybody without tenure is living a fantastically insecure life. He doesn't realize there are people out in the world who actually work for a living."

Littlejohn nodded. "I wasn't always in the ivory tower. I didn't get my Ph.D. until I was over forty. I've broken horses, cut sugar cane, spent more than one night in jail. I even worked as a dressed-up Indian chief at a tourist trap one summer."

"It does build character. I took the other direction, tried the coddled life first. It didn't work out."

We sidestepped a couple sitting crosslegged in a patch of grass, nose to nose. They only had eyes for each other. Littlejohn glanced at them, then at me. "I could cut cane again, if I had to." He paused, and his tone shifted. "Is being a detective really like—like it is in the books?"

I laughed. The inevitable question, the same one Mrs. Redgrave had asked me. I shook my head. "Maybe a little more exciting than sitting in your office with your books— maybe. Mostly I look through reports, sometimes I follow some insurance deadbeat around. I've caught a few folks in the wrong bed, and I've hotwired some cars for the bank that wanted them back. Not what you'd call high adventure."

"I know how to hotwire a car," Littlejohn said. "That's how I saw the inside of one jail."

At the tavern, he directed me to the rear, and we wedged into a small booth with an overhead light hanging from a chain.

"Now for the good stuff," he said.

"The good stuff is what I need," I said, settling back.

"What I've given you are demographics, now we're going to talk about psychographics. And that's the last bit of scholarly jargon you're going to hear, Dr. Cole."

I nodded. Clearly, it would do no good to get in the way of Littlejohn's narrative. His eyes got that dreamy quality that comes of introspective thought, interrupted when a waitress took our order. After our beverages were served, Littlejohn got down to business.

"Dixie and Taylor counties are among the lowest per capita income areas in the state," he began, "yet we've got a number of citizens—some of them without a job even—driving around in very expensive four-wheel-drive vehicles and cruising along in thirty-five-foot Cigarette boats. Why might that be?"

"Let me guess," I said. "They all have inheritances."

Littlejohn ignored the sarcasm.

"There's a lot of folks in Dixie and Taylor counties that are bad, Dr. Cole," he said. "I mean real bad—people who'd kill you for just about no reason at all. Although there are a lot of good reasons for killing there.

"The main cash crop is marijuana. The main import is cocaine. The main businesses are illegal. There's gator poaching and hazardous-waste dumping, gambling and pit-bull fighting, cocks, too.

"The coke trade is down some, since most of the stuff is coming in through south Florida. But they still offload from boats several miles offshore. They used to do that with grass, too. But they've found a better way to supply our needy population with the weed. They grow it out in the woods, using the latest technology. It's called hydroponics, Dr. Cole. A controlled environment, the best nutrients, the most dynamite pot you've ever experienced."

I'd never experienced any pot, but I didn't want Littlejohn to think me naive, so I simply nodded knowingly. That was enough for him. His world had contracted as he talked; it seemed even I was on the periphery.

"Drugs, the kids and the punks and the pushers are going to get them some way," he said in a slightly distant voice. "But there's a worse tragedy going on—I know a lot of people would disagree—and that's the rape and pillage of the environment.

"Toxic waste, nutrient pollution, fish kills, the buildup of radioactive waste under landfills, animals like our Florida panther are becoming extinct, the beautiful lakes drying up and dying, developers who'd build condos on every square inch of coastline. What did Joni Mitchell sing? 'They paved paradise and put up a parking lot.' "

His voice was becoming strident, as it seemed to do about halfway through each of his monologues.

"They are paving our paradise, Dr. Cole, and polluting it and ravaging it and leaving it for dead."

The extraordinary depth of his concern overwhelmed me. I simply said, "Is it really that bad?"

He considered the question. "You see my passion for Florida," he said. "And my obvious anger. Dr. Cole, I am a full-blooded Seminole, but let's put my Native American ancestry and sentiments aside for the moment.

"I am also a native Floridian. I grew up in the Everglades, but I've hunted and fished all over this state.

"I was lucky enough to get a scholarship to a good university, and it wasn't just because of my 'minority' status." He made a face that was a mixture of embarrassment and pride.

"I spent four miserable years in California, and four more

miserable years in New York. I studied European history, if you can believe it. Those were years I wanted to escape from the accident of my birth, and the difficulties of my youth."

He sipped his drink. "But at some point my pride returned, and I also realized where I was happiest. I had to come home, and home was Florida.

"I've got a good job here, and they let me alone to study our state's history." His eyes met and held mine, and his voice got softer. "I don't mean when DeSoto landed, or how Jacksonville's port developed, or how an oddity like Claude Kirk got elected governor. I mean the heritage of our state, its art, its ballad poetry and music, the legacy of red men and white men alike."

The last statement seemed to startle him; he took a sip of tea.

"I don't mean to go on—it's an occupational hazard, I guess. But I do get angry when people don't take care to preserve our state, its history, and its habitat." He gestured broadly with his arms. "Florida is fragile, and what goes on in the area you've asked about is part of what is killing Florida. The wetlands are polluted; we grow enough dope to supply the whole Southeast. There is no law in the backwoods, and what's worse, the people there, people who have grown up there, whose families settled there a hundred years ago—these people *don't care.*" He slammed his fist on the table, causing the glasses to rattle and skitter across the varnished surface.

"They just do not care," he said more quietly. And gave me a sad smile, one man against the march of civilization, a man with passion. I envied and respected him for that.

We'd finished our drinks. He wouldn't let me pay the check. He seemed to have become somber. "I hope I've been able to give you some information that'll help you. I understand you are reticent to tell me what you're looking into, but Keith vouches for you"—he grinned a little—"after a fashion. By the way, he says to take care of his Jeep. Maybe some day you could drop by when you aren't on business and tell me about the detective's life. I'd prefer you come after we've stomped you in the Gator Bowl."

It was well after dark when I got up to leave the tavern. I thanked Littlejohn for his time and for his information. He said he'd stay there for a while—I got the impression his life revolved around his office and his classes, his books and his research, and maybe his time at the tavern. There was no wedding ring on his hand, no place he seemed in a hurry to go to.

I started the Jeep, rolled down the windows, and took the road toward Steinhatchee. It was a starry night; the coastal wind had reached inland and blown the humidity away, and a cool breeze took the edge off the heat.

I thought about where I might have been tonight, probably at my house in Atlanta, a pot of coffee brewed in the kitchen, the desk light on in the study, maybe some time rereading one of the old novels or something out of the latest bookstore bag, whoever the critics were raving about as "the next Hammett." Maybe I'd get lonely, convince Lisa Carmichael to pick up a pizza and come over, talk about nothing at all, sit on the couch just far enough away, but just close enough. Maybe watch a Braves game.

And I thought about where I was headed. I would check into the Hacienda Court. I'd get a few hours of sleep. Then I'd go out and turn things over and see what crawled around. I might not be smart, but I was persistent. And I suspected there were a lot of wormy, crawly things in Steinhatchee that didn't want to be disturbed.

10

I CHECKED INTO the Hacienda Court about eleven, after driving back from Gainesville with a quick stop along the way at a truck stop for a thin, tough steak and some of the best coffee I'd ever had.

The office was dark and locked, so I rang the night buzzer, which eventually awoke a man who lumbered out dressed in shorts and an undershirt. He didn't seem upset at the intrusion; he also didn't seem to really wake up. I paid him sixty dollars in cash for three nights, which perked him up quite a bit.

"I'm Clyde, the owner," he said. "The wife's Etta. You need anything, you let us know." He shifted his glance to the night buzzer, as if he hoped I wouldn't have need of it, handed me my key, and trundled back to his apartment behind the office.

I awoke early, staggered out into the intense morning light, and used the pay phone outside the motel to call the sheriff's substation. A woman answered, and when I asked if Deputy Stubbs was in she said, "uh-huh." When I asked if I could drop by to see him she said, "uh-huh." Then she hung up. Figuring that was as good an invitation as any, I headed to the substation.

The woman at the front desk—I assumed she'd been the talkative one I'd gotten on the phone—looked up at me when I came in. Her look said nothing. When I asked for the deputy she took her pencil and pointed to an open door. So much for clearance and security.

Deputy Stubbs was leaning back in his railroad chair, feet propped up on a desk scarred by years of cigarette butts and boot heels. He was wearing a red flannel shirt, crisp blue jeans, and lizard-skin western boots. A blue baseball hat that said "Jazz Feeds" was pushed back on his head.

At least I figured he was Deputy Stubbs; a little sign on the desk read "Cecil Stubbs, Deputy in Charge" in block letters. But, I cautioned myself, assume nothing.

He appeared to be in his late forties, neither fat nor thin, not in great shape but not gasping for breath either. His face had the creased, leathery look of a man who spent a lot of time outdoors. The sun had burnished red highlights into his dark brown hair, which he wore a bit longer than stylish.

A floor fan whirred gently in the corner behind the deputy, but the room still seemed mildewed and close. Feeble light streamed through a lone casement window covered with years of streaked grime, playing on a faintly translucent haze of dust. Besides the desk and fan, the only furnishings were a couple of battered gray metal file cabinets, an equally battered wooden bookcase with a few volumes of haphazardously stacked law enforcement books and periodicals, a straight-backed visitor's chair, and, near the desk and within the deputy's reach, a metal hat rack with a black leather holster slung over it. The holster held a large Magnum revolver, probably a .44, with a long barrel and black rubber grips.

He held a supermarket-rack tabloid in his plump hands. After a few seconds he glanced up. His eyes were a startling pale blue-gray. They calmly caught and held my gaze. He gave me the slightest hint of a smile.

"Lookee here," he said, tapping the tabloid in his lap. "You find out a lot of amazing stuff by reading this." His voice was a good slow twang, concealing nothing of his rural roots. I figured him as an indigenous species to the area.

"Listen," he said, beginning to warm to his subject. "In this one issue we got a story on how Noah's ark was really a submarine designed by space aliens. We got a one-year-old who weighs a hunnert and twenty-seven pounds—with a picture for proof. We got Princess Di telling her husband he needs to be neutered. Ouch!"

He continued leafing through the paper. "That ain't all. Here's a guy committed suicide with a bow and arrow. Nice touch, huh? There's a giant dinosaur runnin' through the African jungles, even attacking boats. And here's a mama who's proud of her seven homo sons.

"Hey," he continued, turning the page. "Here's a story of interest to all of us law enforcement officers. Tells about why women keep falling in love with serial killers."

"That's incredible stuff," I agreed. "You'd think the popular press would pick up on this more often."

"Yeah," he said, leaning backward so that his seat creaked and stopped at a precarious tilt. "I never read about this stuff anywhere else. But they wouldn't print it if it weren't true, would they?" He gave me a big toothy grin.

"Those big-city papers are just too scared of the truth," I said.

"Chicken livers." He tossed the tabloid on the desk, leaned forward, and brought his feet onto the floor. "Sit down. I'm Deputy Stubbs, Cecil Stubbs. You're from out of town. What can I do for you?"

I lowered myself into the visitor's chair, told him my name and occupation.

Stubbs gave me a long inquiring look. "Private eye, huh?" Then he stared at me some more.

"I understand you handled the investigation into Walker Redgrave's death not too long ago," I said.

"Yeah, that was mine," Stubbs said. "He was a famous book writer, I heard. Never read any of his stuff myself."

"I was wondering if you would tell me about the case."

Stubbs gave me a long look, the kind cops give people who aren't their own. "All about the case, huh? Why should I do that?"

"Because I'm honest and upstanding?"

"That's not good enough," he said without hurry.

"Because if you don't I'll run all around town asking embarrassing questions and being a royal pain in the rear?"

"Better," he said. "One more time."

"Should I just say please?" I said, looking as open and innocent as I could.

"Great to hear a dick stand there and grovel," Stubbs said. "One more question. Why are you poking around in an itty-bitty open-and-shut case anyway? You think there's more to it?"

I shrugged. "I don't assume anything. I have no preconceived notions. I have a client. This is what I'm paid to do."

"And if I ask, you ain't by any chance going to tell me who that client is, are you?"

I said, "Nope."

"I didn't think so," Stubbs said. He looked at me for a moment, as if deciding, then opened a desk drawer and rummaged through some manila folders. He extracted one, laid it on his desk, and opened it up to the sheriff's summary report. I waited while he scanned the pages.

"Case number 90-1467. Suicide," Stubbs said. "Open-and-shut. Victim was found in his motel room by the owner after the maid couldn't get a response, tried the door, and found the inside chain lock fastened. They had to take the door off the hinges.

"The victim was found on his back in the bed, fully clothed. The bed, by the way, was still made. Back door was locked and chained, too. Both windows locked, shade on the front one closed, the one on the back partially open. The overhead light was on. He'd been shot once in the right temple by a .38 revolver. No signs of a struggle—probably wouldn't be since he was the only one in the room. The gun was still in his right hand, one round fired—in fact it was the only round in the gun. His own gun, we checked."

Stubbs flipped a page of the report. "The autopsy determined that the victim had only been dead a few hours. Rigor mortis was just starting to set in.

"No one heard the shot; it was fired point-blank, that'd

muffle the sound, and anyway, around here, even if someone does hear a shot, he's still likely to mind his own business. We're kind of quiet that way, just keep to ourselves. Don't like to make no trouble. You wanna see the pictures?"

Stubbs took out two glossy color prints from the folder and flipped them toward me. They landed on the desk, face up, like a hand of cards.

I picked them up; I knew what I'd find. There was Walker Redgrave, on the bed of the motel room. From the angle of one picture he appeared to be resting calmly in bed, head tilted toward one side, eye closed, looking relaxed and untouched—except for the little blue hole in his right temple. At the edge of the picture I could see part of the gun lying on the sheet.

The other angle showed the carnage—under the side of his head where the bullet had exited there was a gooey mess on the pillow—brains, blood, and matted hair. That eye was open, bloated, and bulging. Some drool had run out of the corner of his mouth and collected on the pillow. The side of his face had been shocked and distorted by the velocity and force of the bullet, which I assumed had come to a stop somewhere in the pillow or mattress.

I handed the pictures back to Stubbs, and asked him whether there were any other ways someone could have gained entry to the room.

The blue-gray eyes considered the question. "Of course the owner and the maid had passkeys, but the chain locks could only have been hooked from the inside. I even tried having our smallest deputy put his scrawny little hand through the opening to see if the chain could be fastened. No way. It was definitely locked from the inside. Same with the window."

Stubbs flipped the folder closed. "Anything else?" he asked.

"I understand there was a suicide note. Can you tell me what it said?"

"Don't see why not," Stubbs said, opening the folder.

"Heck, since you're sort of a law enforcement brother, I don't see why I can't give you a copy." He lumbered out of his chair with the letter and left the room. Standing, he was taller than I realized, something over six feet and probably more than two hundred pounds. The lizard boots squeaked when he walked.

A few moments later he returned and handed me a photocopy of the note. I read it, only a few lines handwritten in a distinct compact script, presumably Redgrave's. That would be easy enough to check.

I folded the photocopy of the note and stuffed it inside my notebook. I'd read it again later.

"By the way, are you carrying a gun?" Stubbs asked.

"As a matter of fact I am," I said.

"Somehow I'm not surprised. What kind?"

"Colt, .38 Special." I didn't tell him it was the same kind Marlowe carried. I didn't think he'd understand.

"That's like a gun, only smaller," Stubbs said. He reached for the .44 and laid it on the desk. He patted it lovingly. "Now this is a gun," he said. He patted it again, then stroked the barrel with his thumb and forefinger. I hoped he wasn't about to make love to it.

"I can't help it," I said. "That's all Georgia allows private detectives to carry."

"Mind if I see it?" Stubbs said. "Just to give it the ol' official check."

I reached inside my jacket, withdrew the Colt, and handed it butt-first to Stubbs. "It's loaded," I said.

He looked at me as if I were stupid. "They all are," he said. He studied the old Colt thoughtfully for a moment, rubbed his thumb over the hammer a couple of times.

"Well, at least you can pistol-whip 'em with it," he said as he handed it back.

I holstered the Colt. "Thanks for your time," I said. "You don't mind if I hang out around here for a little while and ask a few questions? I don't want to raise too much suspicion, so I figure I'm just down here to relax and do a little fishing. You got a problem there?"

"Not so's I can tell. Fishin's good this time of year. I hope you catch something."

I watched Stubbs as he sat placidly in his chair, not even breaking a sweat in the stifling Florida heat.

"I'm curious about one thing," I said. "Usually I meet a fair amount of hostility when I poke around in a cop's territory, especially if I'm using a cover. Why were you so easy?"

"Ain't never had a big-city private eye nosing around these parts, just the occasional DER man or somebody from the drug enforcement office in Gainesville. Besides, you most likely won't find anything that contradicts our investigation. Just don't get shot, that's more work for me, and if by some chance you do find out something interesting, you hop over here and tell me pronto, understand."

I thanked him. "I'm staying at the same place Redgrave bought it, number six. I'll do my best at keeping you informed." I neglected to tell him how lousy my best was when it came to keeping policemen informed of my investigation.

"One more time, who hired you?" Stubbs said.

"That's confidential."

"Sure it is," he said. "Be sure to give my regards to Mrs. Redgrave next time you report in."

"She just wants the truth," I said.

"Don't we all," Stubbs said. "Don't we all."

I got up and turned to leave. Stubbs stuffed the folder back into the desk drawer and picked up the tabloid.

"Wow," he said. "Another Elvis sighting."

11

As bars went, it was a bar. A roadside tavern in a backwoods town, built of aging wood weathered by coastal winds and badly in need of paint. But it would be cool inside, not too loud or too clean, the kind of place you could sit for a while without being bothered or arousing attention. There are worse things that can be said about a place.

It was late evening. After I'd left Stubbs I'd been hit hard with fatigue, so I went back to the Hacienda and got three or four hours sleep. Then I'd asked Clyde where the locals hung out.

"Down the road," he said. "Florida Bar, only place in town."

I pulled off the hard road into the dirt parking lot and nosed the Jeep in between a rusty pickup truck and a late-model Corvette convertible. I cut the engine and walked up to the front porch, which sagged and creaked under my weight.

A hand-lettered sign was taped to the front door. It read:

Welcome to the Florida Bar
No checks
No credit cards
No guns
No fighting
No spitting
Closed Sunday
Have a nice day!

Now that I knew how to behave, I pushed the door open and went in. The interior of the place was pretty much standard issue. The light was dim. There was a horseshoe-shaped bar, the wood polished to a well-worn luster. Four mounted bass perched on the wall behind it, forever caught in the act of lunging at the bait.

About a dozen bar stools lined the bar, all but two of them empty. At one was the guy I figured for the Corvette. He was wearing a brown suit that had been expertly tailored a long time ago. It wasn't shabby, but it was a long way from new.

The guy inside the suit was deeply tanned and had longish gray hair that curled behind his ears. The top three buttons of his shirt were open, and a thick gold chain glittered against the deep brown skin of his neck. Another chain encircled his left wrist. He looked as if he'd known money, but maybe didn't know it as well now. And if you looked closely he wasn't too clean. He sat quietly, stirring his glass with a straw and working on his thoughtful look.

It was hard to see the other man, even if you looked. He was that nondescript. He, too, silently toyed with his drink, slowly working his fingers over the condensation on the glass, making smooth little streaky patterns.

There were a couple of pool tables in an alcove off to one side, a dart board, a few tables and chairs, some neon beer signs. Two men were playing pool. A jukebox stood quietly in one corner, and the clatter of the billiard balls was the dominant sound in the room.

I sat down at one of the stools and signaled to the waitress, who was perched on a stool at the far end of the bar, looking bored. She got up and came around behind the bar.

"What'll it be, mister?" she said when she got close. She was a little wider than she should have been, the type who'd get wider with age. Her blond hair had dark roots, and she had the faintest beginnings of a double chin. But her heavy breasts strained against her low-cut leotard, and the dim tavern light was kind to her skin.

"Do you have spring water?" I asked.

That seemed to puzzle her. "Sprite?" The voice was backwoods; the word came out "spraat."

"No, like Perrier, or club soda."

"Club soda I can do. You want a dozen sliders?"

It was my turn to be puzzled. "Sliders?"

She leaned her breasts on the bar, squeezing them together with her arms and showing a lot of freckled cleavage.

"Y'know, raw oysters on the half shell," she said. "Specialty of the house. You just pop 'em in your mouth and tilt yer head back, they slide right down."

I ordered a dozen oysters and a club soda, which she poured by pushing a button on a nozzle at the end of a hose.

"Oysters'll be right up," she said, heading toward the kitchen.

I watched her walk away, giving me a lot of hip movement and breast action and twist and turns. Still the stuff of teenage dreams of lost innocence and backseat entanglements, I thought. And she would be for a few more years.

"Hey, Stormy," the nondescript man at the end of the stool said, "how's about topping this up?" He waved his empty glass in the air. She took his glass, scooped it through the ice bin and filled it from a bottle behind the bar. She squeezed a tiny sliver of lime into it and sat it down in front of the man.

He picked up the glass, gulped half his drink, and set it back down, a little too hard. Droplets of clear liquid clung to his upper lip. He grinned at Stormy. "So I ask you again, wanna set up some light housekeeping in the parking lot?" His articulation was not superior.

"You know I don't play house with the patrons," she said.

The man grinned; he didn't seem as nondescript now. He picked his keys off the counter, leaned over the bar, and dropped them down the front of Stormy's leotard. They disappeared into the depths of her cleavage.

"I think I lost my keys, honey. You'll have to drive me home."

Stormy looked down into her cleavage for a moment, then

fished her hand into the vee of her top, letting the man see a lot of freckled skin and white bra.

She rummaged around for a while, finally got hold of the keys, and brought them out. Then she came around from behind the bar and walked over to the front door. She opened the door, propped it with her hip as she stepped outside, took a good windup, and threw the keys hard into the darkness beyond the parking lot.

She turned around and gave the man an elaborate shrug. The door banged shut. "I guess you did lose your keys, Jake. But I'm not drivin' you home. You'll have to walk—or crawl."

The pool balls had stopped clattering; the men leaned on their cues and watched.

Jake came off the stool, took three steps, and stood still, arms stiff at his side. "Why, you little . . ." Then he grinned, reached into his pocket, and brought out another set of keys.

"Always keep a spare, babe. Never know when I'm gonna need one." He walked out the door.

"I get all the charmers," she said to no one in particular, going back behind the bar. "He fooled me havin' that extra set."

The man in the suit still hadn't looked up, he just kept pushing the ice around in his drink. Stormy walked over to him and said, "Durel, you ever think about havin' some dress code or somethin' that keeps people like Jake outta this place?"

The man looked up then, and smiled. His teeth were extremely white. "Just think of Jake as a bit of local color, Stormy. He's real boring till he gets drunk, then he's real stupid. It adds comic relief."

The accent was from somewhere else, the bayou rather than the woods, I thought. It was a little bit musical, and a little bit whiskey-edged.

Stormy took the man's glass out from under his straw and headed back to the bar, muttering. He grinned just a little and tapped the straw on the bar. I had the feeling this wasn't the first time they'd had this little interplay.

She finished mixing his drink and walked over to where I sat. Without looking she set the glass down and pushed it; it slid along the bar until it stopped about six inches from the man's hand. He calmly picked it up, slipped his straw in it, stirred a couple of times, and took a sip.

"That's incredible," I said. "May I buy a drink for the gentleman?"

The man looked up and turned toward me. "No need to, sir, though I appreciate the gesture," he said. "I am the owner of this establishment, and so would have paid for that drink already." He spoke with an odd, almost formal, cadence.

He eyed me for a moment. "Have you not been to the Florida Bar before." It was a statement, not a question. "Where might you be from, and on what business in Steinhatchee?"

"Tampa," I said. "Up to do a little fishing. Got a room over at the Hacienda Court. You have any idea where I can rent a good boat that won't cost me an arm and a leg?"

"Smitty will supply you a boat. Just travel back along the main highway as it curves into town. You'll not miss it, it's right on the water. He has gasoline and groceries and fishing supplies, and boats out back. He can tell you all about the waters here, and the fish. He will treat you right."

I remembered Smitty. He'd pumped my gas and given me directions to the Hacienda Court during my first visit to town.

Durel gave me a vague look. "Fishing, huh?"

He seemed to tire of conversation then, and settled back with his drink and his straw and his introspection.

Stormy came over; she was a lot more interested. I'd seen that look before.

"Tampa boy with a Hot-lanta accent?" she said.

That caught me off guard. So much for an airtight cover. "Darn," I said. "I've worked so hard to try and hide it. Do you know that people who've heard me talk have actually accused me of being unintelligent."

I sipped at the soda water and smiled at her. There

was more there, I suspected, than heavy breasts and bottle-blond hair.

I was about to say something else witty when one of the pool players, a tall, skinny—almost emaciated—guy wearing a baseball hat, came over to the bar.

"Lemme have a beer, Stormy," he said. He gave her a grin that wasn't innocent. "You flung them keys outta that door harder'n Jim Palmer. And I bet ya look better in your Jockey shorts, too."

Stormy handed him his beer. Then she reached out, grabbed the bill of his hat, and snapped it down over his eyes.

"Keep dreamin', Troy," she said, " 'cause you'll never know."

12

"You can be from wherever you want, honeybunch. Tampa, Atlanta, N'Ahwlins, Topeka, I don't care. Just so you ain't from around here."

We were on the road out of Steinhatchee, headed east in the Jeep to a restaurant Stormy had suggested, about ten miles out of town over on U.S. 19. The windows were rolled down for the cool wind. I drove; Stormy sat with her head leaned back, relaxed and talking.

"Most everbody around here is from around here. No one leaves, no one moves in; we got sons and daddies and granddaddies sittin' around the farmhouse their great granddaddy built."

She looked out the window; the breeze did things to her hair.

"Life gets real boring when all you know is a bunch of boys grew up pitchin' slop on the family farm," she said. "Or fishin' in the family hand-me-down boat. Or working at the lumber mill like everbody else in their family has or ever will."

"I think I get the point, Stormy," I said over the wind rush. "You don't like it here too much."

"Right, right, right, Cole. I don't like it, I hate it, I'd just as soon be dead as be here, I ain't happy, I'm miserable, I ain't got a husband or even a boyfriend, not even a dog."

She stared out the window, head laid back on the seat, chest rising gently as she breathed. I tried to keep my eyes off the leotard.

Leaving the bar with her hadn't taken much effort on my part. As soon as she found out I was from out of town, she moved in like a boxer sensing a knockout. By midnight I was about to float away on a sea of free soda water, and Stormy, who happened to get off at midnight, had convinced me I could use a bite to eat; a dozen sliders may be good, but they didn't make a meal.

I accepted; I didn't want to go back to the dreary little motel room, and she was a good candidate to tell me more about the little fishing village and its people, information that might give me a clue as to what to do next about Walker Redgrave's death. A talkative woman can shed light on many things.

"Turn here," she said abruptly as I cruised down the two-lane going seventy.

I plowed the brakes, just in time to careen into an all-but-invisible parking lot nestled between two huge clumps of oak trees. Back about fifty yards, visible through stands of oak and pine, was a low log building with a flashing neon sign that advertised, "Buster's Boar Butt, Southern Bar-B-Que."

"God, barbecue," I said under my breath as we parked.

"I was right—Topeka," Stormy said. "Every Southern boy loves barbecue. I dated a guy worked cooking barbecue once, he liked to tell how it was good for you, all that fat gettin' in your veins and slicking 'em up so the blood just rolls through real easy."

I looked at the building. This was the real thing, no Sonny's or Fat Boy's chain so clean the tourists will eat there. The brown paint was weathered and peeling. A greasy film covered three front windows, making them almost opaque. A fourth was boarded up with old planks.

A gray plume of smoke rose from the chimney and was backlit by the moonlight. The smoke hung in the trees and the smell of cooking hog was in the air.

"Maybe they have breakfast," I said hopefully as a high-school-age hostess in a blue-checked apron showed us to our booth. The interior carried on the tradition—built-in wooden booths, checkered oil-cloth tablecloths, old license plates tacked onto most of the available wall space, old pictures of a black man—perhaps the owner, I thought—in a high school football uniform, hanging over a huge brick fireplace. And that pervasive piggy odor.

There were three bottles of barbecue sauce on the table—mild, hot, and another that simply had a picture of a grinning red devil waving a pitchfork.

The waitress took our drink order. I looked over the crowd.

"Eclectic bunch, huh?" Stormy said.

"Eclectic?"

"Whoops," she said, giving me a little giggle. "I must be spending too much time at the library over in Perry."

Maybe it was the word, maybe it was something more indefinable beneath the barroom country facade, but I was beginning to realize there was a depth to Stormy that most people didn't see, didn't even look for.

The waitress came by with our drinks. Stormy glanced around the room, which was packed with people, mostly young or middle-aged, mostly tired-looking, as if they'd been working hard at having fun all night and had come here to recuperate.

"They're all from around here," she said. "I probably know most of 'em, not necessarily by name. You got some secretaries from Floral City, lots of 'em work at the county offices or the lumber mill. The mill's the biggest honest employer in Taylor and Dixie counties." I noted her use of the word "honest" but kept quiet and let her talk.

"There's a bunch from Steinhatchee and some come up from Horseshoe Beach," she said. "You think Steinhatchee's dead, you oughtta go to Horseshoe Beach." She rolled her eyes. "There's probably a coupla people from Gainesville down here slummin'."

"Eclectic," I said.

She took a drink, rattled the ice absently, looked around the room again, and gave me a weary, almost sad stare.

"They're all so tired from having so much fun they can barely see straight. Or maybe it's just they been drinkin' too much."

I got the feeling Stormy spent a lot of nights here, recuperating from having so much fun.

"If you hate Steinhatchee so much, why haven't you left?" I asked.

"Different times in my life there's been different reasons," she said. "Right out of high school I got the hot pants for Cordell, that's my ex. We got married and not more'n a year later Katie came along. Seems like the last few years it's always been somethin'. Money, Katie, Momma bein' sick." She sighed and picked up a bottle of sauce, put it back down. "Always somethin'," she said, almost to herself.

She focused back toward me. "Now I got my job at the bar; Momma's better. She looks after Katie the nights I work. The bar takes up a lot of time."

"So what's so important about staying at the Florida Bar?" I asked.

"Durel Barbour—he's the owner," she said. Her eyes were bright. "I owe him. He fronted me the money to get my house back outta hock after no-good Cordell used it as collateral for one of his—business ventures." She almost spat the last words. "If it wasn't for him I'd have lost the little bit I'd worked so hard to get.

"Durel ain't usin' the loan to force me into stayin'. I've worked for him four years now, done a good job. He thinks I got potential. He wants me to get up to speed, run the place. I'd be a, how do you say it, a 'hospitality executive.' " She gave me that little giggle again. "I read that in a book on restaurant management I got at the library."

I backtracked to something she had said. "What kind of business ventures did your husband get involved in?"

She narrowed her eyes and gave me a suspicious look. Just then the waitress brought our food. Stormy eyed her plate like a vulture on a telephone pole. "Enough about Cordell," she said. "I've talked enough about Cordell Corbin to last me a lifetime." She scooped up a huge spoonful of baked beans. "Let's eat."

And she did—pork, baked beans, two helpings from the salad bar, three refills on tea, and a piece of mud pie to help everything settle. I munched a pork sandwich and watched her put it all away. She was a real barbecue pro; during the meal she gave me a little dissertation on the subtle differences between the main schools of barbecuing—Florida, Georgia, Texas, and Carolina. "It's the sauces," she said. "Georgia's sweet, lots of brown sugar. Carolina is tangy, they use vinegar. But there's another problem—there's two Carolinas. The folks in South Carolina put mustard in the sauce, that's a grave sin in North Carolina. They've been fightin' over that for a hundred years."

Stormy sopped a biscuit through the pork, and continued her barbecue dissertation. "Florida has lemon in it to give it bite," she said. "And Texas is—hot."

She picked up the bottle of hot barbecue sauce. "Buster thinks this is hot, but he's wrong. You want hot sauce, go to Elroy's Hog Heaven in Fort Worth. That stuff'll strip the chrome off a bumper hitch."

About the time Stormy had given up on finding anything else edible on her plate, a black man came over to our booth. He wore an apron that might have been white once, on which he was rubbing his hands. He looked like he might have played football—a long time ago.

"Bulkin' up after a long night at the Florida?" he said to Stormy.

"Gotta get my dose of cholesterol, Buster." Stormy motioned toward me. "This's Bennett Cole, he's from—" She gave me a quick glance. "He's from Tampa, up here to do a little fishin'. Cole, this is Buster, the owner of this fine establishment."

"Out-a-towner, huh," Buster said. "Wait right here." He hurried off toward the kitchen and returned a moment later holding a jar of barbecue sauce. It, too, had a little devil on it.

"On the house, Mr. Cole. If you like it here's a little order blank. I send this stuff all over the country. Even got a doctor fella up in Alaska orders it by the gallon."

I took the bottle. "It's the hot version," Buster said. No kidding, I thought.

"It's hot, but it ain't Elroy's," Stormy said.

"Outta here, little one," Buster said. "Elroy's sauce has shellacked your taste buds. That stuff's like kerosene. You can't even taste hot anymore." He started back toward the kitchen.

As we were leaving I asked a harried waitress for the restaurant phone number, figuring I might want to talk to Buster, since everyone in the county probably showed up here at some point, and he probably knew something about everyone who showed up.

"Can't stop," she said. "We're in the phone book. Look under 'Skip's.' "

"Skip's?"

"Don't ask me. It's always been listed that way, even when it was named the Moo Moo Hut, and that's been fifteen years ago."

"Was it ever named Skip's?" I asked.

"Nope, never," she said.

13

I DROPPED STORMY off at the Florida Bar; her Camaro was the only car in the lot, parked under the sentry light. I waited until she got in and drove away.

Then I drove out and back onto the road to the Hacienda. The lighted sign came into view after a few minutes, but I drove by and continued along the dark highway. I was putting off going back to the drab little room, putting off trying to figure out what to do next, depressed that I had a lousy cover and no plan at all.

I turned on the radio, fiddled with the dial, and found a fairly clear signal from what sounded like the university station up in Gainesville. The announcer appealed for money "from our friends out there who appreciate commercial-free alternative radio." Then he said, "Here's the Dixie Dew Drops, singing 'Your Own Strong Heart.'" I perked up and twisted the volume knob. I was a fan of the Dew Drops—Darla and Dwana Dewcett—had been since I first heard them fifteen years ago at a festival in the Georgia woods, before they got famous.

The song wasn't one of their big country hits, just a cut off an early album. But it was one that had stuck in my mind since the first time I'd heard it. I listened as I drove through the thick Florida night.

> *You've got your father's blue eyes*
> *And you've got your momma's smile*
> *But you've got your very own heart*

And there are secrets there that'll take a while
So listen to the beating of
Listen to the beating of
your own strong heart

Stormy, I suspected, would probably follow her heart, break away and go—I had that sense of the building tension in her. She probably needed to leave, that was clear from our conversation at the restaurant. She wouldn't like a lot of what she found, but perhaps that wasn't as important as the search. And in life, doing something usually beats doing nothing—especially if that something will make you a better person, or the world a better place.

The Dew Drops and their music, and the guy volunteering for the night shift at the radio station, and Stormy with her dreams, and me—each in our own way fighting back against the crawly things that would come out from under the rocks and overrun us if they could.

All of which was a lot of introspection that got me exactly nowhere on my case. I loitered on the back roads of Taylor County for a while, but that just got me a case of insomnia and a frightful case of the blues.

I drove back to the Hacienda; this time I pulled in to the space in front of my room. But I didn't go in, just sat in a flimsy lawn chair on the walk in front of my door and thought about Unit Three—two rooms down. Redgrave's room.

If it was anything like the room I was staying in, it was impersonal, with an impersonal lumpy bed and cheap impersonal prints screwed tight to the wall—as if anyone would want to steal them.

Unit Three seemed to be empty tonight, but there'd be other guests on other nights, people on the way to somewhere and just needing a few hours sleep before facing the highway again. Just people passing through, their minds on some distant destination.

In the predawn silence the presence of the room almost seemed to scream, "Come here!"

I thought about that awhile, sitting and staring at the empty highway and the mercury vapor light on the pole next to the entry drive. Summer bugs kept darting into the hazy aura of the light and slamming into the globe like little kamikaze pilots.

The sound of a car engine grew slowly louder in the distance; a soft light spread on the horizon, popping into sudden brightness as the car crested a gentle rise. The car flashed by with a whoosh of noise and then lights and sound grew dimmer until they vanished around a distant curve.

The bugs kept fruitlessly attacking the light. And the room two doors down kept looming.

I looked toward the motel office. It was dark, as was the owner's apartment in the rear. Clyde and Etta had called it a night.

The whole place was as dark as my mood.

After a while another car crested the gentle rise, whooshed by, and dissolved into the night.

I got up and went inside, lay on the bed, and stared at one of the prints screwed into the wall, a picture of a contented Mexican sleeping propped up against a palm tree while his donkey munched on grass nearby. The Mexican's face was obscured by the world's largest sombrero, but he appeared to be sleeping a big sleep.

So was Redgrave.

I threw one of my socks at the picture; it hit the donkey but he didn't seem to care. The Mexican didn't wake up, either.

And I wasn't sleeping any kind of sleep. So I got up and slipped into my shoes, took a credit card out of my wallet, and went outside. I walked a few feet into the parking lot next to the Jeep and looked back at my room. The curtain was heavy and opaque; no light at all showed from the room even though I'd left two lights on inside.

I padded softly down the walk until I got to the door of the room where Redgrave had died.

I took another look around, then slipped the edge of the

credit card into the little space between the lock and the door jamb. I put gentle pressure on the knob and fiddled with the card. It took me two swipes before the knob turned in my hand and the door swung inward.

I stepped into the room, pulled the door shut, and stood still in the darkness. The air was heavy; an underlying odor of mildew and stale cigarettes hung like something tangible. And I might have sniffed a trace of a lost dream or a squalid sweaty interlude.

I reached behind me and felt along the wall until I touched the light switch. I flipped it upward and harsh light from an overhead bulb filled the room.

I looked around. What a godforsaken place to die. The walls were a faded and splotchy mustard color. The prints were even worse than the ones in mine—a seashore scene that could have been a paint-by-numbers job, and another Mexican, this one grinning and strumming a guitar while a gaudy lady in black sequins whirled in front of him. It was done on black velvet.

No phone, no clock, no television—no lifeline to the outside world.

A thin, flower-patterned spread neatly covered the bed. Two aqua-blue vinyl chairs were on either side of a round Formica table with a lamp pole sticking out of its center. The carpet was brown and riddled with cigarette burns.

No blood, no body, no smoking gun, nothing to suggest that anything had ever happened to disturb the impersonal innocence of the drab little room.

I got down to business.

After half an hour I knew the room well. I'd found dust motes, a tampon wrapper, thirty-seven cents in change, and more dust motes. Under the nightstand I'd found a dirty white sock, a pair of women's bikini underwear, and a dead mouse. A *Reader's Digest* somehow had ended up in the bottom of the toilet tank. There were eight pieces of rock-hard gum stuck to the back of the headboard, and a rusty disposable razor in the medicine cabinet.

There was nothing to suggest Redgrave had ever been in the room, much less died there. There was only emptiness, and those few insignificant remembrances of former passers-through.

Right, I thought forlornly. Conduct a felony breaking and entering of the crime scene itself and can't even find one little clue. Nothing. Zilch. Nada.

Some detective.

Walker Redgrave had chosen to stay here, he had chosen to die here—if in fact it was a choice. Why, and why? Easy questions to ask. The journal of Redgrave's stay in Steinhatchee was filled with blank pages.

I turned off the light, stuck my head out the door, and peered around. Nothing had changed. The night was as still as an empty cathedral. I stepped out of the room and quietly closed the door behind me. Just then another vehicle crested the rise, going fast. It was a pickup truck. I pushed myself back against the wall as the truck roared by, headlights slicing the night. I caught a glimpse of the driver—a man wearing a straw hat, staring ahead. There were fishing poles sticking out of the truck's bed.

I waited until the truck was beyond the curve in the road. Then I shepherded my rapidly beating heart back to my room. I undressed, said goodnight to the Mexican, and got in bed.

When the sun came the Mexican was peacefully sleeping. That made one of us.

14

THE POUNDING WASN'T in my head, I realized finally. There was a voice going along with it.

"Wake up, Mr. Cole, it's Clyde, the owner."

I shook off the fitful sleep I'd been wrestling with. "Just a minute," I said. Actually, that's what I tried to say. It came out, "Jussamint" in a hoarse whisper. I got up and lurched toward the door.

I pulled the door open as far as the chain lock would allow and came eyeball to eyeball with Clyde. His eyeball was winning, but it wasn't fair; he had the bright morning sunlight backing him up. He was grinning with the fresh exuberance of a man who liked the morning time. I hated him for that.

"Good morning, Mr. Cole, and a beautiful morning it is," he said. "I hate to disturb a guest but you have a phone call. You can take it in the office."

He went away down the walk whistling. I gave him my best steely-eyed stare and slammed the door. Take that, Clyde.

I pulled on my jeans and a T-shirt and walked to the office. The phone receiver was off its hook, lying on the counter.

"Hello?" My voice was nearly human. But the cobwebs spun by a sleepless night were there, clustered behind my eyes.

"Cecil Stubbs here. How are you this morning?" he said in a cheerful voice.

"Who knows?" I said. "Listen, is the whole town filled with morning people?"

"Irritating, ain't it?" He laughed. "Actually, I've been up

since five. That was when Deputy Hirst called me after he saw you sneaking out of Redgrave's room at the motel."

"The pickup truck?"

"Hirst loves to fish, goes just about every morning, that's when the bass love to hit those topwater Rapalas. But you bein' here to fish, I don't have to tell you that. Why'nt you come on down and we'll talk about your sleepwalking."

When I got to Stubbs's office he was propped up in the same position as before, reading another tabloid. He gave me a passing glance and pointed at one of the hard-backed chairs.

"Good morning, Deputy Stubbs, sir," I said in my most polite voice. He ignored that.

"Lookee here," he said, stabbing a finger at the tabloid. "Some guy caught a twenty-seven-pound grasshopper. Here's a picture to prove it. I bet that thing'd look great mounted on the wall over his fireplace." He grinned at me for just a moment, then the grin went away and he slammed the paper down on his desk.

"Would you mind telling me just what you're doing in the middle of the night committing a felony B and E in my jurisdiction?"

"Investigating?" I said hopefully.

"Oh, excuse me. Investigating. I should have known."

He leaned over the desk and looked at me. His eyes were not friendly.

"In a rat's behind you were investigating," he said. "You were screwing up is what you were doing."

He looked at me a little longer, for effect. "And, mister big city private eye, what did you find during the course of your, ah, investigation?"

"I found a dead mouse under the nightstand," I said.

"That's it! You've solved it. We country bumpkins were wrong. The mouse killed Redgrave, but then he was filled with remorse, so he crawled under the nightstand and suffocated himself with a dustball. It's a murder-suicide if I ever saw one."

"I didn't touch the mouse."

"Thank God for that. But the question is, who does the autopsy, the coroner or the vet works over at animal control in Perry?"

Stubbs leaned even farther over the desk, which made a deep crease in his belly. His voice got soft.

"Mr. Cole, let's cut the crap. I told you I don't mind you nosing around here on your wild goose chase. I told you if you found something to come and tell me. I did not give you permission to break the law."

"Look," I said. "I'm sorry for that. I was out of bounds. I'm frustrated. I haven't found anything that contradicts your investigation—nothing at all. But I can't shake this feeling that it might not have been a suicide. That's all I have is a hunch. But over the years my hunches have turned out to be right more often than not. Until I can shake this feeling I'm going to keep looking around."

"Look but don't touch," Stubbs said. "I'm not gonna be accused of runnin' you out of town 'cause I got somethin' to hide. But I have a feeling you're gonna give me plenty of good reasons to send you packin'. So watch your step. One more screwup like last night and you aren't out of town, you're in my jail. Understand?"

"Yessir," I said. "I'm sorry."

Stubbs picked up the tabloid. "I already knew about the mouse," he said. "I just forgot to tell the maid."

15

By the time I left Stubbs, it was ten o'clock and the sun was beginning its daily summer siege.

I stopped for late breakfast and more coffee—a lot more coffee. Then I drove out the county road that dead-ended at the shore. There were no clues there that I could see. But how would I know? I never was much good at detecting on two hours of ragged sleep. So I drove back to the Hacienda Court, pulled the light-tight drapes together, and lay for a while in the artificial darkness.

But sleep wouldn't come, only the fractured thoughts of partial consciousness. This was the kind of rest that made you need more rest.

After a couple of hours I gave up and wandered outside. The sudden afternoon heat hit me hard in the face. I stopped by the ice machine, grabbed a couple of cubes, and popped them in my mouth, took another one and rubbed it on the back of my neck, feeling the cold water run down my back.

Still sucking on the ice, I made my way back to the office. Clyde was behind the desk, watching a Braves-Mets game on the Atlanta cable station.

"Braves winning?" I asked. Clyde nodded as if I'd spoken a universal truth. The truth was, the Braves had been bad for a lot of years, until a couple of seasons ago. Worst one year to first the next, two trips to the World Series. Sold-out crowds. Ted Turner and Jane Fonda sitting behind the dugout doing the tomahawk chop. Amazing how quickly we forget—or remember again.

"They are playin' the Amazin' Mets," Clyde said. I looked at the screen. Glavine whipped a looping curve that caught Vince Coleman looking. Third strike, third out, end of inning.

"Ya know, the Braves used to be bad, but the Mets . . ." Clyde let the sentence hang. "Grizzard said once that Ted oughtta apologize for the Braves. But Ted did something else—he built a winner. The Mets, they're headed back to the glory days of Casey Stengel."

"What goes around comes around," I said, as Gant slapped a sharp grounder down the right field line that went through the first baseman's legs, allowing Gant to go into second standing up. McGriff followed with a huge drive to left that cleared the wall by at least thirty feet. The left fielder didn't even move. The Mets manager headed toward the pitcher's mound. He'd probably be headed home soon to do some fishing and collect the remaining part of his contract.

A new pitcher trotted in from the bullpen. The score graphic dissolved to a beer commercial.

"I hate to interrupt this classic moment in sports," I said, "but I need to know if I've had any messages."

"Well, there was Deputy Stubbs, but you got that already," Clyde said. "You settin' him up as a fishin' buddy?"

I ignored the question. And the curious look. "Were there any other calls?"

"As a matter of fact, there was," Clyde said. He ruffled through some papers on the counter, came up with one, and held it at arm's length. "A Stormy Corbin called." He put the paper down and looked at me. "You're real popular for a short-timer around here," he said. "Don't she work over to the Florida Bar?"

"What's the number?" I asked.

He handed me a piece of paper. There was just her name and a phone number, no message.

Clyde turned his attention back on the game. "Guess I might as well watch the Braves administer the last rites," he said as I left the office.

Back in my room I considered calling Stormy but decided against it. Stormy could wait; she'd been waiting in Steinhatchee for a long time.

I cranked up the air conditioner. The room was almost bearable; at any rate it was twenty degrees cooler than the fearful furnace outside.

Redgrave's papers were stacked on the dresser. I'd been avoiding them too long; reading the dead man's words bothered me more than I would admit. It was a little like peeping into a lovers' bedroom.

But a good peeper peeps. So I began at the top of the Redgrave pile.

At the end of an hour I'd peeped my heart out and sorted the stuff into four neat stacks. One contained random notes he'd made to himself, another consisted of plot ideas and character sketches. There was a fairly large stack of article reprints on the craft of writing, and another consisting of letters to his editor, a Ms. Julie Marsh at St. Albans Press.

Seven letters to Ms. Julie Marsh. Letters about the progress of a novel, or inquiries about advances and royalties. Seven letters over a nine-week period, judging from their dates.

I thought about that. Seven letters in nine weeks. Ms. Julie Marsh probably knew quite a lot about Redgrave's literary activities.

Maybe the answer to why Walker Redgrave was in Steinhatchee wasn't in Steinhatchee. Maybe the answer was in New York. Maybe I ought to visit Ms. Julie Marsh.

It wouldn't hurt. Heck, all I was doing in Steinhatchee was wearing out my welcome and almost getting arrested. And, I was sure, trying to get to New York from Steinhatchee promised to be quite an adventure.

16

THE ROOM HAD more chrome than a 1958 Cadillac. Chrome-and-glass coffee tables, chrome picture frames. I was sitting on a beige couch with chrome legs and armrests. There was a chrome vase on the chrome-and-glass end table. There was a chrome sign that told me not to smoke. I wished I had mirrored sunglasses, to blend in with the scenery.

The receptionist provided dissonance. She was all earth tones—brown tweed jacket, light cotton blouse, a necklace of brightly colored wooden beads, long brown hair that hung straight past her shoulders. She even had a tan. She looked as fresh as spring rain, and there was a dainty little blue flower tattooed on her right wrist. She was reading a copy of *Publishers Weekly*.

She put the magazine down as I approached. "May I help you, sir?" She seemed genuinely pleased to see me. So much for her taste in men, I thought.

"So much for your taste in men," I said.

"Pardon me?" she said, still politely.

"Never mind," I said, resisting a temptation to ask her out on the spot. This was business; she'd just have to go through life not knowing what she'd missed.

Her eyes narrowed just a little, and she tapped her nails on the smooth desktop a couple of times.

"Let me try this again, with a more polite affect," I said. "My name is Bennett Cole. I'm a licensed private investigator from Atlanta, and I have an appointment to see Ms. Julie

Marsh. I'm not armed, by the way, so I hope nothing untoward happens."

"I have a feeling you can't sustain politeness for very long," she said, smiling. She picked up the phone and punched two numbers.

"Julie, there's a private detective named Cole to see you. He says he isn't armed." There was a short pause, then she said, "Yes, tall, too."

She swiveled in her chair and came from behind the desk. "I'll show you back, big fella."

She led me down a long corridor, starkly lit, with office doors on either side. She had outstanding legs.

We came to another reception area—more like a lounge—with several doors opening off it. More chrome, more glass, in this case a sweeping view of midtown Manhattan and the river beyond.

A woman came to one of the doors behind the reception desk. My guide said, "You're on your own, fella," and took her excellent legs away.

"Dr. Cole, I'm Julie Marsh. Come in."

She stood to the side as I entered the office. It wasn't particularly large, and it felt smaller because most available flat surfaces were stacked with paper-filled folders—manuscripts, I assumed.

We sat at an L-shaped pit group in one corner. Forty-eight floors below I could see Fifth Avenue, alive with crawling yellow bugs that darted in all directions. It looked like a distant game of bumper cars.

Julie Marsh tucked her legs under her skirt. She had the sinewy, slightly drawn look of a runner. She wore a muted gray plaid business suit along with white running shoes. She looked slightly breathless.

She caught me staring at her.

"I know," she said. "You thought Redgrave's editor would be perhaps a little, ah, older?"

It was exactly what I was thinking. "Not at all," I said.

"It's okay," she said. "I'm older than I look. And I'm good at my job. I've been with St. Albans for more than ten years, and I worked with Walker on his last five books. I have, you might say, been around." Her last comment seemed to fluster her. "I mean around the publishing business," she added quickly. Julie Marsh worked hard to be taken seriously.

"You came up from Atlanta?" she asked, steering the conversation in another direction.

"From Steinhatchee," I said, "and it wasn't easy. The nearest airport is in Gainesville, about sixty miles away. That's where I called your office from. I waited there about four hours for a commuter flight that took me to Charlotte. I was able to catch a Delta flight that got into LaGuardia about one this morning."

I paused. "But the cab ride to the Algonquin was very relaxing."

She smiled and stood up. "My, my, what an adventure. Would you like some spring water, Dr. Cole? I've just come back from my walk."

She went over to a credenza and poured from a plastic carafe. There was a Vassar diploma hanging on the wall behind the credenza.

"I'll pass," I said. "I don't want to take up too much of your time. I was hoping you could help me on the Redgrave case, I haven't come up with much to go on so far."

She returned to the couch. "Redgrave case," she said. "It makes it seem so impersonal."

"It's not meant to be," I said. "Habit. Keep a distance, you won't get involved, or burned. Actually I liked Walker Redgrave, and his work, a lot."

"I've read your books. Why didn't you keep it up?"

"Couldn't stand staring at a typewriter all day. I much prefer staring at empty doorways and parked cars."

"Spare me the details of a private eye's existence. I've had to edit too many mysteries. How can I help you?"

I filled her in on what I knew so far, which didn't take long. She slipped on a pair of tortoiseshell glasses and listened intently, her eyes steady on me. She nodded a couple of times.

"I went through mountains of his notes, but most of it was old stuff, and I couldn't find anything that had to do with what he was working on when he died. I have a bunch of it in my briefcase, but I honestly can't see how your looking at it would do any good. One thing I did notice, though. There was a lot of correspondence with you. I didn't see anything that jumped out as being significant, but the number of letters got my attention. It appears he communicated with you quite a bit on a variety of matters. You probably know more about his work than anyone else. So I came here."

I gave her my most heartfelt questioning look. I'd learned it from a puppy I once had.

Julie Marsh looked at me. Her look was nothing like a puppy's. She took off her glasses and began absently chewing on one of the earpieces. She leaned forward a little.

"I never knew what he was working on until it was well underway. If he was just working on some preliminary ideas or rough plotting, I wouldn't know anything about it. And I've seen the notes he keeps; nobody but him could really decipher them."

She paused and took a sip of spring water. I looked out the window. A jetliner seemed to hang motionless in the distance. Then it banked sharply and began its steep descent into LaGuardia.

"You said he left a suicide note," she said. "I'd like to see it. Do you have it with you?"

I reached into my briefcase and brought out the photocopy Stubbs had given me. I handed it to her.

She put her glasses back on and read the note, looked out the window for a moment, went back to the note. She didn't hurry.

After a second time through, she took off her glasses again and laid the note in her lap. She looked at me.

"Dr. Cole, here is your clue."

"Clue?" I said idiotically, my voice rising and cracking like an adolescent's. So much for reserved sophistication.

"This may take some explaining," she said, "so bear with me."

She got up and walked over to a file cabinet, opened a drawer, and looked inside. She withdrew a manila folder packed thickly with paper and came back to the couch.

She fished around in the folder, flipped through quite a few pages, and at last took out two pieces of paper. She handed one of them to me.

"That's a page from the draft manuscript of Walker's last book," she said. "You can see some of the notes and comments I've made. What else do you see?"

I looked at the page, neatly printed-out words. I remembered the scene. Julie Marsh's edits were in red ink.

"Most of what you've done are notes in the margin," I said. "There's not many edits to the text itself. It all looks pretty ordinary to me."

"I'm not trying to be coy with you, Dr. Cole. I just want you to see the subtlety of this. Forget about the margin notes. What else?"

I returned my attention to the page. "Well, he misspelled a word, 'occasion.' He spelled it with an extra *s*. You circled it. Other than that the page is pretty neat."

She handed me the other page. Again, it was filled with neatly printed text. Again, there were Julie Marsh's margin comments in red. And again there was a misspelling—"occassion."

I looked up from the paper. Julie Marsh handed me the photocopy of the note. "Dr. Cole, what do you see?"

It didn't take me long. "He used the word—'on the occasion of my death.' " I took a deep breath. "He spelled it correctly."

"Exactly. And it's not a coincidence. Walker Redgrave could spell as well as anybody. And he had a spell check program on his computer. He misspelled certain words on purpose."

"Why would he do that?"

"It was an inside joke between us. It took me a while to catch on when I first started editing his books. Finally I asked him. He laughed and said, 'That way I'll know you actually read all the stuff I turn in.'

"In the six years I've been editing his work, I've never known him to spell that word correctly."

She looked out the window, into the hazy air over Manhattan. "Just a joke," she said quietly to herself.

She turned away from the window and looked at me. Her eyes glittered brightly. "Dr. Cole," she said. "Walker Redgrave was trying to tell us something. This is the first time he's ever spelled that word correctly."

17

M‍y euphoria about the clue in the suicide note plummeted about as fast as the elevator that dropped me at the ground floor. It was a New York elevator; it went down without too much regard for the safety of its occupants. At least I avoided nosebleed. I looked out the doors of the lobby; it was the peak of the afternoon rush hour—thousands of determined people were hurrying for the train or the subway, or desperately hailing cabs.

The spinning doors propelled me out onto the pavement. The August sun beat down mercilessly; it apparently had no idea this wasn't Florida. My uncomfortable summer suit clung damply to me. The skyscrapers offered no appreciable shade and blocked any breeze. Just another New York summer afternoon—hot, fetid, still, and crowded.

I was preoccupied thinking that the evidence Redgrave hadn't killed himself didn't really add anything new; it just confirmed the premise on which I'd been operating. I still had no plan, no particular idea of what to do next.

I pondered my options. I could have high tea at the Plaza on Mrs. Redgrave's money. Or I could go back to the Rose Room at the Algonquin and have a nice liver and onions that would be served, no doubt, by a gruff but polite waiter who would take no notice of the dampness of my suit. I opted for the latter.

That in mind, I walked out toward the curb on Sixth, forgetting for a moment what city I was in. A middle-aged man, well dressed in a gray suit, summer hat, and pigskin briefcase, slammed into me, gave me a look of pure hatred, and pushed me out of his way with the briefcase.

I caromed off the pigskin into the path of a young woman dressed in the severe uniform of the female up-and-comer—herringbone-patterned suit cut severely, white blouse with maroon bow at the throat, and the requisite jogging shoes for the five o'clock marathon.

She didn't break stride, walked into me as if I wasn't there, barely wavered, and kept on going, glassy eyes on some distant vision, probably of being promoted to assistant vice president.

I staggered out of the pedestrian throng and stopped to catch my breath next to a hot dog vendor's cart.

"Been here long, Pilgrim?" the hot dog vendor said. "I been watching your little dance with the locals."

I gave him a quick look. "Alabama?"

"Hattiesburg, Mississippi, by the way of Charlottesville." He flipped up the lid over a vat of steaming wieners. "Even on the basis of that one word, I figure you for Georgia, I'd say Atlanta or maybe Macon, not somewhere too far off the beaten path. Wanna dog?"

"An Atlanta boy'll take a hot dog anytime from a fellow pilgrim," I said. "Mustard and relish."

He went through the motions of stabbing a plump dog and cradling it on a bun, ladling on the mustard, and spooning on a dollop of relish. He reached inside another bin and came out with a cold Pepsi, with drops of condensation clinging to the side of the can.

He handed me the hot dog and Pepsi. "On the house," he said.

I tilted the Pepsi can back and took a long cooling drink. "I appreciate the kindness. What're you doing in New York?"

"Why would any Mississippi hick come to the Big Apple?" he said. "I'm here to study for my doctorate in cultural linguistics at Columbia. Got an assistantship and a stipend. You're gonna ask why with all that I'm out here pushin' a doggie cart. You ever try to live in New York on what educational assistantships pay?" He didn't wait for an answer, this was pure monologue. "I'm forking out over eight hundred a month for a flat that's so small I gotta leave when the rats get home."

I said consoling things about the rats, finished off the dog, and drained the last of the Pepsi. I thanked the vendor and stepped off the curb. There was a huge blaring of horn. The hot dog man grabbed me by the back of my suitcoat and snatched me back onto the sidewalk just as a cab roared by doing at least forty.

He straightened my suit and said, "Pilgrim, remember, when you step off a curb in New York, you're in play."

18

I FOUND DEPUTY Cecil Stubbs in his usual position—leaning back in his chair, feet on the desk, reading a supermarket tabloid. Today he was in brown khakis, precisely creased and starched, and black boots polished to a mirror shine. A badge was pinned on the left breast pocket; on the right sleeve was a patch that read, "Taylor County Sheriff—To Serve and Protect." The fan in the corner pushed air around the room.

I figured I owed Stubbs the courtesy of a call after my New York trip. The trip back had been much the same adventure as going there—cab rides, airport delays, connections on flimsy, noisy commuter planes. I was starting to feel that creeping fatigue that goes with too little sleep and too much frustration.

Stubbs swiveled his head toward me as I came in. "Well, well, if it ain't the big-city detective. You ain't been shot up yet. I hear you been in and outta town. Your cover holdin'?"

"Not very well," I said as I took a seat in the chair in front of the desk. "I probably ought to really go fishing. Or maybe I'll try something different, like not using a cover."

Stubbs labored to an upright position and plopped his heavy boots on the floor. He didn't show any outward reaction to the last remark. He flipped through the tabloid.

"More incredible news," he said. "This week we got a fella was frozen for fifty years in a block of ice and brought back to life. We also got space aliens writin' secret code messages on some man's chest."

He turned the page. "Youch. Guy does a do-it-yourself

vasectomy in his kitchen. And here's a tragic story about some poor little Indian girl has a nest of insects livin' behind her right eye."

"Remarkable," I said. "And, oddly enough, I still haven't seen anything in the newspapers on any of that stuff."

"Liberal wimps are afraid to print the truth. They just want to quote Teddy Kennedy and Jane Fonda."

"There is that," I said. I was waiting for an opening, and I could feel patience slipping away.

Stubbs picked up the tabloid and flipped it open. "Wow. A space alien raped some Mexican's electric broom. Pervert."

That was enough. Suddenly I was sick of sitting in the uncomfortable chair, playing along with the deputy's good-ol'-boy routine, sick of the inertia of the case, sick of Steinhatchee, sick of lack of sleep, sick of everything and everybody involved with closing the Redgrave case as suicide.

I said, "Shut up, Stubbs."

That caught his attention. He carefully folded the paper and placed it on the desk. He took his feet off the chair and faced me.

"This better be good," he said. "Or you'll be sittin' in my jail."

I got up and leaned on his desk.

"I have evidence that Walker Redgrave didn't kill himself," I said.

"Do tell," Stubbs said as if I'd just told him the score of the latest Braves game. "Wanna fill me in?"

I told him about my visit with Redgrave's editor, about the misspelling on the note, about the inside joke. About my confidence that there was more than suicide involved in the writer's death.

When I finished I felt a little out of breath. I sat down.

"So?" Stubbs said in the same placid voice.

That brought me back out of my chair.

"So? So you don't care about my little clue? So you don't care how Redgrave died, as long as it doesn't rock your lazy little boat? So you threaten me with jail if I'm not appropriately polite? You think I care, Stubbs? You think I give a rat's rump whether I'm threatened by some two-bit deputy sheriff in some backwater town? Listen, I've been threatened by big-city cops a lot tougher than you—" That wasn't true, but why ruin the effect?

"Go ahead," I said. "Throw me in jail, see what happens. You'll have a whole bunch of boys from Atlanta come storming down here you won't want to see." That wasn't true either, but I'd gone too far to stop.

I gripped the edge of the desk and leaned close to the deputy. "You don't want to hear the truth, I'll have your badge. I'll have your butt. I'll have this town."

I walked over and turned off the fan. "Don't you ever sweat?" I yelled. Stubbs just sat in the chair looking at me. I grabbed the tabloid off the desk, crumpled it up in my hands and threw it on the floor.

"Elvis is dead," I yelled. Shaking, I sat back down in the hard chair. The crumpled newspaper slowly opened, like a flower.

Stubbs didn't say anything for a long time. Then he got up and walked over to the fan, turned it on. The blades began to turn and the air stirred, just a little, in the room. Stubbs bent over and picked up the tabloid. He placed it on the desk and smoothed it out, spreading the crumpled ridges. Then he sat down.

"My, my, he do have a temper," he said. He grabbed a pencil and aimed it at me, as if it were a little pistol.

"Listen to me, *Dr.* Cole. Yeah, I been checkin' on you, I'm probably not as stupid as you think I am. I know a lot about you. I know you're a two-bit investigator with a big-shot degree and no cases worth talkin' about. I also know you're reasonably honest, and you know a lot less about the detective business than you think you do. And I don't know any big-city cops who think you're important enough to bother roughing up."

Stubbs sighed, laid the pencil on the desk, and looked around the room. He still hadn't broken a sweat; the khakis looked pristine.

He picked the pencil up and tapped it absently on the desk. "Let me make my position clear," he said. "I'm sworn to protect the law in Taylor County, Florida. I also gotta live in Taylor County, Florida. I grew up here, my daddy was a deputy sheriff. His daddy was a moonshiner. I got a brother did time for gator poachin'.

"The law here isn't the same as Atlanta, or most any other place. We don't like strangers. We like to be left alone. Folks don't like anyone, especially the law, messin' with their business.

"Which leaves me in a somewhat precarious situation. The law here doesn't go all the way; there's things happen in the woods and the swamps'll make your hair stand on end. Dope. Killin'. Greed. Revenge. Some people don't even declare all their income for tax purposes.

"I'm in charge of the substation here. I got one man. We got nine deputies total in the county. Five of 'em graduated from high school. The sheriff's more interested in gettin' elected than enforcing the law. We got hundreds of miles of shoreline. It's even worse down in Dixie—they got seven deputies total and a highway runs into the middle of nowhere at the coast where dope smugglers land their planes. The drug guys out of Tallahassee and the Marine Patrol are no help at all. They're understaffed, underpaid, and overwhelmed.

"In the woods and the swamps, Dr. Cole, people for the most part do what they want. Sometimes what they do is illegal. I can't stop that. All I can do is see that innocent folk don't get caught up in it. If Redgrave was an innocent folk there's something needs to be done. But I've gone as far as I can. My case is closed."

Stubbs got up from behind his desk and walked over to the window. He adjusted the direction of the fan, though he was still dry—the man didn't have sweat glands. He looked back at me.

"I do care. If Redgrave didn't kill himself I want to know the truth. I just have to be careful how I find out the truth, 'cause I also want to keep my job and not be taken into the swamps and shot, not necessarily in that order.

"So you say that Walker Redgrave came into our wonderful little town and for some reason shot himself in the head, but it wasn't suicide. Fine, you go find out. Maybe you can get away with some things I can't.

"Now go on, get out of here and be glad you ain't in a cell." He gave me a little smile. "And you're lucky I appreciate a dick with a backbone. Now git. And the same advice as before stands—don't get shot, and if you do, see if you can do it in Dixie County. They need the business."

I got to the door and looked back at Stubbs. He had picked up the newspaper and was staring at the front page, but his gaze and his thoughts seemed far away. His fingers stroked at the crumpled newsprint. He seemed to draw inward. Then he slapped the paper down on the desk; the pencil went skidding onto the floor.

"Elvis *is* dead," he said. "I wonder how it really happened." He looked at me. "Maybe you can find out, unless you're busy with something else. See you around."

I know a dismissal when I hear one. I left before I got myself in more trouble.

But the meeting had been a turning point, in my relationship with Stubbs, and my relationship with the case.

I'd walked into the sheriff's substation as Bennett Cole, fisherman on holiday. I walked out as Bennett Cole, licensed private investigator from Atlanta, looking into a celebrity murder. I was sure that would complicate my life in Steinhatchee. I wasn't wrong.

19

I GOT BACK to the motel just as Clyde was putting away his pool-cleaning equipment. If he was suspicious of my odd comings and goings, he didn't show it.

I waved at him. "Any calls?" I asked.

"Stormy Corbin—again. And again. You must be cuttin' a wide swath through this town."

I didn't respond to that; just gave him my best knowing smirk and headed to the pay phone near the road, one of those freestanding, fully enclosed contraptions. It was like stepping into a convection oven.

I dialed a number and opened the door. Just then a tractor-trailer rig loaded with cows pulled to a stop at the shoulder of the road and the driver jumped out and headed toward the motel office.

The cows began to moo. Lisa Carmichael answered the phone. "Hello," she said.

A dozen cows said, "Moo." Loudly.

There was a long silence on her end of the line. I let the cows do the talking on my end. It was too good to pass up.

Finally she said, "This can only be you, Cole. Is this your idea of an obscene phone call?"

"Moo to you, cupcake," I said. The driver swung back into the cab of his rig, fired up the motor, and began to slowly pull out onto the blacktop.

"Hold on," I said. "My backup singers are leaving on the bus."

"This better be good," Lisa Carmichael said. "I've got a

class that meets in thirty minutes. Where are you? If those cows were in your apartment, I'm not coming over to help you clean up." She was starting to giggle. "What gives, Cole? You never call to chitchat, and you don't often call when you're surrounded by so much bovine beauty. What do you want with little ol' me? And, by the way, where are you?"

"Steinhatchee, Florida," I said quickly, as if everybody knew where Steinhatchee was. "Now here's the deal. I need to pick your brain on a case I'm working. I have a feeling I'm about to make a real nuisance of myself and probably get beat up or shot at. I'd like to have a plan while that's going on.

"Seriously," I said. "I do need someone to bounce some things off. I don't have any leads, just a lot of suspicions and hunches. Care to let me probe the depths of your fertile mind in exchange for a night or two at a beautiful Florida resort, my treat, including airfare?" I didn't mention that Mrs. Redgrave would be picking up my treat.

"In a place called Steinhatchee?" She sounded a little alarmed.

"God forbid. Cancel your class, you can do that, you're tenured. Get a flight to Tampa. That'll be easy, there's plenty of flights. When you land, get a cab and ask them to take you over to the Gulf beaches, a place called the Tides. You can be there by tonight if you start now. I'll have a room reserved for you."

"I'll never know why I agree to this foolishness," she said and hung up.

Three hours on U.S. 19 got me to within five miles of the Tides. Then snowbird gridlock set in, and I poked along Gulf Boulevard behind a car with Minnesota plates going fifteen miles an hour. The driver, a white-haired woman who could barely see over the steering wheel, kept riding her brake, causing the brake lights to blink in some inscrutable code only Northerners know.

It was after dark when I pulled into the circular driveway of the motel.

The Tides Motel and Bath Club is a little bit of authentic Florida amid the faceless architecture that has plagued the state recently.

I've stayed at Tides a lot over the years. It was built in the 1920s, and sprawls along more than a thousand feet of white-sand beach. It's old enough to be somewhat seedy—and to have a history. It's said that Joe DiMaggio and Marilyn Monroe honeymooned here.

I wouldn't say the Tides has fallen on hard times; it's still packed with tourists during the season. If you look close, though, you can see the effect of years of relentless assault by wind and water—peeling paint, sagging boards, cracks in the windowpanes, rusty air conditioners.

But the place has class—a class the glass-and-cement highrises can never equal.

I walked into the high-ceilinged lobby. A gentle breeze came in an open door on the sea side—there's no air-conditioning in the lobby. A canary in a hanging cage was singing merrily.

And as usual, behind the desk was my compatriot Billy Harvel.

"Hoowww 'bout then Dawgs," he hollered when he saw me.

"Billy, you know they went three and eight last year. I wouldn't be broadcasting my affiliation too loudly."

Billy's a University of Georgia graduate who got off the fast track a few years ago and moved to the beach. He works the desk at the Tides and hangs out at waterfront bars. It's a low-pay, low-stress life. There are times when I envy Billy's life a lot. I met him about four years ago, when I started making regular visits to the Tides.

"Things haven't been the same since Dooley quit," Billy said as he got me the key to my cottage.

"Billy, you know more than half of Dooley's players never graduated," I said.

"Details, details. What do you want, championship teams or kids who actually learn something?"

"At Notre Dame, they combine the two."

"Please, don't say that name in my presence—you know we don't allow profanity here. Take your key and go away until you can talk civil."

"I hear the University of Florida is going to be a real powerhouse this year," I said as I turned toward the door.

I ducked just in time to avoid the ballpoint pen Billy launched in my direction, and was out the door before he could reload.

I got a one-bedroom apartment overlooking the Gulf. I reserved the one next door for Lisa. I parked the Jeep, and got out my overnight bag and the briefcase containing Redgrave's papers. The beach here is a world apart from Taylor County; there are vast expanses of white and sea oats, throngs of sun worshipers. It is still beautiful, but, like so much of Florida, it is dying, slowly being choked to death by developers and erosion and roads and shopping centers. Maybe I should get a bumper sticker that says "Pave the Beaches" and slap it on the Jeep. Make Hutchins real popular with the university crowd.

I sat on the patio and looked out at the darkened gulf. I could see the lights of a cruise ship on the horizon, probably one of those one-day gambling cruises out beyond the three-mile limit. Senior citizens taking a few dollars they'd saved and throwing it at the tables and games, never to be seen again. Might as well as throw it in the water, I thought.

I looked down the beach. So far I'd used my expense account to stay in a classy cottage in Captiva, a Midtown hotel in New York, a quaint anachronism in Steinhatchee, and now this— one of my favorite places in the South to be. Spending Mrs. Redgrave's money, and not solving any crimes at all.

I hadn't reported in; what was I going to report on, the quality of my accommodations?

I'd about decided to update my vita and look for a teaching job when I heard a knock at the back door.

"Door's unlocked," I yelled through the apartment, and went back to looking at the sea.

I heard the sounds of bags being dropped. Then Lisa Carmichael stuck her head around the open door on the gulf side.

"Your courtesy is as finely honed as ever," Lisa said. I sat in the chair and gave her a morose look.

"Not fair," she said, sitting down in the chair next to mine. "Where's the happy guy who was mooing at me so affectionately? Give you a few hours at the beach and you look like you want to take a one-way swim in the ocean."

"I would," I said, "but I'd probably screw it up." I worked up a semblance of a smile. "I'm not serious about that."

"So Cole wants to embrace life, but life isn't embracing him. What's up?"

I looked at the sea—nothing there but melancholy waves and a deep blackness. I stood up.

"I've spent my client's money on the best resorts in Florida and the best hotels in New York. I might as well spend some more on good food with a good friend." I reached down and grabbed her hand, gently pulling her to her feet.

She rose up—she was nearly as tall as I was—and gave me a little peck on the cheek. "Shucks, massa, this lil ol' colored gal do 'ppreciate yo lookin' afa her."

The burlesque of her parody made me laugh in spite of my melancholy.

"Dr. Carmichael, you're smarter than all the white people I know, and more successful than most of them. But I love it when you bow and scrape."

"Well, you've seen the last of it. Let's eat somewhere real nice, some place they wouldn't have let me in twenty years ago. We can sit around and be smug."

20

WE WALKED ALONG the beach about a quarter mile to a restaurant that served excellent fresh seafood, where shorts and T-shirts were the usual dress and plastic lobsters hung in netting on the walls.

My improved mood was fleeting. I couldn't shake the bleakness that seemed to overwhelm me. Hundreds of seagulls, pecking for tasty sand creatures, scattered and took flight as we approached; they veered in swooping arcs and settled again behind us, cawing and shrieking.

"Some dick," I muttered as we kicked along in the sand.

She stopped abruptly and turned to face me. Her face was silhouetted against the distant lights from the condos and the streetlamps.

"Stop whining, Cole," she said angrily. "Stop feeling sorry for yourself. Either give up or go to work. You're a detective—you think that's easy? You think the bad guys are going to see you coming and fall all over themselves confessing?

"Quit or don't quit," she said, "but stop shuffling around in the sand feeling sorry for yourself."

Her words stung me. I realized that my extreme desire to make headway in the case was having the opposite effect, bogging me down. I was too emotionally involved. And, I was embarrassed to admit, she was right, I had been whining and shuffling.

The embarrassment was compounded because of the person I was with.

Lisa Carmichael hadn't given up, ever. And there had been lots of reasons, lots of opportunities, lots of times it would have been easy to.

She was what she had made herself—a strong-willed, intelligent woman. She also was a product of her environment—growing up black and poor in the worst of Macon's ghettos.

Her father did time at Starke for Murder One. The person he'd killed had been her mother. She'd been raised by an aunt who believed "colored folk" ought to know their own place.

She left her aunt's house when she was sixteen, ran to Atlanta, lied about her age, and got a job in a laundry. Nights she went to school and got her high school diploma, used it to get into junior college.

There she found her niche. She was good—good at the books, good at the exams, good at the politics, good at the scholarships. She'd told me she had used her color to get ahead, but despised herself when she did so.

She took a doctorate from Yale and got a job at Emory, teaching in the sociology department as an adjunct lecturer.

But the subtle stigma of being a black woman in Georgia never went completely away.

She'd told me how she'd been at an Atlanta hotel for a convention and decided to wear a slinky outfit for the evening. Two men propositioned her in the lobby bar; they couldn't believe she'd be anything but a hooker.

She'd told me how she'd gotten anonymous notes in her faculty mail box after she was promoted to associate professor, accusing her—in graphic language—of sleeping with the chairman; how else could a *black* girl get ahead?

She'd told me how the dean got a little tipsy at a faculty Christmas party and, in slurred words, told her "how good it was to have such a pretty minority, and smart, too."

She was more than that, much more. She was smart, she was aggressive, she was published, she was successful.

She'd also told me how she took antidepressants and went through periods when she felt hopeless, defeated, and worthless. Somehow, hearing that made her seem more human to me.

It also didn't get in the way of her upward mobility. Now she was a full professor, and her interest in criminal behavior—she said the ghetto had inspired that—had led her to the criminal justice department. She now was director of a research division that focused on the motives. And she was an often-quoted expert witness at some of the biggest criminal trials in Georgia.

And she was my friend. Perhaps that was the biggest reason the words hurt.

I looked at her a long time. The gulls circled and shrieked. "Let's eat," I said above the cacophony. "I've got an investigation to get going on."

21

During most of the meal neither of us acknowledged the reason I'd asked her to come; I knew we'd get to it, she knew as well. For now, just for a little while, there wasn't a rush.

We moved easily into relaxed conversation, caught up on things, the way people do who are good friends but don't see each other very often.

That's the way it was with Lisa and me. I might not have any contact with her for months, but I'd be able to call her in the middle of the night, wake her up, and ask her to meet me at the Waffle House on Peachtree. And she'd come without hesitation or question. And she knew I'd do the same for her.

Maybe it was the knowing, the knowledge that there was a friend there, that most of the time was all we needed.

And there were the times one of us needed more—like now. The conversation was like a tonic to me. I was just about back to my old self, which Lisa pointed out was "pretty awful to put up with."

About halfway through the main course, the people at the next table began to heat up their language. They were drinking wine and smoking cigarettes and doing some one-upmanship on the decibel level.

A jowly, florid man with a veiny nose was leading the charge, lacing almost every sentence with profanity. He was wearing one of those tight-fitting Cuban-style pastel shirts with lots of buttons on the sleeves and pockets.

Lisa saw me staring at him.

"Oh no, Cole, don't start," she said under her breath.

I saw the man look our way, clearly heard him say "nigger."

I reached into my coat pocket, took out my notebook, tore out a page, and began scribbling a note.

Lisa covered her face with her hands. "Now I remember why I can't take you anywhere," she said. "This ought to be good."

I motioned for the waitress, handed her the note, and asked that she deliver it to the jowly man.

"Sure, sir. Shall I tell him who it's from?"

"He'll figure it out."

The waitress walked over to the table and handed the man the note. He glanced at it, still talking, then stopped midsentence. His eyes bulged open like a guppy. The other three people stared at him. He looked up and scanned the room.

Then he saw me. Our eyes met; I grinned at him and gave a little fluttering wave.

I turned to Lisa. "I don't think the gentleman will be intruding on our quiet little chat anymore."

"No, I wouldn't think so," she said.

The waitress cleared the dishes and we ordered dessert. The jowly man was long gone; he'd exited about thirty seconds after he'd gotten my note. The others at his table had been left to settle the tab. The waitress brought our pie and coffee.

"I'm investigating the death of Walker Redgrave," I said.

"The writer who committed suicide?" Lisa said with polite interest, taking a bite of pie. Then the fork stopped abruptly in midrise and she looked horrified.

"Oh my God, Cole, I'm sorry. He was your hero. You wrote books about him." She put the fork down; it missed the plate by three inches. "I should have called. It never occurred to me. I was swamped with summer session exams and—"

"Stop, it's okay," I said. "I wouldn't have been there anyway. I've been on the road for the past, how long has it been—since right after he died. I'm road-weary and the case has me buffaloed. The best thing you can do for me is listen. So listen."

She sat silently while I filled her in on the details of Redgrave's death, how I'd been hired, and what I'd done so far. All of that didn't take long.

"So I've got a locked-room suicide in a small-time town, a note with a clue that I believe but the law would laugh at, and a bad feeling about the whole thing. Help."

Lisa nodded her head up and down, slowly, thinking. She squinted her eyes while she thought. It made her look cute, but I'd never tell her; I didn't think she was the type of who'd consider cute a compliment.

"So we start with your hypothesis and begin to construct a scenario," she said. "Hypothesis: He didn't kill himself. Do you think he pulled the trigger?"

"Every shred of evidence points to the fact that he did."

"You're not answering the question. Did he pull the trigger?"

"I don't know," I said. "I don't know. He must have, and that makes it suicide."

"Not so fast," she said. "Let's assume he did pull the trigger; in light of the overwhelming evidence it's likely he did anyway, so our working hypothesis begins with these two premises: He didn't commit suicide, and he did pull the trigger. Is there anything, any detail you found out that doesn't fit, or seems out of place?" Lisa asked.

"You've hit on something that bothered me, but I brushed it off. It certainly didn't bother the cops. Now it seems real important. To answer your question: Yes, there was something that didn't fit. There was only one bullet in his gun; Stubbs mentioned that when I first talked to him. I didn't think much of it myself at the time, but I've gotten curious about that. Why would a man only have one bullet in his gun? Where were the other bullets?"

"It only takes one bullet to kill yourself," Lisa said. "In fact, if his only purpose in having the gun at all was to do that, he might not even think to load more bullets into the gun. But let's come up with something that supports my intuition that this particular detail is unusual. Let's come up with a reason there was only one bullet in the gun, and make it support our hypothesis. I don't have an answer. You help me, now."

"Aha," I said. "It would make the gun much more ineffective as a weapon for his own defense. Especially if he's outmanned."

I was starting to feel a tense anticipation that we might actually be on to something. "The gun was a revolver," I said. "Unless you know your gun real well, it takes a lot of thought to put the bullet in the correct chamber. I can't even tell you which direction the cylinder on mine rotates. And I can't believe a person would have the nerve to just put a bullet in and keep pulling the trigger until it fired."

"Does seem odd," Lisa said. "But people who kill themselves do all sorts of odd things."

"That's not all," I said, but I didn't know where that was leading me. "I've read the police report. The bullet concerns me, but I have the vague sense that there's something else. Nothing else jumps out at me as being odd, but there's something there. Like it's there, on the edge of my consciousness, hovering around. When I try to think, it just evaporates."

"That's the problem. You're attacking it head-on. Let it lie, and it might crystallize."

The waitress hovered on the periphery of my vision. Lisa seemed oblivious to her presence. "Sir, would you like something else?" Her tone indicated it wasn't the first time she'd said it.

"If you don't get an answer the first time," I said, "that's the answer."

She looked at me as if I'd said something nasty and huffed away.

"Tip went down," I said.

"Who cares?" Lisa said. "So where does all this lead

us?" She looked at me over her coffee, hinted at a smile. "Inevitably."

"Extenuating circumstances," I said.

She looked at me as if I were one of her freshmen. "Well of course. But that's too vague. Try again."

I tried to narrow the focus; why was it so hard to think? "Extenuating circumstances—a man puts one bullet in his gun, pulls the trigger, he kills himself, yet it's not suicide. If you don't treat that as a contradiction, what's left?"

The light bulb went on. "Duress," I said.

"Precisely," she said, pointing her fork at me. Some gooey pie slid off, slightly blunting the effect.

"He pulled the trigger," she said, "because he was left with no alternative. He had no choice. So how might that have happened? What kind of pressure could have been brought to bear to force him to do such a thing?"

"Now that we've gotten this far, it's easy to make it plausible," I said. "He would have been threatened with alternatives that were less palatable than shooting himself. Threats of horrible torture, threats to his loved ones, who knows? If he truly believed those threats were going to be carried out, and if he believed he was going to die anyway, he might have seen the wisdom, so to speak, of pulling the trigger. He'd have been forced to write a suicide note, one that would have seemed plausible—short, vague. And he'd have, in the last moments, come up with that feeble little clue. What a straw to grasp at."

"It would have had to have been incredible pressure," she said. "And he would have no idea if these people would have carried out their threats after he died."

"At that point, any faint hope is better than none at all," I said. "And besides, what choice did he really have?"

"What torment that man must have experienced," Lisa said.

"There are some really evil people in this world, Dr. Carmichael," I said.

"Sometimes I forget," she said, "up there in academe."

"So now we just have one little problem to solve," I said.

Lisa was clearly proud of having given validity to her "working hypothesis," as she called it.

"What's that," she said.

"Who did it?" I said.

"And what was the threat?" she added.

22

"All right, Dr. Carmichael, what kind of person would kill in the manner we've described?" We were back on the deck chairs at the Tides, watching the waves, drinking coffee out of paper cups we'd brought from the restaurant, and passing a bag of potato chips back and forth. Lisa had changed into some kind of tie-dyed, flowing garment that she proudly called a "BLT—Big Loose Thing. They're all the rage right now, hide every bodily imperfection."

"Stop the academic crap, Cole," Lisa said. "I'm off work and out of town. What you mean is, 'what kind of sick weirdo would kill a man like that?'"

"Yeah," I said. "There's something here that sets this guy apart from your average killer. There's that element of—of—sport. Not that he killed for sport, but that the killing itself was a sporting event."

She looked at me and raised her eyebrows. That made her look cute, too. Just about everything Lisa did made her look cute. "By the way, you say 'guy' but it's just as likely the killer could be a woman. Don't jump to conclusions. But man or woman, we're definitely dealing with a personality type here."

A couple walked by along the beach holding hands. They looked at us, their gazes lingering a shade too long. In the South, it still happens when people of different races engage in emotional proximity. The couple kept going. We'd be subject for a little juicy speculation.

Lisa said, "We're talking about a very specific spectrum of personality disorders."

"Now you're the professor," I said.

"What I mean is, there ain't a lot of dudes that bad and that out of whack," she said. "So go to Steinhatchee, find the baddest and wackiest dudes. Problem is, they might be accountants by day, have wives and kids, go to the Elks Lodge."

"Does make my job a little more difficult," I said. "You're a criminologist; you give me some profiles, what motivates somebody like we're talking about."

"You're going to make me work, aren't you?" she said. "Okay, I've had to do some research for testimony on quite a number of antisocial or sociopathic personalities—that's really what we're talking about, here."

She took on that inward, reflective look, the academic brain kicking in. She began talking, as if to herself.

"Antisocial or sociopathic personality. It's a character disorder, as opposed to neurotic or psychotic behavior, and marked by deeply ingrained maladaptive patterns of behavior and an egocentrically unself-critical cognitive orientation." She glanced up. "Sorry. That was a bit much, even for me."

"It's okay, I had no idea what you meant," I said. "Do continue."

"This type of disorder," she said, "is marked by a deficiency of conscience—that's important—and a proclivity to lying and insincerity." She looked at me. "You with me so far?"

"Reminds me of an old girlfriend," I said.

"You never know," she said. "A sociopath will do what appears most expedient in a given situation, without regard for others. He'll make decisions on what will be best for him, what will give him pleasure, what will ease his pain. Now that sounds like most of us, but what is missing in the sociopath is that regard for the other person or the larger context of right and wrong. Killing, for example, can become the most expedient thing to do in a given situation, so he'll kill—without conscience or remorse."

"So if he has to kill someone, or wants to, he'll do it and not think much about it later?"

"He may not give it any thought at all," Lisa said. "If it

gives him pleasure to kill, he'll kill. If it is exciting to kill in the manner we've talked about, he'll kill that way.

"He or she is truly antisocial, though often appearing to function well in society. You're looking for a person with a major psychological component missing. The sociopath doesn't reject morality; he simply isn't interested in morality. This person, if the sociopathic tendencies are turned toward violence, can be a very dangerous person indeed."

"You sure know how to cheer a poor detective's day," I said. "I thought maybe I'd find a suspect like a meek kindergarten teacher."

"Don't laugh. Your meek teacher could be a cold-blooded killer underneath. You know that. The problem is, there's a lot of sociopaths out there, and they look as normal as you and me." She looked at me. "Well, maybe not you."

The swirling gulls had come in over the beach. I took a few potato chips and tossed them into the air. The birds cawed and snagged them in flight; the pieces that landed were snapped off by birds swooping inches above the sand.

A seagull landed on the nearby balcony railing. He had his dinner, a big chip he could barely keep in his mouth. He sat for a while, his head perched sideways in that perpetual listening pose, trying to down the chip. Then about ten other gulls came sailing out of the night, swooped down upon him. He took flight, the chip fell from his mouth, and the other birds descended to fight for it.

"It seems if I can put the right kind of pressure on the right kind of places, something might break," I said. "Of course, that might be me, when the bad guys get wind of what I'm up to."

We both sat quietly for a while.

"I have no idea where to start," I said. "The only thing I can think of is make myself some kind of Judas Goat, let them come to me. Doesn't sound like too much fun, does it?"

"It'd help if you could reconstruct Redgrave's movements in Steinhatchee," Lisa said.

"No kidding," I said with some sarcasm. "See those

papers back there?" I pointed through the open door to the four stacks on the living room table. "That's just a little bit of what I've gone through. He's got notes about everything in the world, scattered in offices in two states. And not a thing about any current project that would involve Steinhatchee. His editor has no idea, either."

The talk drifted into more idle speculation about the case, and eventually into other subjects. Lisa was starting to yawn. She pulled herself out of her chair, stretched, and said she'd be right back.

"I gotta check something," she said, "see how long I can stay here before I have to go back."

She headed toward her apartment. I listened to the breakers and the sounds of the gulls, more distant now that they'd moved out to sea.

Lisa came back carrying a thick black leather appointment book, the kind with places for dates and meetings, addresses, places for notes, and pockets for receipts. She began flipping through the calendar part.

"I can't even function without this thing," she said, peering in the dim light at her tiny handwriting.

I stared at her, at her notebook, for a very long time.

She must have felt the intensity of my gaze. She looked up at me quizzically. "Are you okay?" she asked.

"You have an appointment book," I said, in a kind of wonderment. "I have an appointment book. Everybody who has any kind of schedule at all has an appointment book."

Lisa looked at me as if I'd lost my mind. I could feel my heart pounding. I looked in at the stacks of papers, mentally revisited the offices I'd rummaged through.

"Where's Walker Redgrave's appointment book?" I asked.

I didn't wait for an answer. I went inside the apartment and grabbed the phone. I glanced at my watch; it was two-thirty in the morning.

I was in luck. No Valerie Simmons was listed with Atlanta information, but there was a V. A. Simmons with a Buckhead number.

I dialed the number, let it ring a long time. I was about to hang up when a very sleepy voice answered with a slurred hello.

"Ms. Simmons, this is Bennett Cole," I said, as if it was the most routine thing imaginable to call up a stranger in the middle of the night.

I could hear little snifflings on the line as she cleared her nose. "Dr. Cole," she sniffed. "Where are you? Why haven't you called? We've left messages with your service for—"

I cut her off. "Listen carefully, I need to know something that could be very important. Did Mr. Redgrave carry an appointment book or notebook with him?"

"Of course, he never went anywhere without it," she said. "I don't understand."

"Where is it? What's it look like?"

"I have no idea where it is. It's black leather, like lizard skin, I think. It's a three-ring binder, smaller than a full-size notebook. Didn't you find it when you went through his things?"

"If I'd have found it would I be calling you asking where it is?" I realized I was shouting, told myself to calm down. "I'm sorry, no, I went through both offices and there was no appointment book or calendar of any kind."

"Well, I don't know then," she said with a trace of huffiness.

"Ms. Simmons, please call Mrs. Redgrave and see if she has it or knows where it is. This is all I've got to go on right now."

Valerie Simmons said she'd make the call. I gave her the Tides number and said I'd wait by the phone. I hung up.

I went back out to the patio. Lisa said, "I heard all that—it was hard not to, the way you were yelling. Who is Ms. Simmons and what did she say?"

"Redgrave's secretary. She said she'd call Mrs. Redgrave and get back to me."

We sat for about fifteen minutes. "I wish I had a cigarette," I said.

"You don't smoke," Lisa said.

"I wished I did right now. It'd be better than watching the hands of my watch go around in slow motion."

The phone rang, startlingly loud in the early morning quiet.

I quickstepped back into the apartment and picked up the receiver.

"Dr. Cole, I spoke with Mrs. Redgrave. She said she thinks it's in Captiva. She remembers the police in Steinhatchee giving her a plastic bag with all his personal things. I drove her back to Captiva before she came back to Atlanta. She says she got his wallet and keys out and left the rest of the stuff in the bag. She thinks it's in there."

"I need the real estate agent's number," I said.

"I'd only have it at the office," she said. "And probably only her work number."

"Okay, listen, sorry to bother you. Tell Mrs. Redgrave I haven't made much progress but I'm hanging in there." I hung up.

Next I called Sanibel-Captiva information. Second swing, second hit. There was an M.H. Lamb listed. Women did that these days, listed only their initials so they'd be safe from pranksters and obscene callers. You see initials and no address in the phone book and it'll be a woman. All the pranksters and obscene callers know that.

Mary Lamb answered the phone almost immediately. It didn't seem that she'd been sleeping.

"This is Bennett Cole. Did I wake you?"

"Actually, no," she said. "I was reading. Besides, I don't sleep much." She didn't express any surprise at all at my call. "How are you doing?" she asked.

"I hope better in a few hours. I need to get into Walker Redgrave's house. It's three o'clock now. I can be there in about four hours."

"Just drive on to the house, I'll be there at seven. If you're late I'll wait."

I threw my clothes in my overnight bag. I went out on the

beach side, where Lisa was sitting. "I have to go to Captiva. Want to come along?"

"Are you kidding? I have a room on the beach, paid for, and a chance to be alone—no offense, Cole. I think I'll stay and spend the day soaking up some rays." She smiled ironically.

"Bye-bye. Feel free to run up a tab."

There was almost no traffic. I got off the beach onto the interstate that spans Tampa Bay and headed south. I had a full tank of gas, a hot cup of coffee, and a heart full of hope. It was all any detective could ask for.

23

The sun was breaking the horizon behind me as I crested the bridge to Sanibel.

I had a disconnected feeling; I'd had to look at a newspaper to figure out what day it was. I wasn't sleeping on any particular schedule; in fact, I wasn't getting much sleep at all.

But now the adrenaline had kicked in. That would sustain me for a while. It would have to. If the trail of Redgrave's death got warmer I wouldn't have the luxury of relaxation.

I stopped at a convenience store for coffee. There were a mix of people already up and beginning to go about their day's business. I was still working on yesterday, they were on today.

A couple of guys were buying ice and cold drinks to throw in the cooler of a trailered Boston Whaler rigged for offshore work—Loran, radios, several depth finders, outriggers, a spotting tower, and no more than a dozen tackle rigs. This thing was capable of doing just about everything but cooking the fish and serving it up with a nice béarnaise sauce. The boat's name was *Acufuncture*. Rich chiropractors, I figured.

I got to the Redgrave house just after eight, pulled into the crushed-shell drive among the vegetation, saw the top story of the house above the trees. Mary Lamb's car was in the drive, and she was leaning on the front fender, trying to look toward the entrance of the drive. She was squinting against the morning sun and holding her hand over her eyes. She jumped when I beeped the horn.

I pulled up beside the car, parked, and got out. I was hit by a steamy blast of humidity; the sea breeze hadn't had time to come up, and the sun was already baking the air.

"Dr. Cole, I was looking right at the drive, but the sun had me blinded," she said. "Your horn startled me." She nodded her head toward the house. "Let's go in. I've only been here fifteen minutes and I'm covered with sweat." To illustrate the point she took hold of the thin material of her blouse and pulled it away from her. There were wet spots on the front, and the whole thing was wrinkled.

The house wasn't much better; still the musty, closed-up feeling, still the uneasy sense of the lack of life—or the presence of death, I wasn't sure.

"Has anyone filled you in on why I'm here?" I asked. I noticed her blouse clinging wetly to her stomach.

"Not in the least," she said, "but I figured if you were willing to drive here in the middle of the night I could sure be here to help you." I caught the odd choice of words; it was as if assisting my mission gave her some sense of purpose. Of course, she had been fond of Redgrave, and I figured the pace of island life could be boring for someone with her energy level. Or maybe she simply found me irresistible, in a humble sort of way.

"I'll open some windows and turn up the air," she said.

"Will that cause your blouse to dry?" I asked.

She said, "Pardon me?"

"Never mind," I said. "I'm particularly interested in finding Mr. Redgrave's personal effects. Mrs. Redgrave said she thought she'd left them here after she got his keys and wallet. Have you seen them?"

Mary Lamb tilted her head to one side. She looked a little like the seagull with the potato chip, only a lot cuter.

"You checked his office. It wasn't there?"

"I didn't see it. I wasn't really looking for that type of stuff, but I think I'd have been interested if I'd come across it. No, I don't think it was there."

She suggested we try the bedroom. "That's what Mrs.

Redgrave fell in love with when I showed them the house. She said she spent most of her time there. It has a veranda and a beautiful view of the gulf." The thought seemed to make her sad. She screwed up her eyes for an instant, then it was gone.

"Lead the way," I said.

We took the stairs to the upper level, went down a hall that led off the central landing, and got to a closed door on the beach side. Mary Lamb opened the door, stepped inside, and stood aside for me to enter.

The room was feminine, clearly dominated by Mrs. Redgrave's tastes. It occurred to me that Redgrave probably only dropped in to sleep. Or did he have his own bedroom? That seemed a slightly lurid thing to think about the dead, and I shoved it from my mind.

The room was white. Three windows and French doors opened to the gulf. Now the beach was in shadow, shielded from the morning sun by the house. There was a wicker dressing table, and a couple of matching wicker chairs with colorful floral-print cushions. A small table held a tea service. There was a dhurrie rug between the table and the bed.

On the colorful bedspread was a plastic bag. The lettering on it said, "TG&Y, Perry, Fla."

"Bingo," I said. The bag seemed to hold a mixture of interest and dread for Mary. She took a couple of steps back, but looked at it intently.

"Oh, dear," she said. "Is that what he had when he . . . when he died?"

"The cops call it the 'personal effects of the deceased,' " I said. "I hate law enforcement jargon. Like calling a child molester the 'alleged perpetrator.' "

I walked over and picked up the bag. It wasn't too heavy or bulky. I dumped its contents on the bed. There were only a few things in it: a pair of sunglasses and his reading glasses, both in leather cases, a couple of ballpoint pens, a map of Taylor County.

And a leather appointment book.

I picked it up. The leather was soft, worn from years of use. Each year the calendar pages would be changed, old ones filed or thrown away, new ones inserted. Times changed, the cover endured.

I opened the book. It was crammed, in Redgrave's pack-rat style, with a multitude of loose papers, stuck in the inside cover pockets or between pages. I dumped the loose stuff on the bed. There were receipts for meals and tolls, wrinkled credit card receipts, a dry-cleaning pickup stub, just the little addenda to a busy life.

There were divider inserts spread throughout the pages. It seemed logical to go to the calendar portion. I flipped there. Each page noted one day. I'd turned to July 27. Two weeks before he died. Not much there, he had a couple of personal appointments in Atlanta, and the notation, "reading time." The next several pages were much the same, Redgrave was obviously mixing social obligations and personal errands with some reading and a little writing. There were detailed lists of inconsequential things for Valerie Simmons to do, check on, or look up.

On August 4 he'd written, "tie things up before leaving." There was also a notation to take back overdue library books, a reminder to "have Valerie check on trip arrangements."

On August 7 he'd flown to Fort Myers and taken a cab all the way out to Captiva. I ruffled through the receipts. There was one from a Fort Myers cab company for forty-two dollars.

I felt Mary Lamb close behind me. It wasn't a bad feeling. I kept at the book.

August 8 and 9 were blank. On the tenth he drove to Steinhatchee. "Hacienda Court, check in by six," he'd written.

The next couple of days were filled with trivia—"drive down the road to nowhere. Alert Clyde to mail. Go by Cr.Cty. Gaines, der man . . . V & L." Idle ramblings, idle thoughts.

Another day that was a blank page.

And August 13, the day before he shot himself. A single

notation. "See Wyndle." Nothing after that, until August 26—three days from now—"call Julie re: advance arrangements" and "haircut."

I flipped back to the last entry. See Wyndle.

The rest of the notebook could wait. I was sick of reading and speculating and waiting.

I'd have to start where Redgrave left off. I'd have to go see Wyndle.

24

"Please do one thing," Mary Lamb said. We were back outside, standing in the heat next to my Jeep. "Would you tell me about it when it's over? Tell me what you found out?" Her blouse, I was pleased to see, had gotten damp again.

"I will," I said. "I promise."

She smiled at me. I got in the Jeep and rolled the window down.

"Aren't you tired?" she asked.

"I don't even know," I said. "I think so, but I'll run for a while. I've got to get back to Steinhatchee now."

She leaned down; her face was close to me. I could smell faint perfume or bath soap.

"Be careful," she said. She reached in and patted my shoulder, left her hand there. "Okay?"

"Sure," I said. Her hand was still on my shoulder. She was staring out beyond the passenger's window. "But I can't leave until you let go of me."

"Oh, gosh," she said, quickly removing her hand and giving me a self-conscious smile. "I didn't—"

"I will let you know," I said. I started the Jeep and U-turned in the drive. I looked back once before I made the turn onto the road. Mary Lamb was staring intently into the sun, shielding her eyes. I beeped the horn, for old times' sake.

Wyndle.

I tried to look at other parts of Redgrave's appointment book while I drove, but stopped after I jumped a curb and nearly ran over an old woman pushing a shopping cart. She shot a bird at me. I put the notebook down and drove.

Coffee. Interstate. Refuel, drive some more, watch the sun climb in the sky. Exit toward the coast. Drive on the two-lane, mostly behind trucks. More coffee. More trucks.

Going to see Wyndle.

Maybe I should call my service, give Mrs. Redgrave a message. What would I say? Maybe I'd gotten fired for not reporting in. Maybe the IRS had decided to audit me. Maybe Shelly had forgotten to feed my cat and he'd died. I wondered if I'd paid my electric bill. Was I still registered at the Hacienda, or would there be no vacancy because of a cow haulers' convention?

Maybe I should stop thinking so much and just go see Wyndle, see what happens.

I stopped just outside Steinhatchee, turned off the Jeep, and unlocked the glove compartment. I took out the Colt and shoulder holster, then stepped outside. I looked to make sure no cars were coming, slipped the revolver in the holster, slung it over my shoulder, and tightened the strap. Then I reached behind the driver's seat, took my lightweight windbreaker off the hook, and slipped it on. I knew I'd look a little silly with a jacket on in this heat, but the windbreaker would be a lot easier to explain than the Colt. The gun felt good, snugged under my armpit. I hadn't felt the need to have it on before; now I did. Going to see Wyndle.

It was just after noon when I pulled in to Smitty's shop. Smitty had his head buried under the hood of an old pickup truck, and I had to tap the horn before he realized he had a customer.

He came out to the pump, taking his time, wiping his hands on a red shop towel.

"How's the fishin'?" he said as I set the pump on automatic. He was still wiping at his hands; I couldn't tell which was greasiest, him or the towel. Maybe they just traded back and forth.

"Better and better," I said. "I need to see a fellow named Wyndle. You know where I might find him?"

His whole demeanor changed. He stopped wiping his hands, leaned over, and looked into the Jeep. His eyes had taken on a harder look.

"Wyndle," he said. It was a statement. "Why you wanna see Wyndle?"

"Let's start with, who is Wyndle?"

"This is gettin' confusing, mister," he said. "First you want to see Wyndle, then you want to know who he is. Don't make sense."

He was still leaning down, peering at me. The interior was beginning to heat up. The automatic pump shut off with a loud click.

"Could we go inside?" I asked.

Smitty didn't say anything, just turned and walked toward the building. He'd begun to wipe his hands again. I got out of the Jeep and followed.

Just as we got in the door another car pulled up to the pumps. Smitty said, "Hold on," and lumbered back outside.

I looked around the place. It was a throwback to a time before fast food, all-night convenience stores, and credit card self-service. The interior was fairly dark, with a pleasant musty odor. The walls were tongue-and-groove wood, the ceiling cracked plaster. A couple of ceiling fans whirred overhead.

I wandered down an aisle. Three or four shelves held food—canned goods, catsup, bread. There were cans of Vienna sausages, sardines, and deviled ham. And sweets such as honey buns and those little powdered doughnuts, twelve to a box. Stuff I'd eaten when I was a kid, stuff I hadn't eaten in a long time. I picked up a honey bun and walked around the corner.

The next aisle held a jumbled collection of automotive supplies—brake fluid, fuses, radiator caps, oil—and fishing supplies, mostly artificial worms, hooks, and saltwater lures. It was all covered with a thin sheen of dust. Smitty didn't turn over his inventory very often.

I walked back to the counter. The register was old, the

kind with the manual keys you have to push down about three inches. There was a huge jar of pickled eggs on the counter. Under a piece of glass were worn and faded photographs of people holding up fish—big fish, little fish, strings of fish. All the people were grinning. All the fish were dead.

On the wall behind the counter were mounted fish, bigger than the ones at the Florida Bar. There was also a collection of fan belts hanging from racks near the ceiling. Underneath the belts was a double-barreled shotgun, its stock shiny with wear. The blueing was perfect. Next to the gun was a framed photograph of a man—a very young man—in a crisp marine parade uniform. He had the serious look all marines strive so hard for. The picture didn't look recent.

I dropped the honey bun on the counter. I was wondering if local protocol allowed self-service on the pickled eggs when Smitty came back in. He'd had time to think; he seemed a little more composed.

"Mister, I'm sorry I snapped at you out there," he said. "It's just that strangers don't usually just drop by asking for folks like Wyndle. Took me by surprise, that's all."

That struck me as odd; people don't usually react as suspiciously as Smitty did—unless there's a reason.

"Folks like Wyndle?" I asked. The jar of eggs was making me hungry. I realized I didn't remember when I'd eaten last. "I've got to have one of those eggs."

"Help yourself. Folks like Wyndle Bledsoe don't get many outsiders visitin'. The Bledsoes ain't what you'd call our model citizens." He kept his voice steady. His face looked as though he was in pain.

I munched an egg. It was probably the best egg I'd ever had. I finished it and fished out another one, speared it with a fork, and shook some salt on it. Next I'd be asking him if he had any cans of Spam.

"Trouble?"

"Wyndle owns lumber mills down in Dixie. That's his business, leastwise his honest one. I hear the mills do pretty good. But that ain't the big money-maker for Wyndle."

"What is?"

The suspicion had returned. "You gotta have a reason for askin'. Maybe I ought'n to tell you anything else until you tell me somethin'."

I wasn't ready to do that. As it was, my conversation might be all over town by nightfall.

"Let's leave it at that," I said. "I would appreciate your telling me where he lives. That's not a secret."

"It might be," Smitty said. "Truth is, he mostly lives up on some land south of here, about twenty miles. They say he owns two to three hundred acres." He got a map from under the counter. "Here, it'd be easier to show you."

Just then a young woman came into the room. Her eyes were bright with interest.

"What's he want with Wyndle Bledsoe?" She talked to Smitty, but she looked at me.

She was pale creature with strawberry red hair and freckled skin that seemed almost translucent. She had narrow shoulders that seemed to hunch forward a little, and breasts that were disproportionately large for her small frame. She might be in her twenties; around here it was hard to tell.

"None a your business, Mickey," Smitty said.

"What's he want?" she said again, this time more sharply. Was she the woman I'd heard singing behind the window when I'd been here before?

"Do you know Mr. Bledsoe?" I asked innocently.

That was as far as I got. She opened her mouth to speak and Smitty said, "Out!" Her mouth snapped shut. She looked at me. She looked at Smitty. She looked intently for a moment at the picture of the marine. Then she turned and walked out of the room.

Smitty watched her go, his jaw clenched, the muscles tensing and relaxing. I thought I saw him cast a rapid, furtive glance at the picture. "My daughter Mickey," he said. "Never did mind me worth a durn."

He turned his attention back to the map. "You got to go

back through Jena, pick up this road." He jabbed a dirty finger at a line that looped south from here, curved a few times, and dead-ended out in the middle of nowhere on the coast. All there was near the last few miles of road was twisting coastline and lots of space.

"Wyndle lives back in here," he said, putting his finger down about half an inch from the end of the red line that marked the road. "Ain't no way it's marked, you're on your own."

25

I THANKED SMITTY for his time. He hadn't pressured me to tell more about why I wanted to visit the man, but he was clearly curious.

I nodded at the picture. "You got a boy in the marines?" I asked.

Smitty looked at me for what seemed a long time in the hot stillness of the store. "Dead," he said finally, and closed down, as if there wasn't anything else that could ever be said.

I paid him for the gas, the honey bun, and the eggs and got back in the Jeep. I glanced at the trip meter. Keith would not be happy; I was driving his car right out of warranty. And I'd noticed a slight pinging in the valves. When I gave it back to him I'd have to suggest he get it tuned up.

South of Jena the road opened up. There were a few houses and trailers, but they petered out a few miles beyond the town. Then there was just scrub land. There were electric lines, however, strung along one side of the pavement—a sure sign of life out there somewhere. Occasionally there'd be a conspicuous sign nailed to a tree, warning against trespass. One read, "Trespassers Will Be Prosecuted"; another, "Trespassers Will Be Shot."

The road straightened out; I remembered what Henry Littlejohn had said. This road would make as good a landing strip as any pilot could ask for.

Occasionally there were ill-defined dirt roads branching off the hard road. Electric lines ran down a couple of roads, trailing off into the woods out of sight. I suspected Wyndle lived down one of these, but which one? I respected the trespassing signs, and there was nobody around to ask.

I noticed a side road that looked interesting, made a U-turn, and was parked along the shoulder, peering into the brush, when a marked sheriff's cruiser came into view, coming from town, wavering like a mirage in the heat haze. As it approached the Jeep, the cruiser slowed down. When it neared I could see who was driving—Deputy Hirst. No fishing hat this time; now he was wearing a baseball hat with the Taylor County Sheriff's Office insignia on the front.

He cut across the center line and pulled alongside. I rolled down the window. The window on the sheriff's car slid down smoothly, powered by its electric motor.

"Well, well, well, if it ain't the detective," Hirst said. "I hope you're not lost. This road only goes in two directions—out to the dead end and back to town."

"I must be lost," I said. "I thought I was in Dixie County, and I run into a constable from the adjoining county. Aren't you out of your jurisdiction?"

"When you're as undermanned as we all are, you help out. Dixie radio had a report of a suspicious vehicle out here. It's amazing how quick folks are to notice strangers. There wasn't a Dixie deputy handy so I drove out. And found you. Are you out here acting suspicious?"

"I think just being here qualifies as suspicious in these parts," I said. "Actually, I was looking for Wyndle Bledsoe's place. Can you help me?"

Hirst stared at me for a long time, expressionless. Then he broke into a wide, toothy smile.

"Wyndle Bledsoe! This oughtta be good," he said. "What in the world you want with Wyndle?"

"Stubbs said I could poke around as much as I wanted as long as I didn't get shot and cause his paperwork to mount up," I said. "I just happen to be poking toward Wyndle Bledsoe, whoever he is."

Hirst wanted to know more, but he was a cop. And his superior had given me some latitude. Hirst would have to live with that. He didn't have to like it, though.

"Turn around," he said. "Drive out past where the electric lines end, go about a mile. There'll be a small stand of pine trees on your right, you go in there. It's been dry, you probably won't hardly see the road. Follow the tracks into the woods as far as you can. Then get out and walk another quarter of a mile. Then you can say hi to Wyndle."

"No electricity?" I asked.

"Generator," Hirst said. "I've never figured out how Wyndle gets the gas out there to it, but he does. He don't need much juice anyway, just his lights and the refrigerator." He grinned. "And the battery charger for his cellular phone."

I followed Hirst's directions. The side road wasn't that hard to find. There were even some tire prints in the ruts, faint but apparently recent.

It wasn't any cooler in the woods; the sun cut through the thin shade and made the air sultry. I drove as far as I could, about a half mile, and stopped where the trees simply got too close together for a vehicle to pass between. There was a clear space off to my left; in it were parked a battered pickup and a new-looking Jeep Wagoneer.

I parked behind the truck and got out. The light was hazy, and there was a constant sound of buzzing bugs.

Had Redgrave come out here? If so, why? There had been a reaction each time I'd mentioned Wyndle Bledsoe's name. Wyndle and Redgrave, tied together only by an entry in an appointment book.

I walked down an overgrown path and came upon the rusted hulk of an overturned car. A little farther along was a small clearing where trash and garbage had been dumped—sacks that had been torn open by animals, the contents spread around, old cans mainly, and jars and paper. There was an old mattress lying half against a tree, and a number of large drums, the kind oil comes in, were lined up in fairly neat rows. The pine needles made a thick, pliable carpet underfoot.

I walked a little farther. There was a faint sound; I couldn't place it at first, but as I listened it became more distinct. The sound of waves.

Then I saw the house, set in a small clearing. It was made of wood and set up on blocks, the way cracker houses were built. The roof was rusted sheet metal. Over the years the house had settled into the soft coastal sand, and now nothing was plumb; the whole thing tilted and sagged at odd angles.

On the front of the house was a sagging porch. And on the porch was a man. He sat in a chair that looked like it had once been a bucket seat in a car. He sat placidly, chin on chest. He couldn't have weighed more than three hundred pounds. He looked as large as a hippopotamus, and just as pretty.

I was partially obscured from the man, behind a tree heavy with hanging moss. I stood still, not moving from my feeble camouflage.

After a while he seemed to raise his head. Then he stared in my direction, not moving at all.

I moved behind the thick trunk of an oak tree. I felt the weight of the Colt under my arm.

I eased my head out from behind the tree. He might have turned his head a little, that was all. I could see his eyes, deep-set in fat and wrinkles.

I said, "Are you Wyndle Bledsoe?"

He might have nodded ever so slightly, but there was no way to be sure.

I stood for a moment, and when he didn't speak, I said, "I was wondering if a man by the name of Walker Redgrave had come out to see you."

Still the stare, and nothing else. When he breathed, his distended belly pushed against his shirt, forcing the spaces between the buttons to gap widely. Little tufts of gray hair stuck out of the gaps. I walked across the clearing and up the steps to the porch. I stopped a few feet from his chair. It had a headrest, so it must have been out of a fairly new car.

Now I could see behind his bulk. There were crutches lying on the floor behind him. And the cellular phone.

He kept his eyes narrowed, making him look half asleep. There was a coffee can at his side. He reached down and picked it up, held it up to his mouth, and spat. He set the can down. A rivulet of brown drool ran down his stubbled chin. He didn't seem to notice.

"Did he come to see you, Mr. Bledsoe?" I heard the faint sound of a motor turning on. The generator, most likely.

He might have smiled then, but I could have been wrong about that. I might as well interrogate a side of beef. Might do better, even.

"So you'd remember if Redgrave came out to talk to you," I said. "Mr. Bledsoe, are you there? These aren't hard questions."

He spat, this time directly on the porch. His eyes had taken on a predator's look. He made an almost imperceptible gesture, and suddenly there was a pistol cradled across his fat leg.

"Git."

I got.

▽

26

So much to do, so little sleep. But ultimately sleep wins out. I headed back to the motel room—heck, I could knock off a couple of hours, try sleeping on the installment system.

It didn't work. I had just taken off my clothes, hung my holster over the chair, flopped on the bed, and started to doze off when someone started knocking.

I got up, feeling disoriented and slightly stunned, opened the door a couple of inches, and peered out. And came eye to eye with Stormy Corbin.

"You play hard to get more'n anybody I ever knew, Cole."

"I didn't know we were having a relationship."

"Give a girl a chance. At least call her back."

I realized I was still keeping the door cracked, as if I were holding something at bay. Maybe I was. Reluctantly I opened the door wider, but I still blocked the entrance. I didn't feel up to conversation, my brain was still playing catch-up.

"I had to leave town. I just got your messages."

"And you were just getting ready to pick up the phone, right." She laughed to show me she wasn't taking this as serious as it seemed. Just then an eighteen-wheeler drove past, sending a backdraft of wind, dust, and noise swirling across the parking lot. "I may be a small-town girl, Cole, but I still like a guy with manners. You gonna keep me standing out here?"

My brain was still dragging like the middle beat of a mazurka. I stepped to the side and nodded my head. Stormy walked inside.

And saw the Colt hanging on the chair.

"Oh, my," she said. She looked left, then right, a little wildly. Then she leveled her gaze on me. "Up here to fish, huh? You gonna hook 'em or shoot 'em?"

"I'm not fishing for fish, Stormy."

"Startin' to seem pretty obvious." She walked over to the gun, looked at it closely.

"That's like cops wear." She gave me a measured stare. "You a cop?"

"Private. By the way, you were right. I'm from Atlanta. I was going to tell you."

"That's what they all say," she said. "Okay, so you're a private cop. I don't care." She looked like she cared a lot. Her bottom jaw trembled a little. I realized she liked me, and now I wasn't what I seemed, an innocent stranger in town for innocent reasons. Another small-town letdown for the small-town girl.

The jaw stopped trembling. She sat on the edge of the bed and crossed one leg over the other. She gave me a weary smile.

"So you ain't what you seemed. Why don't you tell me why you're here." She gave an expansive gesture that seemed to be meant for all of Steinhatchee. "Any excitement'll help around here."

"I'm looking into the death of Walker Redgrave, the writer who shot himself here."

"Oh, Lordy, right here at the Hacienda." She looked around. "Was it in this room?"

"Two doors down, as a matter of fact," I said.

"He shot himself."

"Yeah."

"Person shoots himself it's suicide the way I figure it."

I shrugged.

"Don't tell me everything at once. It'll spoil the excitement."

"That's the problem. I don't know much. You folks around here aren't real talkative."

She took on a serious look. "Look, I don't mean to make

fun. That writer, he was a nice guy, came in the Florida a few times. He was always askin' questions, but I didn't pay much attention."

"I know, he was married."

I'd meant it as a lighthearted jab, but it clearly stung Stormy. She set her jaw and started to say something, then stopped. Her eyes moistened a little.

"Are you married?" she said.

"No. And that's the truth. I'm sorry for making that crack. You've been nice to me. And I know you want out of here."

She let the jaw relax. "Forget it. Tell me more about Redgrave."

"Sure," I said evasively. "Can you tell me anything about the Bledsoes?"

Her eyes widened. "You don't pussyfoot around, do you? Have you met any of 'em?"

I told her I'd met Wyndle.

"Then why're you askin'? What you see is what you get. And what you get is mostly bad news."

I sat on the bed, not too close to her. "Bad how?" I asked.

"Bad everyways. Bad to the bone, leastwise he used to be. Now he's old and crippled, all he does is stay out at that cabin a his and count his money."

"Is he rich?"

"He owns three lumber mills," Stormy said. She looked down, pulled at the fabric of her slacks, thinking. "I don't see why I shouldn't talk about this, it's common knowledge around here. It's just that we ain't used to tellin' strangers our business."

I patted Stormy on the knee, taking my hand away before she could read too much into the gesture. "Stormy," I said. "I need your help. I suppose I could go to Stubbs and ask him, but I'm not ready to report every angle I'm investigating to the local cops. I don't have any leads except two—I know Redgrave went to see Wyndle Bledsoe before he died. And I know he didn't commit suicide."

"Not suicide? But—"

"It's a little hard to explain, but I'm confident the information I have will stand up in court." That was stretching the truth, but why sweat a small detail? "You said it yourself. You folks here don't talk to outsiders. I'm an outsider. So who's going to talk to me, especially after they find out why I'm really here?"

I paused, pasted on a look of deep concern.

"I need to know about people like Wyndle," I said. "And I need to set the record straight about Walker Redgrave's death." I paused, took a deep breath, and went for the throat. "His poor widow hired me to find out the truth. The way it is now is killing her."

"Oh my," she said. "That poor woman, her husband shooting himself and her knowing it wasn't suicide." She paused and scratched her nose. "That's really confusing. How could he—"

I got up off the bed, walked over to the chair, and picked up the holster. She seemed to shudder slightly. "Okay, you win, just put the gun down."

I laid the holster on the dresser, came back to the bed, and sat down. Still not too close.

Stormy took a deep breath. "There's all kinds of stories about Wyndle and his boys. Truth is, they got money and nobody knows from where. Wyndle's pretty much out of commission, but his boys, that's another story."

"Tell me about his boys."

"Troy and Tiny, birds of a feather, but different as night and day."

I resisted pointing out the two clichés in one sentence. "Hmmm," I said, and waited.

"Like I said, Wyndle was a terror in his time, but he's been real quiet for the last few years. Just sits on his farm mostly. I know he owns hundreds of acres of woods.

"Troy's the oldest—and the smartest, which ain't sayin' much. He has jobs here and there, but nobody'd accuse him of overworkin'. Works some drivin' a truck for a haulin' company. He's usually hangin' around, throwin' money right and left, showin' off his newest toys.

"Tiny—his elevator don't go even near the top floor. An' he don't even pretend to have a job.

"They both live in the woods, probably on the land daddy owns. Troy's place is in Dixie, close to Wyndle's. Tiny lives north of here, close to the water, way out in the middle of nowhere.

"I've never been to either place, myself," she said a little self-consciously. "I just heard."

My hand was resting on the bed. Stormy put her hand on it, an absent gesture. She leaned toward me. "Cole, these boys got one thing in common. They don't give a rip. They don't care about nobody but themselves and they barely tolerate each other. They ain't nobody you want to know."

I was beginning to think I would like to know them better. I knew Redgrave had contacted Wyndle. Wyndle had a couple of bad boys, boys who, from what Stormy had said, could be capable of killing. They had money but no jobs. And I didn't think they were living off their investment portfolios.

There was something else. They sounded a lot like the kind of people Lisa and I had talked about that night on the beach. I could justify giving some attention to Tiny and Troy.

"So how do I get to meet these nice young gentlemen?"

"You've already seen 'em, you just don't know it," Stormy said. "They were in the Florida the other night. Most likely they'll be there again tonight. You just come on down, watch the show."

27

After Stormy left I gave up on sleep's installment plan, took a long shower that took the raw edge off my fatigue, and headed to a nearby restaurant to eat. I had a few hours to kill before the nightlife of the Florida Bar would swing into high gear.

I ordered iced tea and eggs from a waitress who looked a lot like most of the waitresses at home-cooking restaurants throughout the South—plump, blond hair aggressively teased, a graduate of the Tammy Faye Bakker school of makeup application, bra working overtime. The place was cool, and I'd almost stopped sweating in the jacket I wore to conceal the Colt.

She brought my tea, popped her gum, and sat down at a table with two other waitresses. They all were smoking.

I was beginning to feel detached and isolated from the world outside the Florida backwoods. I went outside for a newspaper.

The *Constitution* wasn't available. One of the great tragedies of our time. I bought a *Tampa Tribune* from an orange vending machine and took it back to my table.

I scanned the pages. Trouble in the Middle East, with the United States threatening to withhold aid or give more aid, it was hard to tell which; more on the banking scandal; three AIDS stories, one of which cautioned people about their choice of dentists. Some guy in the Midwest had dismembered a number of young men and kept their remains in his apartment as souvenirs. His neighbors had characterized him as "quiet, a little weird but never caused any trouble." They did, however, think the sound of an electric saw at all hours of the night was a bit odd. An ex-government official was questioned in a complicated probe of an issue completely incomprehensible to the average person. And the Braves had lost.

I glanced at the masthead. It was Thursday, just over a week since Alexandra Redgrave had walked into my office. I'd been to Captiva, Tampa, Steinhatchee, Gainesville, flown to New York, and ended up back in the Florida swamps. And I still hadn't solved the perplexing death of one Walker Redgrave, although I was being paid handsomely to do so.

But at least I had a trail to follow now.

My eggs came, with a double helping of grease. Somebody ought to do a study of arterial disease around here. Maybe I could read about it in the paper.

I had the sense that I was in a small window of time before the pace of my case accelerated. So far I'd moved somewhat sedately; it was frustrating but I hadn't any choice. Now I was stepping from behind my flimsy cover and soon all of Steinhatchee would know about the private eye from Atlanta. I wanted to see Troy and Tiny before the news reached them—it might already be too late.

I paid for the eggs, left a tip commensurate with the lack of tea refills, and walked out into the heat. Did it ever cool down here? Did the locals have their sweat glands removed? Is that how they spotted strangers, by the perspiration rings under their arms?

I glanced at my watch. Stormy would be at work by now. It was time to go. I felt that anticipation that comes when anything can happen and probably will.

The Jeep was sitting rather forlornly in the parking lot. It was caked with layers of dust and mud, and there was a large ding on one fender where somebody had opened a door into it. This would be a true test of my friendship with Keith Hutchins. I hoped he was drag racing the Volvo.

There was a pay phone on the corner of the building. I

looked in the phone book. No Wyndle Bledsoe. No Troy Bledsoe, no Tiny Bledsoe. No Bledsoes at all. I thought about going back in the restaurant and asking. The waitress would probably become offended, produce a large firearm from beneath her apron, and shoot me.

The parking lot at the Florida Bar was beginning to fill up when I arrived. More trucks than cars, even a couple of semi rigs parked in the back. A couple of trucks had boats hooked on the back, work boats piled with nets, the motors mounted in a well toward the front. The Corvette was there.

Twilight at the Florida Bar. Who'd notice inside, anyway? I wondered if they had a happy hour. And what would it matter, since I'd get all the club soda I wanted free from Stormy? But should I tip her? This was getting awkward.

The place was more crowded than the last time. Most of the stools at the bar were occupied, mostly by off-work fishermen and laborers, even a couple of girls in tight shirts and tighter jeans. There was loud talk, some backslapping and glass clinking, nothing too rowdy. Three men in sweat-stained T-shirts were at the pool table, playing a game of cutthroat. The smoke was beginning to create a faint haze; it'd take on the aspects of ground fog by night's end.

One man detached himself from the group by the pool table and went to the jukebox. He stuffed it with coins and Hank Williams Jr. sang "If Heaven Ain't a Lot Like Dixie" five times. Stormy, behind the bar, was moving fast. I watched her fill three glasses she held in one hand, slide them down the bar, and go to work building a couple of drinks, stacking empties in a big plastic tub. Durel Barbour was in the corner seat, quiet again, staring at his drink. He saw me, smiled, and motioned me to have a seat next to him.

"You are still here doing the fishing?"

"I'm hoping the fish'll start biting real soon," I said.

The comment brought a raised eyebrow from Barbour, but no more. "Stormy," he said, "serve Mr. Cole what he desires, on my tab of course."

Stormy snapped up the seltzer nozzle. "This critter can

hold more soda'n any man I ever seen. I tried to pop him the other night but he held it."

That brought a raised eyebrow from me, but I didn't detect anything like sarcasm in her voice. She slid the glass of soda toward me.

"I've been meaning to ask you, Mr. Barbour, how you came to own a bar here," I said. "You don't appear to be a local."

"No, no. Coonass, my friend. From the swamps. Not around here, backwaters of Louisiana." He gave me a wide grin of very white teeth.

"Swamp to swamp," I said.

"With a couple of stops along the way," he said vaguely. He drained his drink. "And with that, I am off."

He slipped off his stool, and said to Stormy, "Little one, you are in charge," and headed for the door.

"That means if the register doesn't tally it's my butt," she said without malice. It was obvious she liked the responsibility.

She aggressively polished the bar where Barbour had sat. "Just wait, honeybunch," she said, "and you shall be rewarded."

"Shall?"

"Cole, that's really startin' to get old."

"You're right, I'm sorry," I said.

Stormy flashed me a big "it's all right" smile. Then she looked over my shoulder and said under her breath, "Showtime, Act One." She drifted over to the other end of the bar, whistling slightly.

I turned around as unobtrusively as possible. The door was open and in it was the silhouette of a tall, thin man. He stood still for a moment, his head swiveling right and left, then entered the room. The screen door banged shut behind him. The pause and the entrance were clearly calculated.

He moved away from the door, passing from silhouette to full light. Zane Grey would have called him a long drink of water. He was beyond rangy, all arms and legs, slightly concave chest, stringy, shoulder-length brown hair. His body gave off a sense of placid relaxation.

He walked without hurry toward the pool table, exchanged words with the men playing, picked up a cue, and sighted down it. Then he moved to the wall and leaned against it. He looked like he'd been leaning there all his life.

Stormy came by carrying a drink. "Troy," she said.

She headed toward the pool table and handed the drink to Troy. He took it without looking at her, nodded his head slightly. Stormy made her way back to the bar and busied herself with some dirty glasses.

Not much happened for a while. I drank soda water. Waylon Jennings's "Good Hearted Woman" played at least half a dozen times. Durel Barbour came back in, went to his stool, and looked inquiringly at Stormy. She made his drink and slid it along. He gave her a small nod and raised the glass to his mouth, took the smallest of sips, put it back down, and went into his staring act.

Troy played pool, appearing to win easily each time. I alternated drinking soda water and going to the bathroom. People shuffled in, people shuffled out. Another night at the Florida, mecca of polite society in Steinhatchee.

About nine o'clock the door slammed open hard against the wall and a very large man lumbered into the bar.

"Showtime, Act Two," Stormy said.

Different as night and day. He was fat, but not in a soft way, more like a big-bellied wrestler. His hair was a wild mass of curls, his face was a pockmarked, pasty white. He had narrow shoulders that sloped sharply away from his neck. His fat nose angled off to the side like it was trying to make a left turn.

This one didn't stop to survey anything, just heaved himself inside and came directly to the bar. He had on filthy jeans and a T-shirt that said "Eat Mo' Possum."

"Brew," he said to Stormy. He talked like he had rocks in his mouth. She tapped one up for him. He took the glass in a pudgy hand and blew the foam so it flew off and landed on the bar with a wet splat. He giggled and walked off. He didn't pay for the beer.

Stormy took a rag to the bar. "Tiny Bledsoe, a real Southern gentleman," she said. She finished wiping up the mess, held the rag between two fingers like it was dirty, and tossed it in the sink.

Tiny wandered off toward the pool table and took a stool against the wall. Troy was absorbed in a game of eight ball. Neither appeared to acknowledge the other. Troy ran the table; Tiny sat with his belly sticking out, squinting at his beer.

After a little while Stormy drew a couple of a large glasses of beer and took them to the brothers. Same scenario—Troy took his without comment or eye contact, Tiny blew the head off his and giggled. It was like a redneck Laurel and Hardy skit.

I drank some more soda water. Surveillance sure can make a man thirsty. Tiny and Troy didn't appear to take any notice of me.

About 10:00 P.M. the phone behind the bar rang and Stormy answered. Her face got a thoughtful look. She caught my eye and winked. She said, "sure," and put the receiver down. She walked over to Troy and said something.

Troy got a pouty look on his face, like a youngster told to come home just when he was having fun. He left the table and came around the bar, picked up the phone, and said, "Huh." He listened for about a minute, said "uh huh," and put the phone down. He was maybe five feet away from me, and as he put the receiver down he turned his head in my direction.

I met his gaze. His eyes were startling behind hooded, drooping lids. They were not the eyes of a rangy cowboy. They were the eyes of an animal, deep and black, watchful. He stared at me unhurriedly for perhaps twenty seconds. Then the left corner of his mouth arched upward. It might have been a grin. It lasted maybe a couple of seconds, then the face settled back into a sullen repose.

Then Troy moved around me, walked over to Durel Barbour, who was still staring intently into his drink, and tapped him on the shoulder. When Barbour looked up, Troy nodded his head once, sharply, and jerked a thumb at the receiver. Barbour, who clearly had been caught off guard, raised his eyebrows at Troy, got off his stool, and went around the bar to the phone.

Troy walked over to Tiny, leaned close, and said something. Tiny's mouth slowly sagged open and he began to chew on his lip. He heaved himself off his stool and set his glass on the green felt of the pool table. One of the players looked up, started to say something, then saw who it was and snapped his mouth shut. He gently picked the glass off the table, put it on the windowsill, and went back to his shot.

Tiny lumbered toward the door, Troy drifting behind. They went outside. Barbour hung up the phone and went back to his seat, picked up his straw, and rapidly drummed it on the bar.

"When daddy calls, the boys jump," Stormy said to me. She glanced at Barbour, got a thoughtful look for a moment, then put a mask on it.

I got up and wandered over toward the door, hesitated a moment, and went outside, looking as innocent and inconspicuous as possible.

A four-wheel-drive pickup truck, perched high above its huge tires, backed out of a space on the far side of the lot. It was a new model, bright red, with chrome running boards.

Troy was driving. He changed gears while the truck was still backing, and the tires spun dust and gravel. The truck lurched forward and lumbered out of the lot onto the road, the tires still clawing for traction.

Nice set of wheels, Troy. Probably set you back twenty thousand dollars. Not bad for a guy doing odd jobs. Not bad at all.

I waited until the truck was out of sight, then started toward the Jeep with the idea of tailing the truck.

Then I stopped. Something was wrong with the Jeep. It appeared to be sitting too low to the ground. I walked across the lot and took a closer look. All four tires were flat.

I leaned down and examined a rear tire. There was a deep slice across the sidewall above the steel belt. Each of the other tires had a similar slit.

There was something else. On the dusty driver's window, someone had written, "go way."

"Hello Troy, hello Tiny," I said. "Nice to meet you both."

28

I RETURNED TO my seat at the bar and smiled smugly at Stormy.

"Anything could have happened tonight, and it did," I said.

Stormy said, "Say what?"

"Never mind. I need a tow truck," I said happily. "My tires have been slashed."

"You are weird, Cole. This is the first time I ever seen someone happy their tires were cut. Aren't you worried?" She looked worried when she said it.

I fended off any further questions. I scanned the room; the place was crowded but nobody seemed to be paying any attention to me. Barbour had left the room.

I borrowed the bar's phone book and looked under towing services. The closest one with a twenty-four-hour number was in Chiefland, about fifty miles away. Sure, they'd come and tow my car. It would only cost slightly less than a first-born child. Sure they could be there in only a couple of hours. Sure, I'd have the cash on hand. Reluctantly they agreed that travelers checks were just like cash.

Stormy kept a wide-eyed stare on me, but when she started to speak I shook my head. I got a to-go cup full of soda water and went outside.

I walked down the street a little way, away from the glare of the streetlight in the parking lot. The air had cooled down, and a good sea breeze had cleaned the air and cooled it a bit. I breathed deep—no pollution like I was used to in Atlanta.

I looked up and saw the stars, thousands of them, shining brilliantly in a cloudless sky.

Not a bad place, really. Mostly people did what they do most places, went to an honest job, came home to the family, saved their money, went to church, tried to have a little fun. Henry Littlejohn probably was right about the bad stuff that went on in the swamp, but you wouldn't know it driving down Main Street or eating the good home-cooked food at Carol's Café.

I thought about the people I'd met. Stormy, with her desire for knowledge and sense of responsibility. Smitty, who seemed to care about his business and helped me even though I was an outsider. Stubbs, who was letting me go farther than he could officially go in the investigation. Why? He'd said it would be interesting to have me snoop around, but there was more to it than that. Behind the good-ol'-boy facade was a savvy lawman, I thought. It was probable that Stubbs knew about things he couldn't act on—officially. He might be watching me work; he might be quietly manipulating me. But that was okay, as long as he didn't try to prevent my investigation.

I sipped on the soda water; it felt clean and good. It was starting to happen. Walker Redgrave had shot himself, but he hadn't killed himself. I'd gone to see Wyndle Bledsoe. Wyndle had called his boys. I'd had my tires slashed and been told to go away. From the looks of them, Troy and Tiny were capable of rough stuff. And slashed tires and writing in the dust didn't qualify as rough stuff. I had no evidence they'd had anything to do with Redgrave's death, but one appearance at Wyndle's sure had gotten their attention. So, I wondered, what would a little more pressure accomplish? Might get me nothing. Might get me killed. If they had anything to do with Redgrave's death, it might make them jumpy, even do something incriminating. That was worth the risk.

I wandered back to the Jeep and sat on the back bumper and settled in to wait for the tow. Every once in a while somebody would come out of the bar. A couple of them nodded their heads at me, but no one spoke and no one mentioned my squat-looking Jeep.

It was a little after midnight when the tow truck pulled into the parking lot. The driver had come in a big flat-bed model, the kind they haul your car on with a winch. Only way to tow a vehicle with four flats.

As he tilted the bed and hooked up the winch, he said, "Don't look like wear and tear on them tires. You jump in the wrong set of arms?"

"No such luck," I said. "I must have been fishing in somebody's spot."

"Sure," he said.

Just as the driver was strapping down the Jeep the lights on the bar's sign went out. The last of the customers came out in one group and scattered to their trucks and cars. There was a sudden cacophony of engines and gears, and then the lot was empty, except for the Corvette and Stormy's Camaro in the far corner.

A moment later Stormy came out and locked the door. She saw the Jeep up on the truck and came over. There was a hard edge of concern in her expression.

"Durel's closin' up. How 'bout I give you a ride back to the Hacienda?"

"I'd appreciate that," I said. I turned to the driver. "Can you drop this off at Smitty's garage? It's right on the way out of town headed to Perry."

The driver nodded. I signed the travelers checks and handed them over, and he fired his engine and drove out of the lot. The Jeep squatted forlornly on the rocking bed of the truck.

We walked over to the Camaro. Stormy unlocked her side, got in, and leaned over to unlock my door. Stretching heightened the effect of her cleavage.

I got in and she gunned the motor, fishtailing out onto the pavement. Something was lurking under the hood that belied the benign exterior of the car.

Stormy straightened the car and powered through the gears. "This tire slashin' ain't no coincidence, Cole."

"I hope not," I said.

"What's that supposed to mean?"

I looked at her, the way she stared straight at the road, both hands on the wheel. There was no flip demeanor, and I felt uneasy. People like Tiny and Troy, whether they had anything to do with Redgrave or not, played tough. Now I'd brought Stormy onto the fringes of the game. She was a valuable source of information, but this wasn't Atlanta, where anonymous sources could blend safely back into their environment. Anything that happened here was showcased on the small-town stage.

We were close to the Hacienda when Stormy said, "Let's go to Buster's, okay? I feel a little rattled."

We passed the motel; three or four cars were in the lot, and the lights burned in number five. The office was dark.

We drove a little ways in silence. Stormy made the turn onto the road leading toward Route 19 and opened up the Camaro a little. She took it up to about seventy, and I could feel the strength of the motor; there's no substitute for a big American V-8.

My thoughts were drifting, and I was enjoying the night air and the gentle pulse of the engine when Stormy said, "I might be paranoid, but there's a car behind us, a long ways back. It pulled out behind us after we went by the Hacienda and it made the turn behind us. I speeded up and it's still there, about the same distance back."

I turned in the seat. The lights were quite a ways back, keeping a pace steady with us.

"Slow down a little," I said.

Stormy throttled back the Camaro. The car behind us must have eased off too; the lights seemed to remain about the same distance behind.

"Step on it," I said.

Stormy waited a moment—was this decision time for her?—and suddenly mashed the accelerator hard. I'd underestimated the motor. A four-barrel carburetor kicked in, and dual exhausts burbled to life. The force pushed me back into my seat and the speedometer needle climbed swiftly up to about ninety.

"What do you have in this thing?" I said.

Stormy was smiling now; she was comfortable with the speed and power of the car.

"Three-ninety-six, Holly four-barrel and Cherry Bomb glass packs. It's got competition headers, heads are ported and polished, and I got a three-quarter race cam. This here—" she patted the shift lever—"is a Hurst Mystery Shifter. You wanna hear about the limited-slip differential ratio?"

The needle was at a hundred and ten. "You can ease off a little," I said.

"It goes a lot faster."

Stormy eased off, though, and I turned around again. The headlights were still back there, much more distant, but back there. They weren't as far back as they should have been.

"How far to the highway?" I asked. I had to raise my voice above the Cherry Bombs and the wind.

"Not far," she said. Then I could see the red blinking intersection light. Stormy was still going about seventy; she hardly slowed down as she ran the light and swung right. The tires squealed but hung on and she powered out of the turn. "Modified suspension, anti-sway bars, and Goodyear Double Eagles," she said above the roar of the accelerating car.

"Quick, pull into a driveway or something," I yelled.

A mailbox and gravel drive came into the beam of the headlights. Stormy suddenly braked hard, downshifted, and whipped the Camaro hard right. The drive led back into a thick stand of trees. "When you get into the trees stop and cut the motor and lights," I said.

The car stopped and in the sudden darkness I opened the door and ran back to the tree nearest the road. I hunkered down behind the trunk and listened. It was quiet in the way a deep woods is quiet—no sound at first, then you realize you can hear the buzzing of thousands of insects, nature's white noise.

A minute later I could hear the sound of a motor, distant at first, then growing louder. The road began to get lighter as headlights approached. I took the Colt out of the holster and squatted behind the tree.

I don't know what I expected, maybe the pickup truck. But it wasn't a truck that whooshed by, going fast. It was a late-model Corvette.

I waited until the Corvette's taillights passed out of sight beyond a rise and walked back to the Camaro. Stormy had gotten out and was standing by the rear fender, peering at the road. The metal of the motor ticked and crackled as it cooled.

"Oh Lord," she said when I got close. She was staring at my hand and I realized I was still holding the Colt. I slipped it back in its holster under the windbreaker.

"Sorry about the gun," I said. "I really didn't need it."

I took a step closer. Stormy stood with her hands at her side. The euphoria of speed was wearing off and she looked disoriented and a little wild-eyed. Maybe she was shaking a little bit. I took another step and she moved toward me, flung her arms around my neck, and held on tight.

I closed my arms around her gently, just held her close for a little while. I could feel her chest rising and falling; she'd burrowed her head against my neck. A small-town girl in a big-time situation.

Finally, she said, "This is scary, Cole, this is for real."

"You don't have to be a part of it."

"Wrong, honeybunch." Her words were muffled against me. "By tomorrow the whole town'll know about you seein' Wyndle and gettin' your tires cut. And they'll know we've been together. You and me'll be an item. Now I'm safer with you than away from you. Rats."

She was right. I'd underestimated the rapidity with which the case was intensifying. I could only hope that the Bledsoe boys were spooked for the right reason.

She held on tight. "I thought when I talked to you, you'd just—I dunno, find the bad guy. It's not that simple, is it?"

"Not usually," I said.

"And now, all the people here, they've seen me talkin' to you. This is gettin' tense. Troy and Tiny are not nice people."

I smoothed her hair. It smelled of shampoo and smoke. "Let's get some barbecue," I said. "It's the only thing that'll save you."

"No, Cole," she said, still holding on tight. "You gotta save me."

29

No one followed us as we drove to Buster's. No one jumped us as we parked in the lot and went inside. No suspicious characters lurked in the shadows. We weren't stared at as we entered. Our barbecue wasn't poisoned.

I didn't mention the Corvette, and Stormy didn't mention anything about the events at the Florida or on the trip over. She did tell me about the Camaro.

"Cordell used to race late models all the way over to Lake City every Saturday night. He spent all his money on his Ford. Named it Katie. But he never won, ever.

"He let me drive it one night in the powder-puff derby, though, an' I was hooked from then on. He wouldn't ever let me drive it again, but after he hit the road, I went out and got the Camaro. Had a guy over in Cross City do the motor and took it over to a speed shop in Gainesville for the suspension work and tires. It looks pretty stock from the outside but I've run high thirteens at the Lake City drag strip."

I finished my coffee. Stormy sipped her tea. The couple at the booth on one side of us finished their meal and left. Two women at the other adjacent booth kept getting tea refills and talking about their boss. It wasn't a pretty conversation. From what the women said, I'd only met a man that evil once, on death row at Starke. Scary to have the guy running around loose.

"Loan them your gun," Stormy said. "Maybe they'll leave and go finish the guy off."

"He made me go buy *condoms* as a gag gift for his wife," one of the women squealed.

"You'd think they'd just quit their jobs if it's that bad," I said.

"For most people, that's easier said than done," Stormy said. "Besides, they probably enjoy all this. Beats sittin' home and watchin' soaps while they wait for their ol' man to get home from the bar."

When we left I paused on the porch. Nothing out of the ordinary in the parking lot. The Camaro seemed okay. After we'd gone a mile down the road I looked back; nothing trailed behind, just dark empty roadway. It was almost three in the morning.

Stormy paced the car through its gears, downshifted expertly as she made the turn onto the road to Steinhatchee, accelerated, and leveled it out at seventy-five. The engine muttered contentedly. Stormy rolled the window up and turned on the air-conditioning.

"What's going on, Cole?"

"You know most of it already," I said. "I went to see Wyndle. He showed me a very large gun and I left. I came to the bar to meet Tiny and Troy. My Jeep developed flat tires and somebody was interested in seeing where we were headed."

"You think this has any connection with Redgrave's death?"

"I know Redgrave went to see Wyndle the day before he died. I know Wyndle ran me off right after I mentioned Redgrave's name. And I know Tiny, Troy, and Wyndle are all perfect gentlemen who wouldn't dare stoop to tire slashing and direct threats."

"Folks around here are real touchy you poke around in their business," Stormy said. "The Bledsoes are touchier than most. This might not have anything to do with him killin' himself, nothin' at all."

"That's true, but it's my lead—the only one I've got—and I'm going to follow it. And after what happened tonight, I think this is getting too rough for you to be involved in."

We came around a gentle curve on to a long stretch of straight road. Stormy toyed with the accelerator, then slammed the shifter into second. The tires fishtailed and squealed, and the car took off. Stormy took it up to the redline in second, speedshifted into third with another squeal of tires, and rocketed down the road. She shifted into fourth and the Camaro just kept accelerating.

I looked at the speedometer; the needle was well past a hundred and ten and climbing rapidly. Then Stormy tapped the brake pedal a little, suddenly mashed it hard. I felt myself surging forward against the seat belt. She double-clutched and hit third; the tires chirped and I felt the car lurch hard to the left. Another downshift, hard acceleration, and I was pinned immobile against the passenger door. I was starting to get disoriented, could see the needle headed upward again as we straightened out, see Stormy staring intently ahead, expressionless, see the road disappear into darkness beyond the Camaro's bright headlights.

"For God's sake, will you please slow down!" I yelled.

Stormy took her foot off the gas pedal, flicked the car into neutral, and suddenly we began to decelerate into a quiet rush of wind noise.

"What are you trying to do, kill us both?"

"There's ways you can scare me, like with the gun back there. And there's ways I can scare you. You think you're mister detective know-it-all and I'm some little punk from the woods. But you need my help. I know this place and you don't. After today, ain't nobody else in town gonna talk to you anyhow. So—" she slipped the shifter into third and blipped the gas—"you're stuck with me."

I looked at her silhouetted face. Some of the bravado was forced, but not all of it. Scared was there, but so was excitement. And excitement was winning out. But Stormy had never gone head to head with people like the Bledsoe boys.

And neither had I.

"I tell you what," I said. "Let me figure out what I'm going to do next. I'll let you know; in fact, I'll most likely need more information from you. I'm willing to let you help if you back off when I say so."

Stormy didn't say anything to that, but she didn't terrorize me with the Camaro, either. I took that as an affirmative answer.

By the time we reached the Hacienda, Stormy was driving at a reasonably sedate pace. The lights were out in all the rooms and the office. She cut the lights and coasted the Camaro into the parking space in front of my room. As we eased to a stop I said, "Something doesn't look right. Flip the headlights on."

She did, and the front of my unit was bathed in bright light. There were in fact a couple of things that didn't look right. One was the shattered front window of my room. The other was the bloated dog carcass lying in front of the door.

"See there," I said. "Just another idle threat. Nothing at all to worry about."

▽

30

I TOLD STORMY to wait in the car. She didn't look happy about it, but she didn't put up an argument.

I walked to the motel office. When I got close I could see the flickering light of a television behind the closed curtains. I knocked and heard Clyde tell me to come in.

He was sitting behind the motel desk, drinking coffee and watching another Braves game on television.

"Why are the Braves playing so late?" I asked.

"Game was earlier," Clyde said. "Me and Etta was out so I set the VCR. She's in bed, I can watch the game in peace—or thought I could."

The camera atop Fulton County Stadium panned the Atlanta skyline. It was twilight, and the city looked pristine. Nice illusion.

Clyde said, "The wife made me take her to Atlanta once, to shop in the big malls. I lasted about three days. Then I started askin' people where was the middle of Atlanta."

"Why's that?"

" 'Cause I figured there's one nice thing about bein' in the middle of Atlanta," he said. "No matter which way you go, you're headed out of town."

We watched the opposing pitcher retire the top of the Braves' order with two strikeouts and a slow grounder. "I wonder how we'd go about findin' the middle of Atlanta—it ain't like the city's square," Clyde said. Then, in a sweeping non sequitur: "I heard a story once about a guy tried to find home plate of Crosley Field, that's the old stadium the Reds played in, been torn down for years. He looked at old plot maps and pictures, talked to folks living in the neighborhood. He finally figured out the exact spot, it was next to a booth in the back room of a bar. He'd go sit in that booth for hours, he worshipped the place. He said he'd stand there, right in the same place Ted Kluszewski used to step up to the plate, and look out toward where right field used to be. Right field's a factory now. He'd take his stance, knock an imaginary ball through the wall over the factory. Then he'd jump around and try to high-five people. The regulars were used to it, but it took the first-timers by surprise." He paused a moment, then said, "I have no idea if that story's true or not."

"Doesn't matter. It's a good story. I used to listen to Reds games on the transistor radio I hid under my covers at night, the kind with the little earplug speaker," I said. "I'd love to step up to the plate at Crosley."

We watched the Dodger leadoff batter rip a fastball down the first base line for a stand-up double.

Clyde said, "You'll have to leave."

"I'll pay for the window," I said.

"And you'll get rid of the dog. I surely ain't. Have you smelled that thing?"

I nodded.

"Was funny, though," Clyde said. "It musta happened maybe a couple of hours ago. I didn't hear a thing, what with the TV goin', but the guy in number five, it woke him up. He didn't see nothin', just heard the crash. It like to scared him to death. He came down and banged on the door."

Clyde chuckled. "Turned out he's from Gainesville, been comin' down here to see some local guy's girlfriend. He thought it was the guy come to get him. Maybe he'll straighten up now."

He stared at the game, tapped his fingers on the desk counter. Then he turned back to face me.

"We put up a good front here, Mr. Cole. But it's a front, and now you're lookin' behind it. That ain't gonna bring nothin' but trouble. I don't know who you are, but I don't think you're here on a pleasure trip—" He put up his hands in a placating gesture. "I don't mind you not bein' straight up with me. But I can see what's comin'."

He got up from his chair and leaned on the counter. "Listen, it was terrible that man shootin' himself here. And now you're here, and things start happening. What gives? What're you doin' here stirrin' things up? It's pretty obvious he shot himself dead."

"I have evidence to support a finding other than suicide," I said, sounding more official than I intended.

Clyde raised his eyebrows and stared at me. I could hear the County Stadium crowd booing. A Dodger was trotting around second base with his fist raised. Not a good sign, especially in a pennant race.

"It's complicated," I said. "I can't go into all the details."

"Don't sound like you think it's an accident."

I shook my head.

"What're you?"

"Somebody who wants to find out the truth about Walker Redgrave."

Clyde reached over and shut off the television set, throwing the room into darkness. "Put 'em out of their misery," he said, and flipped on a desk lamp. "Look, if he did get murdered—and I can't figure out for the life of me how it'd be murder—I sure hope you get the sorry snakes that did it." He shook his head. "But you gotta get 'em somewhere else. Stay until the morning. I figure whoever's got it in for you's already done their thing for tonight."

I thanked Clyde for his hospitality and walked outside. Then I paused and returned to the office. Clyde was reaching up toward the television switch, but stopped when I came in. He didn't say anything, but his eyebrows arched a little.

"Clyde," I said. "I'd like to ask you some questions, about Walker Redgrave."

Clyde sighed and gave me a weary look. "It's late, and I already answered about a million questions from Stubbs and

Hirst." When I didn't move he sighed again and said, "Why should I talk to you? You won't even tell me who you are."

I didn't say anything.

"Are you going to just stand there?"

I just stood there.

Clyde finally shook his head wearily. "Okay, shoot."

I sat down. "How long was Mr. Redgrave here before he—" I let the end of the sentence hang.

Clyde scratched his thin stubble of beard. His sparse white hair stuck out in tufts. "Four, five days, I could find out for sure." He didn't sound as if he wanted to find out for sure.

"Close enough. Do you recall anything unusual about his movements during that time?"

Clyde took another swipe at his chin. He glanced at the darkened television a moment, probably wondering what malady was striking his team now. Then he turned back to me.

"He was pretty active with his comin' and goin'. He was real friendly, let me know right away what he did for a livin' and why he was here, but he wasn't uppity about it at all." He smiled at me sadly. "Even gave me an autographed book he wrote."

"Why did he say he was here?"

"Said he was workin' on a book gonna be about these parts. He didn't say much more'n that."

I said, "Did he ask any unusual questions, anything that caught your interest or seemed out of the ordinary?"

Clyde did a job of thinking. Finally he nodded and said, "He asked what went on in the woods. I told him about lumberin' and fishin' but he stopped me and said, like bad things, illegal stuff, did I know anything about that."

"What did you tell him?"

"Mr. Cole, I'll tell you what I told him. I run a motel here, have for thirty years. I've lived my whole life in Taylor County. So'd my daddy. I ain't never broke the law, leastwise any important laws. But I hear things, we all do around here. Maybe we know more than we'll admit. And we know there's bad folks livin' in the woods. Why, we sit elbow to elbow with 'em at Buster's and Carol's, and go to the same banks and gas stations—probably even the same churches. But we don't really know 'em. We don't really want to know 'em. They got their lives and we got ours."

He stopped, as if suddenly aware of the intensity of his monologue. He shook his head once. "Anyway, we hear the talk about dope smugglin' and moonshinin' and there's guys don't work a lick show up with new trucks and bass boats costin' twenty grand."

He gave me another sad smile, like a man who wanted to be proud of his hometown but couldn't quite summon pride. "That's what I told Mr. Redgrave."

"Did he ask about anything or anyone in particular, or did anybody call or come by?"

"He got a few calls from his wife, he took 'em here in the office. He'd chuckle and talk low in the phone for a while and hang up. They seemed to get along. He told me a couple of times his wife was a great lady. There wasn't anybody else, he was gone a lot."

"Did he ask about anyone else around here?"

Clyde considered the question, absently stroking the stubble. He frowned and shook his head, thinking.

"Wyndle Bledsoe?" I prompted.

His eyebrows shot up. "Wyndle? Wyndle Bledsoe? Mr. Redgrave didn't ask me anything about Wyndle, that's for sure."

Suddenly Clyde snapped his fingers. Maybe he really thought of something; maybe he was just trying to steer the conversation away from the lovable Wyndle.

"He did get a letter, though. I remember Etta sayin' it was different him gettin' it. We hardly ever get mail for the guests, they don't stay long enough for the most part."

"Maybe from his wife?"

"Naw, I remember it special because it was on some fancy envelope with lotsa names in the corner, all done up in silver letters. Real fancy."

So Redgrave got a letter. That didn't have to mean anything. Except that I'd found so little to connect him with this case. I wondered where the letter was.

Clyde broke into my thoughts. "It's right after that he asked about Barbour."

That startled me. "He asked about Durel Barbour?"

"One an' the same," Clyde said. "Asked if there was a lawyer in town named Barbour. I said no, what little we need one for we go up to Perry. Then Etta reminded me about Durel, him bein' a lawyer and all besides runnin' the Florida. I'd clean forgot."

"Did Redgrave go see Barbour right after that?"

"Jumped right in his car, seemed real happy."

"Okay, Clyde, this is important. Do you recall what day he received the letter?"

Clyde attacked the stubble again, and looked out the window. He said at last, "Hadda been the day before they found him dead. 'Cause I remember, that's the last time I ever seen him." He shook his head sadly. "Next mornin' we found him dead."

So Redgrave had gone to see Durel Barbour on that last day, maybe around the time he went to see Wyndle.

And Durel Barbour was a lawyer.

I left Clyde and walked back to the Camaro. Stormy had locked both doors and was staring intently at the broken window. I tapped on the passenger door and she threw both hands in the air and turned toward me, startled.

She reached over and unlocked the door. I got in.

She said, "You're scarin' me to death." The statement clearly encompassed more than tapping on the door. She was trying not to look at the dog.

"Serves you right, for the way you drive," I said, but the attempt at humor fell flat. She reached for the ignition key, reflexively, but I put a hand on her arm.

"Stormy, listen, I have to ask you something. First of all, do you know anything about Durel Barbour being a lawyer?"

She looked at me, a little puzzled. "Sure, Durel's a lawyer.

How'd you know that? He don't usually tell his business to strangers. But I guess it ain't a secret. Why?"

I evaded the question. "Does he still practice?"

"You mean, does he do any lawyerin' besides runnin' the bar? I guess so, he gets some calls that sound like lawyer stuff, and he gets some mail addressed to Durel Barbour, Attorney at Law. But it don't seem to take up much of his time. That's about all I know. You gonna tell me why you want to know?"

I sidestepped that one, too. No use for her to get suspicious of her boss. Things were confusing enough for her now.

"Do you have any idea how Barbour ended up here?"

"All he ever said was he bought the Florida from a client of his, some guy I think lives in Jacksonville. That's all I know."

"Okay, another question. You said you wanted to help, right?"

"Sure."

"You said you were in this with me, right?"

"I'm not scared, Cole. I wanna help."

"So if I ask you to do something for me, you'll do it?"

"Cole, I said I'm in this and I wanna help, okay?"

"Stormy, I need to borrow your car."

"No!" she said. "No way. No."

"Okay," I said in a flat voice. "I thought—well, I'll have to make other arrangements."

"No, wait," she said. She was thinking while she stalled for a few moments. Then she sighed and said, "You're a rat, Cole, a low-down rat. Will you at least tell me what you're gonna do with it?"

"My plan is to put some real pressure on the Bledsoe boys. That's probably going to involve some surveillance. I need a car, and I don't know when the Jeep'll be ready. Besides, they're sure to spot it. They might recognize the Camaro, but if I stay low, I might be able to pull it off."

I patted the shifter. "And if not, I can outrun them."

She closed her eyes and leaned her forehead down on the steering wheel. "Please, please don't wreck her."

"There's one other thing," I said.

Stormy said, "Oh, Lord."

"This is serious. I want you to leave town for a few days."

She was talking before I finished. "I can't do that. I can't just leave. I've got my job and—Cole, there's no way I can leave."

"I have a bad feeling about you staying here, Stormy," I said. "This thing's going to escalate pretty fast, I think."

"But I don't see why they'd—"

"Stormy, look at the dead dog."

"Oh, God, the dog," she said.

I asked her if she'd ever seen Troy or Tiny get in a fight.

"Oh, man, yeah," she said, remembering. "Hasn't been for a while, but they been kicked out of the Florida more'n once. One time Tiny was playin' team pool with Moelner Hall and Moelner scratched on the eight ball. Tiny took to beatin' Moelner over the head with a pool cue, had to take him to the hospital in Chiefland. Troy thought it was funny."

"Let me guess. Moelner didn't press charges. And he doesn't come around anymore."

"I don't want to leave." Her voice had a tremor of fear in it now. "I got my job at the Florida and Katie's in summer school."

"It's your only choice, Stormy."

"Then it ain't a choice."

"You have a point there. I'm glad you're starting to listen to reason."

She was backpedaling now. Her tone was a confused mixture of anger, fear, and frustration.

"Oh, Cole," she said. "I'll—I'll probably, I mean, maybe I'll—"

I cut her off. "Great, I'll call Lisa. You can drive the Jeep up to Atlanta as soon as the new tires are put on. And I promise I'll call you anytime I need information."

I reached over and twisted the starter before she could say anything else. She'd halfway agreed. That made me feel halfway better. I'd feel a whole lot better when she and Katie were out of Steinhatchee and safely stashed with Lisa in Atlanta. Of course, I had no idea how Lisa would feel about having a couple of unexpected houseguests.

"I'll drive you home and come back here," I said. She started to answer but I put my hand up. "I'll have Smitty get the Jeep out to you tomorrow as soon as it's ready. Clyde said I have to check out tomorrow, so is it all right if I stay at your place?"

She nodded. I got out of the car and walked to the door of my unit. I stared at the dog, which stared back at me with filmy, lifeless eyes.

"C'mon, Fido, heel," I said.

"Cole, that's incredibly sick," Stormy said.

31

It was storming hard when I woke up, just after sunrise. I pulled the curtain open and peered out. Rain pelted the Camaro. There also was a large puddle of water on the inside of the windowsill, courtesy of the hole in the glass.

The broken window brought back the events of last night into sharp detail—being followed, the high speeds on the back roads, then the broken window and the dead dog. I was okay with that, but I worried about Stormy; this was uncharted territory for her.

I jogged through sheets of rain across the puddled parking lot to the phone booth and called Smitty. He answered at once.

"It ain't tire wear," he said.

"You're the second person to make that observation."

Smitty didn't say anything about Wyndle. He told me the tires would have to come from Perry, and the Jeep wouldn't be ready until midafternoon. He agreed to run it out to Stormy's place. His wife could follow him and drive him back to town.

"Mr. Cole," he said before I hung up. "Be careful. If you're messin' with the Bledsoes, you're messin' with trouble. Bad trouble. And there ain't near enough law to help you if you get into it."

I told him I appreciated the concern and hung up. Then I called Lisa, who had been asleep. I told her about Stormy. She sighed and said, "Are you asking, or is she halfway here already?"

One more call, this time to Stormy. She picked up the phone but didn't answer right away. She was talking to someone else in the room. I heard her say, "If you don't take your bath, I'll break both your legs." Then, into the receiver, "Hello?"

"This is Cole. I promise, I'll take my bath."

She was embarrassed. "It's just a little game we have."

"I'm sure Katie will live to dance the ballet," I said. "The Jeep'll be out sometime this afternoon. Lisa's expecting you. What about Katie?"

"Momma's comin' by to get her this morning. She's out of school, so momma's going to take her with her to Gainesville to visit her sister. She was plannin' to go anyway, and they all spoil Katie rotten."

That was good—fewer people to worry about. I gave her directions to Lisa's place in Atlanta, told her I'd call her, and hung up before she could protest.

I went back to my room, packed my bag, and left a hundred-dollar travelers check to cover the window.

Then I got in the Camaro and fired the V-8. So far, driving Stormy's car had been about the only perk I'd gotten on this job.

I was dressed to follow—dark gray work shirt with black buttons, black stone-washed jeans, and dark high-top hiking boots. I had a cloth watchcap beside me, and sunglasses.

I knew Wyndle and Tiny lived out on that long county dead-end road. That seemed as good a place as any to start.

I was right—and timely. I stopped at a convenience store to fill my Thermos with coffee, drove to the intersection where the road came into Jena, and parked well off the pavement behind a couple of pine trees. The rain obscured the car, and I slumped down in the seat to wait.

I didn't have to wait long. About fifteen minutes later, the big red pickup came rumbling along. As it crested a small rise and drove past me I could see Troy Bledsoe driving. Probably coming back from a nice family visit.

I started the Camaro and eased out onto the road. I picked

up speed until I was about a hundred yards behind, then set my speed to match the truck.

Troy drove through Jena, then through Steinhatchee. He didn't stop at any stop signs, and he ran the red light at the road leading toward the coast. He just kept driving steadily, as if he expected anything else on the road to move aside. He didn't drive like a man who knew he was being followed. And he certainly didn't pay any attention to the innocuous beige Camaro following at a discreet distance.

And he went where every red-blooded good ol' boy goes in the morning—to a home-cooked breakfast. He wheeled into the lot of Carol's Café, jumped out in the rain, and trotted inside.

I pulled over across the street from Carol's, in the parking lot of a Baptist church. I had my suspect in sight.

Or almost in sight. The red four-by-four was parked squarely in front of the café. Lights shone brightly through the windows, but they were steamed and foggy; I couldn't see where Troy was sitting, or who he might be with. I hadn't seen any sign of Tiny.

So Troy sat inside, eating a nice breakfast. I sat in the Camaro, in the steaming rain. I could smell the bacon frying, even from across the street.

Every few minutes I'd flick the wipers and they'd take a swipe at the raindrops gathered on the windshield.

I liked the rain. It would make my job easier. And my job this morning was tailing Troy Bledsoe.

For that, the rain was a great help. Shadowing a suspect, especially in a small town like Steinhatchee, is difficult at best, highly risky at worst. To do the job right, you need several operatives connected by two-way radio. You need backup vehicles, binoculars, and additional operatives to come on duty when you become too tired or numb with boredom.

I didn't have any backup—just me, Stormy's Camaro, a Thermos of coffee, and the rain, which would shield and obscure my movements for a while. I figured I might get by with a day, maybe two, before my presence became too obvious.

I poured a cup of coffee from the Thermos and thought about my plan, which didn't take long since it was extremely uncomplicated.

I would follow Troy Bledsoe. I had nothing better to do. The Bledsoes were my only lead. And they clearly didn't want me nosing around in their business, whatever their business was. Which was an excellent reason for nosing around in their business.

And, I figured, my opportunity for shadowing wouldn't last long. It was only a matter of time before I was spotted, but I was hoping for a day or two, at least, to monitor their activities. Then I'd know whether the Bledsoe boys were real, or if I needed to go to Plan B—which was no plan at all.

So I sat in the rain, watched the rain, and said aloud, "Troy, I hope you all killed him. I sure do hope you killed Walker Redgrave."

Carol's parking lot was full, mostly with pickup trucks; a few had boats hooked on behind. There were two gray-and-black Florida Marine Patrol cars and a Taylor County sheriff's car, all parked together.

I hunkered down in the Camaro, peered through the foggy windshield, and waited. There's a lot of waiting when you're following someone. Surveillance is an odd combination of boredom and anxiety. A lot of the time you're waiting, but you can never let down your guard. It can be unnerving and fatiguing. But shadowing a suspect kicks in adrenaline, and I felt tense with anticipation.

I'd switched to a lurid fantasy involving French toast when Troy Bledsoe came out of the door and got in his truck. I started the Camaro, switched on the air conditioner to combat the windshield condensation, and waited for him to pull out.

Troy eased the pickup onto the street, driving a lot more placidly now, and began driving east. The rain was coming down steadily, and I turned the wipers on high and settled in about ten car lengths behind him.

We drove steadily through the rain, passed through Steinhatchee, and got on State Road 51 heading inland. We passed Tennile Airport, and at U.S. 19 Troy turned to the north, still keeping a moderate pace. I let a rock truck get between us on the four-lane stretch of road; I could pull out partway into the lane and catch a glimpse of the pickup. Troy didn't drive like a man being followed.

The rain held, and after about twenty-five miles we came to the outskirts of Perry. Just past a McDonald's, Troy slowed and turned onto a side street. By the time I eased around the turn, I caught sight of the truck pulling through the gate in a chain link fence in the next block.

I hesitated, then decided to chance a drive-by. There was a sign on the fence that said, "V and L Hauling, Inc., Perry." Troy's truck was parked next to a small frame building that looked like an office. On the other side of the little building was a larger truck with dual rear tires, an enclosed cargo area, and a power lift gate. We used to call them box trucks when I was growing up in north Georgia. I could see "V and L" painted on the side of the truck. Troy was on the front porch of the building, talking to two other men; they were all wearing jeans and work shirts and one man was holding a clipboard with a sheaf of papers.

I drove to the end of the block and took a position next to a propane fill station. The rain continued in a steady drizzle. I opened the Thermos and poured; only about half a cup of coffee was left. To run to McDonald's or not to run to McDonald's?

I crushed my Styrofoam container and threw it out the window. I sneered at the empty Thermos. I sneered at Troy Bledsoe. I turned around and sneered at the McDonald's.

I was covertly sneering at an old man walking his dog when the bigger truck lumbered out of the fenced yard. I couldn't see whether Troy was driving, but following the truck—following anything—was better than sitting in the rain. I followed.

The truck turned toward the highway; I caught a brief glimpse of a man in the passenger seat. The truck came to a slow stop, then turned into the parking lot of the McDonald's and parked. Troy Bledsoe and another man got out and went inside.

I did what any thirsty detective would do under the circumstances—I went through the drive-through.

I made sure I wasn't visible to the patrons at the front counter. I slipped down as low as I could in the seat. I put my baseball hat on. I kept the window rolled halfway up.

When Troy and his partner came out I was waiting in the Camaro, parked behind a dumpster, armed with my old Colt, a Florida map, and four large cups of coffee.

Troy hauled himself into the driver's seat, started the truck, and headed up 19. I followed.

And for the rest of the day; I followed. It wasn't hard. In the rain, I was just another obscure vehicle in the distance, and Troy could only see behind him through rain-streaked mirrors.

And so we went. We went east to a little town called Mayo. The truck stopped at an auto body shop where Troy and his partner loaded two fifty-five-gallon metal barrels onto the power lift and into the truck, shook hands with a man at the shop, handed him a piece of paper, and drove away.

There was enough traffic, and enough rain, that I could keep a discreet distance without fear of losing my prey. From Mayo we drove to another crossroads called Branford, where the same scenario was repeated at a dry-cleaning establishment in Fort White.

We continued on to High Springs. A stop at a lumber mill; one barrel into the truck.

By now it was almost noon. The McDonald's coffee was long since gone. Maybe they'd stop for lunch. Maybe I could go to the bathroom. Maybe they wouldn't spot me going to the bathroom and beat me silly in a toilet stall.

We did stop at a Burger King in Alachua. Troy parked and went in. I watched them get their food and sit down, then I wheeled around the building and went through the drive-through. Three hamburgers and four cups of coffee. Again I was armed and dangerous.

The boys hit it big at an electroplating facility outside Alachua. Seven drums went into the truck.

South of Alachua we came to Gainesville. The truck made four stops there—at a Chevrolet dealer, a medical laboratory, a boat manufacturing plant, and commercial printer. Eight more barrels went into the truck. From there we went south on Interstate 75 to Micanopy. One small garage, one barrel. Then to Williston, another stop, three drums.

It went on like this for the next four hours. The truck stopped in little towns with romantic names like Archer, Otter Creek, Old Town, Citra. We stopped at two more car dealers, another printer, four body shops, two inscrutable industrial facilities, and a photo-processing facility.

It was still raining when, shortly after six o'clock, our little caravan of two rolled back into Perry. The truck pulled back into the fenced lot, and I again hid behind the propane tank and checked my notes. Seventeen stops. Possibly as many as forty drums—a good day's work, I suspected, for V and L Hauling.

I got out of the Camaro and peered over the propane tank through the rain. I could see at an angle inside the gate. The back of the truck was visible. Troy was there, and so was Tiny, horsing a barrel off the electric lift gate into the cargo area.

I got back into the Camaro, incredibly weary from that combination of boredom and anxiety. I hadn't been spotted, I was sure, but all I could figure I'd witnessed was a routine day in the hauling business.

Until the box truck lumbered back out of the yard. And it wasn't Troy who was driving, it was Tiny. Why was the truck leaving again? Why was Tiny driving?

With great reluctance I started the Camaro and followed, like a runt puppy trying to keep momma's hind tit in sight.

32

It had rained throughout the day; it was raining during the night. There are days like that in Florida when it rains and rains. Not afternoon thunderstorms, just low, heavy clouds and steady, steady rain.

I felt cramped and tight in the Camaro as I made my way behind Tiny, south from Perry, over to Steinhatchee, back through Jena, and onto the road to nowhere. Heading home, probably, or on out to Wyndle's.

But tired as I was, there was something working against the fatigue and the aching muscles. It was a feeling that something wasn't right here. I didn't know what it was, but there was one way to find out. Follow.

So I followed, feeling very small in the vast Florida darkness. It was fully night now. I dropped back again and shut off my lights; with the rain and cloud cover, the going was much more treacherous than the night before.

And as I drove, keeping a discreet distance behind Tiny, something else joined the game. Fear—vague but unsettling fear—wrapped itself around me like a cloak. I rolled down the window and spat, realized my throat was dry and constricted. Now the gun felt bulky and oppressive against my ribs.

And there it was, the fear crystallized—the realization that I was playing a rough game against rough men. This was no insurance deadbeat or errant husband I was tailing. These were, I suspected, men who would kill, had likely killed before. There was no answer in a book that would help me now, and I realized I had no trust in my wits, none at all. There was no precedent for any of this.

I took a constricted breath. "What a dick'll do for a hundred a day and expenses," I muttered, but the words rang hollow.

Then, suddenly, the brake lights of the box truck flashed up ahead, and the headlights swung left, illuminating trees and brush. I breathed deep, shook off the cloak of my thoughts, and downshifted the Camaro. I let the engine work against the car's forward momentum—too chancy to flash the brake lights in such darkness.

The taillights silhouetted the back of the truck, and I could see it slowly turning as it backed off the road. The headlights beamed on the blacktop, then on the trees across the road. Then I couldn't see the headlights themselves, just the beams bouncing and jumping. I could faintly hear the whine of the engine as Tiny revved it in reverse. Then there was silence, followed a moment later by darkness; Tiny had switched off the lights.

I coasted slowly until I saw what appeared to be a dirt road. There was an electric line leading back into the woods.

Tiny's place, no doubt. Uptown compared to the old man's. Power straight from the electric company's lines. No mailbox, though. I stopped and pulled off the road.

I was in far too deep to stop now. The Camaro was still quietly idling. I slipped it into reverse and began a slow backward journey into blackness. I must have backed up a hundred yards when I saw, through the passenger window, a break in the tree line. I took a chance, eased the Camaro into the place between the trees, and flipped on the parking lights for a moment. I could see a clearing that narrowed into a little path curving off into the woods, probably used by hunters. I shifted into low gear and drove through the mud and potholes into the path, drove around the curve in the path, shut off the motor, and stopped. I was surrounded by blackness and rain, and felt very, very small. The night crickets screamed.

I got out of the Camaro and sank ankle-deep in muck, which intensified the eerie, oppressive feeling. I stood for a moment, shifting from foot to foot in the sinking sand, then moved a few steps forward, felt the ground firming up, and ran blindly into a low tree limb.

My eyes began to adjust to the darkness; the uniformity of the blackness dissolved into shapes and shadows, still eerie, but negotiable.

So I moved back toward the road and began to make my way along the tree line. The drizzle wet my face, and my shirt stuck to my skin. But the rain held the mosquitoes at bay. I figured I was about a hundred yards from Tiny's road.

I made my way slowly, going as quietly as I could, as fast as I dared, scurrying along the ditch next to the trees, slipping along the muck. Once I fell on my butt, sliding a couple of feet on the incline of the ditch bank. I threw my hands back for support, and they sank into the ooze. It would not be difficult, I thought wildly, to lapse into a terrified inertia.

But I got up and went on. For a while there was only the rain and the screams of the insects; then I could hear distant noises, scraping and clanging. Then there were men's voices, drifting indistinctly through the woods. Which only made me feel smaller and more lonely.

I moved forward, staying close to the shoulder of the road, and the noises and the voices got louder. I got to Tiny's road and listened. The voices were a bit more distinct now, and I thought I could make out the parking lights of the truck about a hundred yards away. I couldn't chance the dirt road; I'd have to go through the woods to get closer.

There was no even footing, but there was enough light that I could pick my way between the trees. The underbrush was thick, but that wasn't the problem. The problem was the flies—thousands of them, out for a spin in the drizzle, taking a keen interest in me. They swarmed around my face. One flew in my ear; another got in my mouth, which was open from breathing hard. This was miserable work.

But then there was a ghost of a breeze, and the flies went away, and the ground got firmer, and the dim outline of the box truck took shape through the trees.

And a scene materialized that had all the earmarks of something criminal, something clandestine, like a dope deal. But there was no dope. There was no buyer to haul anything away. There was just Tiny. He was grunting as he horsed the metal barrels into a smaller pickup truck backed up to the box truck. A shotgun leaned against the fender of the pickup.

I crouched down, huddled behind a huge dripping oak tree, and watched. The process went this way: the scrape of metal on metal; the sound of the lift descending, ending with a solid clank as it came down on top of the pickup's tailgate. More scraping, then loud grunts as Tiny rolled and wrestled a barrel into the bed of the pickup. All during this, I could hear Tiny muttering, meaningless conversation with himself.

This had been going on for about twenty minutes when I heard the sound of a motor approaching. I took out the Colt, which made me feel only slightly less lonely.

The sound of the motor got louder, and then headlights flashed between the trees and brush. The beams bounced and wavered as the vehicle turned into the dirt road and approached the clearing. I hunkered down in my hiding place and waited.

Troy's pickup truck drove into the clearing, slipped by the box truck, and went into the trees. Now I could see beyond the truck's headlights, could see a cabin or house illuminated. The truck drove up to the front of the cabin and the lights went off. Then I heard a door slam.

And a minute later Troy Bledsoe walked into the clearing. Tiny didn't say a thing, just kept muttering and horsing the barrels along.

Troy leaned against the pickup, a couple of feet away from the shotgun. There was a cellular phone stuck in a holder in his belt. Umbilical cord to daddy, or part of the security during this operation? The thought suddenly hit me—were there others out here, maybe somebody stationed down at the Jena end of the road, to warn of interlopers? Or were there others in the nearby woods?

Two more barrels were hoisted into the smaller truck, which filled the bed. There were maybe twelve barrels in the bed. Tiny got in the driver's side; Troy closed the tailgate, grabbed the shotgun, and jumped up on top of the cargo. The truck's engine came to life and off they went, with their parking lights to guide them into the cavernous darkness.

The taillights winked a few times and disappeared. I walked over to the box truck, warily, even though I was pretty sure all the participants in the loading operation had headed off in the pickup. There was no sound other than the woods' noise. I peered inside the cab. There was a stack of papers on the seat, but it was too dark to see any further detail.

I walked to the rear and looked into the cargo area. A number of barrels were still inside, probably two or three loads for the pickup. Some were labeled with white stickers, but I couldn't make out any of the lettering.

I looked and listened. There was no sound, except for the noises of the deep woods. The cabin was dark. I scurried among the trees and made it to Troy's truck. I tried the passenger door; it wasn't locked, but when it swung open there was a sudden harsh glare from the dome light. I risked a quick glance in, but the seat was empty. I closed the door, and in the sudden darkness I listened to my rapidly beating heart.

I scurried a little farther, until I was by the porch of the cabin. It was dark inside, no lights behind the curtains. And now wasn't the time to find out more about Troy's living arrangements. I hurried back to the box truck.

I was about to hop into the back of the truck when I heard the sound of an engine. I scurried back to my hiding spot and waited.

The pickup truck came through the woods, crunching underbrush. The driver exacted an amazing three-point turn among the trees and backed expertly up to the box truck.

And the same loading procedure was repeated, only this time Troy actually helped a little.

So now I knew they unloaded large barrels in the middle of the night, in the middle of nowhere. So what did they do with them? So how would I find out?

The sound of the pickup's engine rattled the night, startling me, and I realized I'd let my mind drift—a potentially fatal mistake out here.

I hunkered down. My breath came in shallow spasms, and I shivered in the hot night. The pickup eased out of the clearing. I waited until it was out of sight. Then I left the small safety of my hiding place and forced myself to move in the direction the pickup had taken, as fast as I dared, as quietly as I could. I could see the flattened underbrush that marked its trail. The going was easier than before, and the ground was firmer. But I was headed deeper into the woods, into strange and forbidding territory. I would have wished myself anywhere but here. But I was beyond making that choice.

I completely lost track of the truck for a while, then heard its engine rev up and quit. I caught a glimpse of lights flashing about a hundred yards away, in the direction I was heading. I slowed down, moving more cautiously now in the incessant drizzle. My face had been whipped and scratched by low-hanging branches. My clothes were drenched with a mixture of sweat and rain. I could smell myself.

Then I saw something else, off to my right. The distant lights of a house or cabin, dim and shimmering through the wet woods.

And then I heard it, softly, the sound of surf. We were near the gulf's edge.

I was in a complicated morass of tangled weeds, branches, cypress knees, and palmetto bushes. Ground was turning into marsh, and the foliage was extremely thick. Easier to follow the path the truck had made.

I came to a little clearing at the water's edge, surrounded by a canopy of high trees and thick brush. There was only a few feet of shoreline where the water showed, and in that place was tied the strangest airboat I'd ever seen, nuzzled upon the shore amid the mangroves. Most airboats are made for speed and not much else. This one was made for something else. The bow, in front of the raised driver's seat, was wide and flat. It would make for ungainly going; it would make for excellent hauling. And what it was hauling tonight was a load of drums; about ten of them were lined up on the bow. There was room for perhaps ten more, about one pickup load.

Which is what was being loaded on the airboat. When the cargo bow was fully loaded, Troy took a rope and lashed the barrels together, then looped the rope securely to metal tie-downs along the bow.

I moved with extreme caution now, but my breathing seemed to rattle harshly. Couldn't they hear it? Wouldn't they suddenly spring toward me? I held the gun against my thigh; it felt cold against my sweaty palm, cold and small, not really much protection at all. I clenched my teeth and willed the rattling noise back into my throat. How could they not hear me?

But they were oblivious to my intrusion. While Troy busied himself with the cargo, Tiny sat down, took a huge pinch out of tobacco pouch, and jammed it into his cheek. He chewed a couple of times, then spit a wet stream. I was in the bushes, only about twenty feet away, and I felt like an intruder in a bad dream. But I didn't feel small anymore; I felt large and awkward, an invading presence in these people's place. I stood motionless, barely breathing, wondering why simply standing still suddenly seemed such an effort.

I was watching Tiny with a fearful fascination when the silence was shattered with the roar of the boat's aircraft engine. Troy was at the controls.

While the engine idled, Tiny lumbered to his feet and moved to the boat. He waded into the shallow water among the mangroves, not taking his shoes off, and began to push the airboat back into the water. Then he grunted and gave a huge shove, and the airboat drifted away from the bank.

As soon as the boat was free of its mooring, Troy gunned the motor and engaged the propeller. The engine screamed like a World War II fighter, the cumbersome boat lurched around and straightened out, and the shore was buffeted by the prop wash.

The boat was out of sight in seconds, and I listened to the sound of the motor grow dim as Troy guided it out into the gulf. Then the sound went away, and there was Tiny, grunting softly as he heaved himself out of the water. He made it to a patch of firm ground, fell forward on his stomach, and flopped over onto his back. Just laid there, soaked by the drizzle, his eyes closed, hands placidly at his side. Then he spit, a long dark stream that arched into the air and back to the earth about a foot away from his leg. Tiny let out a big contented sigh; life was good. He began to snore.

I'd learned all I could in the woods tonight. I moved away from the little clearing.

As I made my way back toward the Camaro the tension began to dissipate, and I felt a dragging fatigue. I thought about Troy, wondered what he had been doing while Tiny heaved barrels.

I got back to the clearing where the box truck was parked. Everything looked the same, still and dark. I skirted the truck, looking down in the dim light to make my way over the uneven, muddy ground.

And saw the piece of paper in the mud, near the front wheel of the truck. I bent down and picked it up; it appeared to be some kind of printed form, but that's all the detail I could see. I wiped some of the mud off it, then folded it a couple of times and stuffed it in my pocket.

I got back to the Camaro. I was considering how loud the Cherry Bombs would sound when I heard a low sound in the distance—the airboat, returning to shore. I let the sound build, then hit the starter and rammed the car into gear. The wheels clawed at the mud, and I spun wildly as I backed out onto the blacktop road. I straightened out, rammed the car into first, and accelerated.

I drove a ways in the darkness, my lights off. I could feel my heart beating hard against my ribs. My throat was raw, and sweat was cold on my neck. I clutched the wheel with one hand, the Colt with the other, and began to shiver. The cloak of my fear, I realized, had not left me at all.

33

I WAS IN a scene I'd read a thousand times.

I pulled into Stormy's driveway and everything was wrong. When I drove past the high bushes that obscured the trailer, I saw the place was dark. Stormy had told me she would leave a light on for me.

Then I swung my Camaro around the little bend in the drive and my headlights illuminated the front of the trailer. And there was the Jeep.

I cut my lights and stopped. The hair stood still up on the back of my neck and I felt chilled, even in the steamy heat. This was way wrong. I took out the Colt and felt in my bag for my flashlight. I backed up until I was near the bushes and cut the engine. There was no sound but the night noises.

Middle of the night. Dark trailer. Jeep out front. Not a good combination. All wrong.

I got out of the car and put the keys in my pocket. I eased the door shut so the dome light would go out, heard the gentle click as the first phase of the lock engaged. I felt weary, tired of so much lurking about in the strange woods.

I moved toward the house, keeping low. I had about a hundred feet to cover, across a thick carpet of soggy pine needles. The rain had passed, and the clearing clouds let some moonlight through.

Then I was at the edge of the porch and I could barely make out something else that was very, very wrong. The front door was standing open about a foot.

I stood against the wall just to the right of the door. I could hear my breathing. I could hear the night noises.

Then I could hear something else. It was soft whimpering, like that of a lost kitten, coming from inside the trailer.

There was nothing else to do. I took a deep breath, held the gun poised in my right hand. I moved to my left, kicked the door open with my foot, and dropped to a crouch. I leveled the Colt and flicked the harsh beam of the flashlight inside.

And saw Stormy Corbin, tied to a chair in the middle of the living room. I could see the gag, I could see the blindfold. And I could see the tears mixed with the blood on her face.

She was very still, her head slumped on her chest, not moving at all. I resisted the urge to barge in, but stayed close to the doorframe and played the spot around the room, looking and listening. I turned to scan the yard behind me, went back over the interior with the light.

Then I went in, moving quickly, until I was next to her. I didn't touch her, just whispered, "Stormy, it's Cole. Can you hear me?"

Her head had snapped up then, moved from side to side, looking blindly. There was one huge whimper.

"Stay quiet," I whispered, and she made herself be quiet.

"Are you okay?" I asked, and she nodded. There was a lot of blood on her face.

I tucked the flashlight under my arm and gently pulled the blindfold up from her eyes. Then, in the wavering beam of the flashlight she looked at me, seeing now, and began to cry.

I pulled the gag down, tugged it over her chin so it lay around her neck like a scarf. It was white, wet with saliva and wet with blood.

"I have to look around. I'll be right back. Stay quiet." She nodded again.

I went back to the front door and locked it. Then I moved through the house, keeping Stormy in sight, until I was sure there was no one else inside. Then I turned on the kitchen light, came back to Stormy, and untied the ropes holding her wrists. I held her head in my hands. There were cuts at the edges of her mouth, as if she'd been struck with a hand, and a deep gash over her left eye.

"Are you hurt anywhere else?"

"Hit me hard in the stomach," she whispered. "Hurts there." Her breathing was shallow and rapid. Her eyes looked like those of a deer startled in the headlights.

I got her ankles untied and helped her to the couch. She stumbled, clutching her abdomen, and lay down. I went to the phone and dialed the operator. I hated to make the call, but I hated more not to.

I was put through to the ambulance service. A unit would be there in about ten minutes, I was told by a woman with a flat, detached voice. As I hung up I could hear her calling on the two-way radio.

I went to the bathroom and ran cold water over a washcloth, went back, and wiped her face with it, carefully dabbing around the cut above her eye. The cut was deep, but it wasn't ragged; I didn't think it would leave a scar.

"We've got a few minutes before the ambulance gets here—"

"I don't wanna ambulance," she said through clenched teeth. "Boy, my stomach hurts."

"Too late," I said. "You're going to get checked out. How'd it happen?"

"I was doin' what you said. Momma came and got Katie, and I was packed and everything. But there was this and that to do around here, and it was almost dark before I was ready to leave.

"I took my suitcase out to the Jeep and opened the tailgate. Next thing I know I'm on the ground with my face in the dirt and then I'm pulled up and held from behind. He covered my eyes with his hand and started shovin' me inside. Wasn't no use kickin', he had me around the waist and was just pushin' me along."

I could hear the low wail of a siren in the distance, faint but building. I moved the chair back in its place by the table, then picked up the rope and the bloody gag and blindfold and then stuffed them in the trash under the sink. Then I came back to the couch.

"Then what happened?"

She was beginning to breathe more regularly. "He drug me inside, he still had his hand over my face. He threw me down in the chair, he's still behind me, and wraps this—thing—around my eyes. Then he moves in front of me and leans on me, he just pushed all his weight on me, while he ties the thing real tight so it hurt."

I said, "And then he held you down while he tied you up."

She started to cry. "He was so strong, wasn't no way I could get loose."

"Tell me the rest." My voice was thin and light. The siren was louder now.

"Oh, Cole, he just started—started hittin' on my face, an' then he just punched me hard right here." She pointed to her stomach, just above the waistband of her jeans.

I noticed something about her hand.

"Why is there blood under your fingernails?" I asked her.

She looked at her hands, as if they were someone else's, and shook her head. "I must've got hold of him when he was pushin' me. I was fightin' back," she said defiantly.

"Did he—"

She patted my hand. 'No, he didn't do nothin' like that."

Some tension seemed to release at her answer. "I know you didn't see him," I said, "but do you have any idea who—"

The question was interrupted by two paramedics, who barged in the room, aloof and professional, took a look at Stormy, and went to work. I was told to move away from her. One of them gave me a sour look, like I might be a wife-beater.

"Know how this happened?" he said.

"Nope," I said. Stormy shook her head. The paramedic,

who'd seen too many domestic brawls, looked at both of us and said, "Sheez," under his breath.

After a minute one of them went out to the ambulance. I could hear the two-way radio crackle a couple of times. Then the ambulance door slammed and the paramedic came back in and joined his partner.

I went to the kitchen while they examined Stormy. They talked to her in low tones, and I couldn't make out any words. A couple of times she shook her head, and then one of them raised her blouse up on her stomach, just beneath her breasts, and began to gently probe the area of her abdomen. Once Stormy said, "Yipes," but the guy went on prodding. While that was going on the other paramedic tended to her face, applying a butterfly bandage to the deep cut and dabbing her face with a cotton swab.

After a while they both stopped, moved a few feet away from Stormy, and confided in voices too distant to make out.

The one who had taken care of her face came over to me.

"Not nearly as serious as it looked at first. Only the one deep cut on the forehead, but it's a slice. I don't think it'll require stitches. She'll be bruised around the eyes and there's some scratches, like from a ring, but they'll be fine. She does have a chipped tooth." He paused and looked at me, like I might be a little bit leprous. "Someone worked her over pretty good."

I asked him about the pain in her abdomen.

"Deep bruise. I don't see any signs of internal injury, and she's already feeling a lot better. She was knocked silly, that accounts for her grogginess." He looked at me again, suspiciously. "She ought to be watched for any signs of internal injury, but I don't see any need to transport."

Stormy said from the couch, "I ain't goin' to any hospital, you hear? I'm going to Atlanta."

The paramedics began packing their medical kits. Stormy went to the bathroom. Outside the open door the red lights of the ambulance pulsed rhythmically, painting the night in stop-action, like a crimson strobe.

One of the attendants slipped into the driver's seat and cut the emergency lights, and darkness descended like a hammer.

Only to be replaced by the distant pulsing of a blue light, coming fast. I went back inside, just before the Taylor County sheriff's cruiser came careening into the yard.

The cruiser braked to a stop in front of the trailer, next to the ambulance. Stubbs got out and sauntered over to the paramedics. He leaned on the driver's door while Hirst got out of the other side of the cruiser, walked a few steps toward the porch, then stopped, as if he didn't want to ruin his boss's entrance.

I walked to the door. "No problem here, officer. Nothing at all."

Stubbs snapped his head around. If he was surprised to see me, he didn't show it. He said something else to the ambulance driver and patted him on the shoulder.

He headed toward the trailer and passed Hirst, who stepped in formation one pace back. Sort of like the royal couple, only even weirder.

The ambulance drove away. Stubbs came in and saw Stormy, who had come back from the bathroom and was sitting on the couch. "So what happened to her?" he said.

"She tells me she fell down in the dark and hit her head."

"I don't like that one. Try again."

"Maybe she got the tiniest bit scared and that caused her to fall."

"I like that a little better," he said. "I'd like it even better if it was the truth."

"You're right, I was making that up. Actually, I haven't the foggiest." I gave him the most honest shrug I could dredge up.

Stubbs gave me a sour look. Hirst, who had been eavesdropping, went over to the refrigerator and poured himself a glass of milk. Stubbs went over to talk to him.

I sat down by Stormy. I looked at her beaten face. She looked up at me. Her eyes were bright.

I looked down at her, and felt ashamed. "You could have been killed." I put a hand on her arm. "Stormy, do you have any idea who it was?"

She shook her head. "I dunno. There was somethin'—somethin' familiar with him." She shook her head again. "Isn't nothin' I can say for sure. Just somethin'." Her voice trailed off. "I dunno," she said, very quietly.

"What made him leave?"

"I don't know. He was beatin' on me, just hittin' me and not sayin' anything, breathin' real noisy. Then there's a knock on the door and he stops. There's another knock and I hear him run out through the den. He musta gone out the back door. Then I got sick and next thing I know you're here."

Stubbs came over. "Go outside, dickie boy. I want to talk to the lady."

I went out and stood beside the Camaro, looking into the woods, really looking at nothing. After about ten minutes Stubbs came out.

"She said she fell down in the dark and hit her head," he said.

"See there."

He looked at me and his face might have gotten a little red. He reached in his shirt pocket and took out a flat gold case, opened it, and extracted a toothpick. He rammed the toothpick in his mouth and snapped the case shut. I'd never seen anyone carry toothpicks in a gold case, but then again, I'd never seen anybody like Stubbs, either.

"You're pushin' it, Cole," he said.

"I hope so."

He glared at me. "Who beat her up?"

"I have no idea."

"What were you doin' out here?"

"She's a newfound friend. I came to visit."

Stubbs was starting to work the muscles of his jaw. He looked into the Camaro and saw my hat and bag.

"Why're you drivin' her car?"

"Have you driven it? It's incredible. I talked her into it so I could relive my misspent youth."

"Crap," Stubbs said and spit his toothpick out. "That story's as solid as a sinkhole."

"It's the best I can do right now," I said. "I'm a little preoccupied."

Stubbs studied my muddy, filthy clothes. "Where've you been, anyway?"

"Out and about," I said.

Stubbs suddenly did a half turn and grabbed my shirt with one meaty paw. "Where have you been?"

I stood rock still for a moment. What I wanted to do was knee him in the groin. What I did was slowly bring my hands up, grab his wrist, and pull his hand away.

"Out and about," I said. "Turning over rocks, seeing what crawled out."

We stood together, faces only inches apart, my hands still encircling his wrist. Then he jerked his hand free. He said, "You're real close to gettin' yourself killed." He leaned in close. I could smell the mint flavor of his toothpick. His voice was a soft, brittle whisper. "Don't expect me to save your butt. 'Cause maybe I can't. Or maybe I won't."

He walked to the cruiser, got in, and slammed the door, hard. About ten seconds later Hirst came trotting out, went by me and tipped his hat, and got in the car. Stubbs didn't waste time getting out of the driveway.

When they were gone I went back inside.

Stormy stood in the middle of the living room, holding her overnight bag.

"Where do you think you're going?" I asked.

She gave me a brave grin. "Atlanta, honeybunch. I never thought I'd feel safer there than here," she said. "But I do now."

34

I HEARD A scrabbling at the door, almost an animal sound. I eased the Colt out of its holster and knelt down very quietly behind the bar separating the living area from the kitchen, wishing everyone would leave me alone.

There was a little more scrabbling and then a solid knock on the door, then another knock until it turned into full-fledged door knocking.

I moved quietly to the door and got beside it. The knocking had stopped but I might have heard breathing. I put my hand over my mouth to muffle my voice and muttered, "Who's there?"

"Stormy, it's me, Mickey. Are you all right?"

I opened the door, and there was Mickey, framed in the moonlight. She was dressed for the night—dark jeans, dark pullover, strawberry hair damply framing her face.

She was also holding a large blue-steel revolver, which she absently pointed in the general direction of the ground, as if she'd forgotten she had it.

Her eyes widened when she saw me. "You're not Stormy," she said.

"No kidding." I stuck my hand out. "This is getting to be way too much for one night. Give me the gun, please. I'm keeping all the guns tonight."

She looked down at the gun as if it were some strange thing that had suddenly shown up there. She raised it and pointed it toward me.

"Not that way," I yelled. I took a quick step to the side

and grabbed her wrist with my free hand. She didn't resist, just stood there calmly holding the gun.

I slid my hand along her wrist to her hand, and over the cylinder of the revolver. She let go and I took the gun away. And breathed again.

I looked out into the dark yard. Nothing moved. The trees glistened wetly in the moonlight. I motioned for her to come in.

She looked as if she'd been out in the night for a while. Her clothes were damp; her hair clung wetly to her cheeks and shoulders. She looked confused, like a pet who'd wandered too far from home.

She walked to the middle of the living room, stood with her back to me for a moment. Then she turned to me and pushed the hair out of her face.

"Where's Stormy?" she asked.

I told her. She sat on the couch, picked up a bloody cotton swab, and stared at it. She was in way over her understanding.

I put my gun back in its holster. I put Mickey's gun on the kitchen counter, where it would take her three leaps and a bound to get it.

When she didn't say anything for a while, I asked conversationally, "What did you want Stormy for?"

She said, "I came to ask her to—if she'd help me—" she searched for the right words. I waited.

Then she said, "I needed to see *you*," as if that explained everything.

I realized I was looming over her, so I sat down on the edge of the coffee table, a few feet away from her. I offered her coffee.

She shook her head and said, "This is real hard."

"The easiest way," I said, "is just to start."

That took a little while, but then she said, "You know I overheard you lookin' for Wyndle. And then I hear people talkin' around town, not knowin' what you're up to, thinkin' it's strange your bein' here."

There wasn't anything to say to that.

"Mister, there's somethin' I gotta talk to you about," she said suddenly. Then, once again: "This is real hard."

That was as far as she got. She sat and looked at me hopefully.

I took a long shot. I remembered the first time I'd met her, remembered the way she looked so intently at the picture of the young marine. "Is it about your brother?"

She looked at me as if I'd lifted the heavy burden of disclosure from her. She nodded her head up and down, several times, earnestly.

"Your father said he was dead."

She nodded again. "Mitch," she said. "Dwayne Mitchell Smith. Everybody called him Mitch ever since he was little."

"Did he die in combat?"

"I wish. It'da been better for everyone. Father says he's dead but we honestly don't know. He—he just disappeared."

I said, "As in missing?"

"As in he just went away, didn't tell no one, didn't leave no note." She suddenly looked angry. "Didn't even tell me."

"How long ago?" I asked.

She gave the ceiling a thoughtful look. "October 16, 1982."

"And you've never heard from him again?"

She shook her head, and a thick tear ran down her cheek.

"People do leave," I said gently. "For all kinds of reasons. Reasons that seem important to them at the time."

"No! Mitch wouldn't do that. I'd know. He'd tell me. He would. We—we were buddies."

I took another tack. "It was after you heard I was looking for Wyndle Bledsoe that you wanted to see me about Mitch. Is there a connection?"

Again the look like I had helped her past a rough spot. "Mitch was workin' with Troy Bledsoe when he disappeared."

"At V and L?"

"Yeah. Look, let me tell you about Mitch, help you understand."

I nodded, gave her my patient look.

"Mitch was in 'Nam, he was a captain, up through the ranks. He was in lots of fightin', even got the Bronze Star for bein' a hero. Got a big write-up in the paper for it." She looked off in the distance. "He carried that medal with him everywhere, called it his lucky charm. He could be proud of himself, even if nobody seemed to be proud he'd gone over there and fought."

She pulled at the ends of her hair, absently wrapping it around her finger. "When he came back he wasn't the same. He used to be happy and full of livin'. After the war he didn't care much about nothin'.

"Anyway, he didn't do much of anything for a long time, just took a few vocational courses in Perry and some odd jobs. Said he couldn't get his mind on work. Finally he started workin' as a driver for V and L. Did that for more'n two years. First time he'd worked steady.

"The work agreed with him. He started savin' his money, got a real nest egg laid away. He'd been accepted up to Santa Fe Junior on the G.I. Bill. One night, just after he'd gotten the letter from Santa Fe, we was out on the dock talkin'. He looked at me, and I thought I saw real happiness in his eyes. He told me he was turnin' his life around, gonna go to school, make somethin' of himself."

She started crying, little whimpers that escalated into huge racking sobs. She sat there, hands at her side, head hung down, hair over her face, and kept sobbing.

Tentatively I reached over and put a hand on her shoulder. She didn't resist, and the sobbing began to subside. I patted her shoulder, a helpless, inadequate gesture.

She looked up at me through tears and strands of wet hair. "That's the last time I saw him. Next day he went to work and just didn't come home." She shook her head. "Never came home."

The connection hit me hard. Walker Redgrave had been full of life, full of plans, full of expectations, and suddenly he was dead. Mitch Smith had been depressed, then got interested in life, began to look for happiness. And then, suddenly, he disappeared. Redgrave had visited Wyndle. Then he was gone. Mitch had worked with the Bledsoes. Then he was gone. A collision of facts that superseded coincidence.

I could have asked more, but there was no need. I knew the answers. The family would have frantically called the law and been told to call back after he'd been gone longer. They'd called back and the law had looked into the matter, half-heartedly, and told the family that there was nothing could be done when an adult just took off, no signs of foul play.

"I'm sorry," I said.

"There's somethin' else, ain't no secret." She said it like she wished it was a secret. Her voice was very small now. "I was married to Troy Bledsoe. I was the one helped Mitch get a job there."

A single tear ran down her cheek. She wiped it away with the back of her hand and said, "Maybe he is dead. Maybe he's dead and Troy had somethin' to do with it. He told me he didn't trust 'em, even said that me bein' Troy's wife, but the money was good. He was lookin' to quit." Almost as an afterthought she said, "I was separated from Troy when Mitch disappeared. It wasn't no good."

She put some strength back in her voice. "They done somethin' bad to him, Mr. Cole. I know they did. I know it. You gotta go find out what they did, please would you find out what happened to Mitch?"

Her eyes got bright with meager hope. "Stormy said you was some kinda detective. I got money, I can pay you." She pulled some wadded-up bills out of her purse.

She shoved the bills toward me, and I put up my hand. "I don't want your money, Mickey. I'll see what I can find out about Mitch. I'm investigating the Bledsoes, and I might be able to find out something."

"Thank you," she said in a very small voice. It was hard to tell if she was talking to me or God.

35

I GOT MICKEY'S money safely stashed inside her purse, and got her in her car and back on the road to town. It was very late, that time in the morning when dawn seems far away, and the day past seems distant as well.

I got in the shower, turned the water hot, and stood for a long time under the rushing stream. So someone had come out to Stormy's, beat her senseless, and trussed her up. For what purpose? Did he want information? Not likely, he never said a word and avoided letting Stormy see him. Another warning to me? Mostly likely, which pointed right at the Bledsoes. The brothers were used to getting their way; they didn't know much about me, only knew that I had inquired about Walker Redgrave and then not left town when they told me to.

But the Bledsoes weren't running scared—far from it. I'd watched them conduct what appeared to be business as usual. And roughing up Stormy—I was morally sure they were responsible—was just a part of their business. I was an annoyance to the Bledsoes, they weren't scared of me.

They would be soon.

I was at the end of my ability to stay awake. I lay down on Stormy's bed, got a gentle whiff of her perfume, and remembered nothing until I woke up seven hours later.

I took another shower and put water on for coffee. I felt old and creaky. While the water was heating, I sat at the kitchen bar and picked up the phone.

My first call was to Lisa Carmichael's house. After four rings Stormy answered the phone.

"This is Cole. I only have a minute, just wanted to check and see if you got there safe."

"I'm here," she said. Some of her usual good humor had returned. "Cole, that Jeep's a mess, the tires are all out of balance. You gotta—"

I cut her off. "Bye bye. Have fun shopping. Guard the Jeep with your life. Atlanta drivers are murderous."

Next I called the Florida Bar—not the one in Steinhatchee, the one in Tallahassee.

Durel Barbour was an enigma—put-on swampy accent, oddball clothes, driving a Corvette in four-by-four country.

And professionally, what was he? A lawyer, but he intimated that the folks who regulate lawyers weren't too happy with him. Was he still licensed? If he was, was he practicing any law in Taylor County, or just living high off the proceeds of his Florida Bar?

An operator answered and connected me to an officious-sounding woman, who put me through to a clerk, who said it was the wrong extension and transferred me back to the operator, who landed me back with the officious woman, who seemed irritated at me for being put back through to her.

"You sound irritated at me for having been put back through to you," I said. She said, "Hrumphh," and the elevator music came on again. Time passed. The water all boiled away. A nifty violins-and-guitar version of "Eleanor Rigby" began playing. During the bridge another woman answered.

I said, "Could you put me on hold for one more minute? 'Eleanor Rigby' is one of my favorite songs."

After a little more of this and that, and two more musical intervals, I found out that: Yes, Durel Barbour was a member in good standing of the bar, fully licensed to practice law in the great state of Florida. Yes, he had been disciplined, suspended for a short time, in fact. It had happened in

Jacksonville six or seven years ago, and had to do with accepting a fee he knew involved drug money. No, the woman at the bar didn't have any more details, but if I'd like to write for more information, she'd be happy to look right into it.

Before she could hang up I asked one more question: Did the bar list areas of expertise for its members? That required another transfer, so off I went into Muzakland for a few moments; then I was connected to a perky woman who said yes, the members could and often did list their areas of practice. I mentioned Durel Barbour. Then I got to listen to some more musical favorites.

She came back on the line and said: "Mr. Barbour certainly does list a couple of areas of expertise—environmental and criminal."

Before I hung up I told her she'd made my day.

Environmental. Criminal. What a lovely combination.

Next I called a friend who taught engineering at Georgia, whom I remembered did some environmental consulting for developers, much to the chagrin of his liberal friends.

That got me a contact at the Environmental Protection Agency in Atlanta, where a man told me I should probably talk to somebody in the Florida Department of Environmental Regulation, which got me through to a man in the Gainesville office. He'd been a bureaucrat long enough to be cagey, and after I told him who I was, he said his name was Smith.

Mr. Smith took the time-honored governmental stance of waffling. But he did mention that there was a man who worked in the environmental section of one of the electric companies who might be willing to talk to me.

"His name is Weems. Tell him Smith at DER referred you," he said.

I dialed the number Smith gave me and was told Mr. Weems would be back in just a few minutes.

So I called state information and got connected with the

agency that oversees corporations. I got a clerk by the name of Bedford Prather, and asked him if he had any information about V and L Hauling, Inc.

I heard his computer make little computer noises. It wasn't long before he said, "Got 'em right here, sir. V and L Hauling, closely held corporation located in Perry."

"That's the one," I said. "Do they list a board of directors or major stockholders?"

I heard the computer click and whir a couple of times. "A Mr. Vernon Gash and Lonnie Driggers are the principal stockholders. You wanted directors, let's see. Yes, Mr. Gash and Mr. Driggers, and a Wyndle Bledsoe. Also, there's a Mr. Durel Barbour, listed as director and corporate counsel."

Bingo. A tangled and seamy web indeed.

I called Weems again, this time got him directly. He sounded happy, almost exuberant, like a man who enjoyed his job too much.

"Smith again," he laughed. "Wanting me to be his mouthpiece. So you're a detective. Just don't quote me. What do you need?"

I explained a little about trucks and barrels and pickups at such places as dry cleaners and paint shops.

That was all Mr. Weems needed. He talked and talked, explaining the myriad of nooks and crannies of environmental procedures. He was particularly helpful in deciphering the intricacies of the form I'd found in the mud. He'd never talked to a real live private investigator. He loved having such an audience.

And I loved the information he gave me. I came away with enough stuff to put the Bledsoes in Starke. But not for the murder of Walker Redgrave. I'd have to get that on my own.

Which is what I decided to do.

36

I WAS BEHIND the propane tank again, watching the activities behind V and L Hauling's fence. The late-morning sun was high in the sky, burning hotly.

There wasn't much to see. The box truck was gone, and the only vehicle in the yard was a nondescript Olds Cutlass.

I watched the Cutlass for a while. It didn't move. I left my little hiding place and drove to McDonald's for coffee, then drove back by V and L. Everything was the same.

I drove to the end of the block and found a phone booth. V and L Hauling was only in the white pages, just a phone number. I dialed it.

Three rings and a woman's voice said, "V and L Hauling." I said I had the wrong number and hung up.

I sat in the Camaro and drank coffee in a paper cup. Nothing to do except watch and wait. A peeper's life.

I was fantasizing about how it would be pleasant to be away from all this, be on campus, heading to teach an early-afternoon class, when I was saved from that sort of madness by the Cutlass. It drove by slowly, eased into the McDonald's lot, and parked. A nondescript woman—perfect match for the car—got out and went inside. It was shortly after noon.

I got back in the phone booth, called V and L again, and got an answering machine. A man's voice, distinctively Florida, said, "Hi, you've reached V and L Hauling. We're not here to take your call and we're sure sorry. You can leave a message, or you can call Glenda between eight and twelve every day. Have a good one, and keep on haulin'."

Surely Glenda was the woman in the Cutlass. Surely she worked mornings. Surely she'd be going about her business now, far away from her morning job at V and L Hauling.

I finished the last of the coffee, crushed the paper cup and tossed it into the back of the Camaro, suddenly felt bad about doing that to Stormy's car, and reached back and retrieved it. It dripped coffee onto my jeans, so I placed it carefully on the carpet at my feet.

I drove back down the block. No cars or trucks at V and L. I parked behind the propane tank again and got out. There was no one at the propane filling station. There was no one anywhere around.

I walked across the street, directly up to the door of V and L, and knocked. No one answered the door. I knocked again to make sure, then cast a glance toward the street. Nothing and nobody.

I took out my wallet and extracted a credit card. The lock on the front door looked insubstantial, the kind that only keeps honest people out.

I put pressure on the doorknob and carefully swiped the credit card between door and frame. On the second try the lock popped open. So much for honesty. That swipe of the credit card could get me time in Starke.

I opened the door and went in, closed it behind me, and locked it again. I looked around; I was in a typical small office of a typical blue-collar small business. A couple of battered metal desks stacked high with stacks of papers and file folders, railroad chairs, four or five green file cabinets, fan in the corner, a metal wastebasket overflowing with wads of paper. The answering machine was next to the phone on one desk, and the message light was blinking.

There were two doors leading off the front office. One was closed, and there was a name plaque on it that simply said, "Lonnie." The other door was open.

I walked to Lonnie's door and opened it. The room was

bare except for a clean desk, another railroad chair, and a file cabinet. I walked over to the desk and opened a drawer. Empty. I went to the file cabinet and pulled a drawer open. Empty. I looked around the room. Just an empty office, not Lonnie's office anymore.

The other office had a human connected to it. The plaque on the door said, "Vernon, President." They weren't big on last names around here. It was, like the front room, overrun with papers and the clutter of inhabitation. There was a wooden desk, a big leather high-backed executive chair, pictures of a woman and a couple of kids, one four-drawer file cabinet.

In an office with file drawers, the answer is usually in the file drawers. That's where I began.

Vernon was not neat. He had no filing system. Everything was crammed into folders, stuffed in drawers, piled in stacks.

Just like Walker Redgrave.

I got to work. I started with the bottom file drawer—check ledgers going back ten years. Next drawer up—check ledgers, ten to fifteen years back.

Third drawer—every receipt, it seemed, he'd ever obtained for work on the box truck. That took up the whole drawer.

The top drawer—things got more interesting. There was a thick book of government regulations. It appeared to cover statutes on hazardous waste. There was a federal section, and one entitled "DER Rules." I thought about taking that but decided against it.

Then I got a pack of preprinted forms—three copies and carbons to each form. The heading on the forms said, "Hazardous Waste Manifest." Just like the one I'd found in the mud.

At the back was a small box crammed with similar forms, but these were filled out. I pulled one at random and looked at it.

According to the form, four barrels of something called PERK had been picked up at the Clean 'n Dandy Dry Cleaners in Alachua. The drums were assigned a DER number. And, according to the manifest, they were delivered to a designated receiving site in Arkansas.

Fat chance those drums went to Arkansas. Good chance they were lying in thirty feet of water, or under four feet of muck.

I folded the manifest and stuffed it in my shirt pocket. I sat down at the desk and opened the top drawer, found it full of pencils, paper clips, stapler and staples, scraps of paper, receipts—all the odds and ends of a working man's office. I closed the drawer.

The front door opened.

Instinctively, I dropped behind the desk, and listened. Whoever had opened the door was humming, a woman's voice. I heard the door close, heard feet scuff on the old wood floors, heard a drawer open.

I had the Colt, but it wouldn't look good for me to blaze my way out of a place I'd broken into in the middle of the day. I kept the Colt in the holster and listened to the sounds in the front room. Probably one person.

Another drawer opened, then closed. Silence for a moment. Then a voice said, "I bet it's in Vernon's."

I stood up and grabbed a clipboard lying on a table, made a little noise so she'd notice.

When she came in the room I was standing with clipboard and pencil, making notes and scrutinizing a wall.

"Good morning," I said heartily.

She looked at me and opened her mouth, backed up a few steps. At least she didn't scream. "What're you doin' here?"

"Why, measuring the place to be tented for termites," I said.

"I don't know nothin' about this," she said, looking scared and suspicious at the same time. "They'da told me."

I shrugged. "Just doing my job, lady. I can't help what your boss tells you or doesn't tell you."

"Where's your car?" she snapped.

"Why, across the street, of course," I said as if the answer were totally adequate. "Vernon let me have a key, said you'd be gone in the afternoon."

I was skating, but I didn't have much to lose. I looked around the room again. "I thought Troy might be here, but I didn't see his truck."

"Vernon picked him up, they's on a run today."

"What about Lonnie?" I asked innocently.

She glared at me. "What's Lonnie got to do with anything?"

"Never mind," I said, keeping the innocent voice working. "I need to see Vernon or Troy about this." I gestured vaguely at the room. "Give 'em my quote. When will they be back?"

"Not till late. They all the way up to Jacksonville today." Then she stopped, as if she was giving away too many family secrets. "You best go." She looked at the phone. "You come around when Vernon's here."

I said I'd do that and sauntered out into the afternoon sun.

37

I WALKED BACK to the Camaro as if I didn't have a thing to hide, never looked back to see if Glenda was watching.

Clouds had begun gathering in the west. The humidity created a vicious, overpowering mugginess, and it was both hot and cool at the same time. Just another summer afternoon in the paradise we call Florida.

I got the motor started and turned the air conditioner on high, then eased out onto the road and drove sedately toward McDonald's. Nothing to hide, nothing at all.

There wouldn't be much time now. But time enough for something to drink at McDonald's. A little time to think.

I pulled through the drive-through and parked the Camaro in a shaded corner of the parking lot. The coffee tasted good, even in the heat, and I could feel the solid draft of the air conditioner on my face.

Glenda would try to get in touch with Vernon. You don't confront a stranger in the office and not tell the boss.

But Vernon was out on a run, with Troy apparently. She might be able to leave a message at one of the pickup sites, if she knew the precise itinerary. At least she would leave some kind of note at the office.

She might try to call Barbour. She might try Tiny. She might wheel around the corner, jump out of her car, and shoot me dead with a large gun. Anything seemed possible by now.

I drained the coffee and crushed the cup. It was probable that Troy and Vernon wouldn't get back from their run until the end of the afternoon. Plenty of time to go see Barbour. A lot better than hiding behind a propane tank in hundred-degree weather watching an empty building.

I rummaged through Stormy's tapes stashed in the console, found *Honky Tonk Heaven* by the Dixie Dew Drops and plugged it in the tape player. I got the Dew Drops right in the middle of the bridge to "Hello Lonely, Goodbye You."

I turned the tape low, aimed the car toward Steinhatchee, and considered my latest felony. What had I learned at V and L Hauling? Not much that I didn't know—or could at least infer—about the hazardous waste, about the bogus dumping operation, about Barbour's involvement in the company.

But one thing nagged at me. Lonnie. Where was Lonnie? His office was bare, completely cleaned out. So he might have just resigned, happens all the time in small businesses and partnerships.

By why had Glenda responded so oddly when I'd mentioned Lonnie's name? What was there in the tone of her voice? Suspicion—there was some of that. Surprise, that I had mentioned his name at all. And perhaps some undercurrent of embarrassment. Glenda clearly wasn't comfortable talking about Lonnie.

Lonnie and Vernon. A falling out among thieves? I wasn't sure why, but it seemed a good idea to find out a little more about Lonnie.

I stopped at a phone booth on Main Street in Steinhatchee. A huge thunderhead had formed just offshore, and I could feel the building strength of the cooler wind that would bring the rain. But the mugginess was still overpowering, and I was getting sick of wearing the windbreaker to hide the Colt.

There was a Lonnie J. Driggers in the phone book, with a Bronson phone number. I fished out a quarter and dialed.

A woman with a very small, fragile voice answered. Young children squawked in the background. I could hear the sounds of a television.

I made my voice official: "Mr. Lonnie Driggers, please."

She didn't say anything. The children shouted. The television droned. There was a little static on the line. Lightning popped in the thunderhead.

I waited an appropriate time, then said, "Is this the residence of Mr. Lonnie Driggers?"

Still no answer for a moment, then the little voice said, "Who's calling?"

"My name is Dalmas, with the Department of Toxin Recovery"—I made that up on the spot—"needing to talk to him on some routine administrative matters regarding, let's see here, V and L Hauling."

"Vernon handles that," the little voice said.

"Yes, but there's no answer at the office and Mr. Driggers was kind enough when we last spoke to give me his number. There is a deadline, you know, for filing this information and I'm just trying to help Mr. Driggers avoid a substantial fine and penalty. Is he not home?"

She started to cry. This was happening a lot to me lately. Cole shows up and women start to cry. Stormy, Mickey, why not add one more to my list?

"Is something wrong, ma'am?" I said, much more gently this time. "Are you Mrs. Driggers?"

She said yes, through teary little hiccups. She didn't hang up. I asked: "Is there anything I can do?"

"What can you do when he just up and leaves, mister?" she said, her voice much harder now. "You tell me, what can you do?"

She still wasn't hanging up, so I kept on. "Oh my, Mrs. Driggers. That's awful. A man shouldn't leave a wife and family like that. But maybe he's just gone to get away for a little while and he'll show right back up."

"You call a month a little while? You think after a month he'll waltz in here and say, 'Hi honey, I'm home'?"

"I did notice they'd cleaned his office out."

"*They*, Vernon and Glenda, *they* cleaned it out less'n a week after he was gone, said they knew he wasn't comin' back. How'd *they* know that?"

I realized she was probably going to talk about as long as I'd keep prompting her. But I didn't have the heart to probe this sad woman anymore. I told her I'd call Vernon, told her I was sorry about Lonnie, and hung up.

The sky had darkened quickly while I was talking to Mrs. Driggers, and when I left the phone booth I felt the first drops of the coming rain. The sky was that odd juxtaposition of deep purples and grays over the water and blues and billowy whites to the east. Soon the sun would descend behind the angry clouds and there would be the deepest of purples and jagged rays of pink. The blue would fade to gray and then dark gray, and wind and sheets of driven rain and thunder and lightning would be everywhere.

I quickstepped to the Camaro just as the raindrops began to splatter the windshield, tracing descending paths in the dust on the glass.

I drove to the Florida Bar. No cars in the lot. I drove to Carol's Café and parked. No Corvette there. I looked up Barbour in the phone book in the booth on the restaurant's porch, but he wasn't listed.

I went in Carol's and took a seat at the counter. I ate a huge piece of key lime pie—best I'd ever had—and drank two cups of coffee. The clock above the kitchen door said 4:00 P.M. There was thunder outside, and the steady pecking of the rain on the restaurant's tin roof.

I drove back to the Florida in the intensifying storm, and saw the Corvette parked near the entrance. No other cars. I parked and went to the front door and knocked.

"Open," a voice said from within. I turned the knob and the door swung inward. I walked inside.

There's nothing quite like a bar that's just been opened up after being shut all day. There is no smell quite like that of stale beer and cigarette smoke and old sweat.

But the place was cool, and that was welcome after the hours I'd spent in the heat. Barbour was sitting on his stool, and there was a stack of papers and a pocket calculator in front of him.

"Stormy's friend," he said, as if he were genuinely glad to see me. But, I reminded myself, he was a lawyer. Take nothing for granted.

"Have you heard from Troy?" I said.

"Troy? You mean Troy Bledsoe? Why would I be hearin' from Troy Bledsoe?" He smiled benignly. "You would like a drink, perhaps?"

I didn't say anything, went around the bar, and found a glass. I scooped some ice into it and filled it with soda water from the dispensing hose. I came back around the bar and sat two stools away from Barbour. I took a drink and smacked the glass down on the bar.

"Hot out there," I said.

Barbour nodded. "Is everything okay, sir?"

"Fine," I said. "Fine and dandy." Suddenly I wondered if I was looking at a killer.

I knew he knew some about me. He knew I'd been to Wyndle's. He'd followed Stormy and me. He probably knew I'd been warned off by the Bledsoes. I also knew he wouldn't be forthcoming with such admissions.

"That's a nice car you have," I said. "Probably the only red one around these parts." The smell inside the bar didn't seem as intense.

Barbour pushed the calculator away and said, "Thanks." He seemed clearly puzzled, unable to tell which way the conversation was headed. And I was determined to keep him puzzled.

"I might have seen one like it out toward Buster's place the other night. You live out that way?"

"What? No, no. I live down at Horseshoe Beach, opposite direction from there. Why do you ask?"

I dismissed the question. "I hear you used to be a lawyer."

"Not used to, sir, am," he said. I could hear the pride in his voice, and an arrogance if you listened close.

"Environmental, right?"

"Why—yes," he said. "I once specialized in environmental law, as well as—"

"Drugs, too, I bet."

His mouth dropped open, but before he could say anything, I took off on a new tangent.

"Does the name Mitch Smith ring a bell?" I asked conversationally.

There was just a second of fear, of naked terror, before the mask of his face closed up. He even tried a grin, but it came out lopsided and grotesque.

"The—the young marine who went away?"

"That's the one. I understand he worked at V and L for a while. Then he just up and left."

"The young ones, they do that sometime."

"Sure they do," I said. "But I heard he'd just enrolled in college. I heard he was starting to get excited about life. I guess he got so excited he just couldn't stand boring old Steinhatchee anymore, right?"

It wasn't fear in Barbour's eyes now. It was hate. He got up and went around the bar. He took a glass and poured from a bottle of Jack Daniel's. He looked at me, ever the venerable host, and waved the bottle. I shook my head and he put it back on the counter.

"Make yourself at home, sir. I will be right back." He walked into the kitchen.

I got up and walked around the bar, picked up the dispenser hose, and poured another soda water. I moved close to the kitchen door and listened: soft words, silence, then more words. One side of a telephone conversation. I moved back to my seat.

Barbour came back from the kitchen; he seemed more agitated now. He sat back down at the bar and turned on the calculator, saying, "If you'll excuse me, sir, I've got to—"

"I understand Walker Redgrave came in here. Stormy told me. Did you get his autograph? It might be worth something, now that he's dead."

"A terrible thing," Barbour said. Almost as terrible as the conversation he was having with me, no doubt. "Sir, what is the purpose of your visit?" There was a hard edge to his voice now.

"I'm lonely," I said. "I haven't caught any fish yet. But you never know when you'll land a big one. You know, fishing's a strange thing. You can't see the fish. But you know they're there, under the water. Sometimes they can see you, and they're easy to spook. You have to go slow. So what do you do? You bait a hook and you dangle it in front of them. Sometimes that doesn't get you anywhere, not for a while, anyway. But you keep at it, keep dangling that hook with the right kind of bait and suddenly—" I slapped my hands together—"you have him, the one you wanted. The big one."

I leaned back a little on the stool and grinned. "Right?"

"I don't fish. I wouldn't know."

"One more thing," I said. "Have you ever noticed how fish of the same kind stick together? Schooling, they call it. I bet there's all kind of interesting schools of fish around here. Big fish, bad fish, just hanging together, taking care of each other."

Barbour had had enough. "You talk crazy, sir. I'll have to ask you to leave."

I noticed that his accent had diminished greatly. Probably the stress of the conversation made him forget his roots.

I got up off the stool, finished the last of my water, and slammed the glass down. "Boom, the big one bites," I said.

I headed toward the door. "Say hi to Wyndle," I said over my shoulder.

I took a few steps and turned around. Barbour was staring at me, not moving.

"I forgot," I said. "Stormy said for me to tell you she wouldn't be in today. Pretty surprising, a hard-working girl like that. Must be something pretty serious to keep her away. But the young ones, they do that sometimes, don't they?"

38

I DROVE ABOUT a hundred yards and parked behind a dumpster in the parking lot of the hardware store. A rangy cat hunkered under the dumpster's overhang and looked at me like I'd butted in on his cafeteria line. The storm was in full fury; thunder rumbled and lightening cracked across the clouds.

I let the motor idle and kept the wipers on. So far, I thought, it had been a productive day. I'd run up Stormy's long-distance phone bill. I'd committed at least one felony. I'd met the lovely Glenda. I'd talked with the distraught wife of the missing Lonnie. I'd braced Durel Barbour. And I still had the whole evening ahead of me.

The wipers slapped away a sheet of driving rain and I caught a glimpse of the red Corvette leaving the Florida Bar. The car straightened out on the road and the retractable headlights came up. The Corvette passed me, going fast, wheels kicking up sprays of water. I saw Barbour for a moment, staring straight ahead. He was heading in the direction of Jena. Which led to the road to nowhere. Not much of a surprise there. I let him go.

It was suppertime. I drove back to Carol's Café. And saw the box truck parked squarely in front of the restaurant.

No time like now, I thought, figuring any pretense at cover had been blown by my encounters with Glenda and Barbour. Maybe the boys were huddled inside Carol's, already scheming about how to do away with the pesky detective who'd intruded on their profitable little business. Or maybe they were just eating.

Tiny and Troy sat facing each other at a four-top table in the back dining room, sitting silently with their dinners and iced tea. Troy was reading a newspaper; Tiny flipped the pages of a comic book.

I passed a waitress just as she was coming away from their table, shaking her head resignedly.

I got to the table and pulled out a chair, turned it around backward, and sat down. I said, "Howdy do, Mr. and Mr. Bledsoe," and gave them the biggest grin I could muster.

Troy had his tea glass raised halfway between table and lips. It hovered there, and Troy eyed me silently.

Tiny noticed me. He said, "I seen you."

Troy said, "Shut up, Tiny." That was all Tiny needed; he closed the comic book, scooted his chair back a few inches, and started looking from me to Troy and back again, like a spectator at a tennis match.

I snuggled into my chair. Troy carefully folded the paper and put it to the side. He looked at me and said, "Soldier, I seen you in the Florida Bar."

"Yessir," I said. "And I've seen you lots of places."

He looked at me for a time, nodding his head slightly. "Where's that?"

"Why, all those places you drive your truck. Mayo, Alachua, Bronson, Gainesville, Perry. You do get around."

His expression hardened. "Where else, soldier?"

I looked thoughtful. The waitress came by and said, "You havin' dinner, honey?" Her most distinctive feature was her makeup, a cross between Degas and Sherwin Williams. "Special's fried mullet, collard greens, and cheese grits, comes with hush puppies, pie, and a drink, three ninety-five."

"Tea only," I said. "I don't know if I'm in the proper company to enjoy a good home-cooked meal."

She went away with my tea order. I glanced at Tiny, who was trying to catch a fly in his hand.

I said to Troy, "I assume you're the spokesman for the both of you."

Troy said, "Get to the point, soldier."

"How's Lonnie doing?"

There was no immediate response.

"How's the waste hauling business?"

Still nothing, just the cold-eyed look.

I said, "Ever read anything by a writer I know, Walker Redgrave?"

The chair scraped back harshly. Troy rose about six inches, then sat back down. Tiny was still after the fly.

Troy did a lot of thinking. Tiny played with the fly. Troy sipped tea.

"Soldier," he said, "you're in way over your head."

"That's the problem," I said. "Everybody's been saying that. Cops, victims, robbers, innocent bystanders." I grinned. "But here I am."

The fry cook yelled, "Order up, three on a raft, sink 'em, side a grits." A waitress got up from the counter, stubbed out her cigarette, and wandered listlessly to the cook's station.

"Git outta here," Troy said. Tiny finally caught the fly, which caused him great glee.

"Your daddy said the same thing. And here I am." I grinned at Troy.

Troy tensed and made a move to get up. I said, "I wouldn't do anything irrational, Troy. I've got a gun. I would like nothing better than to shoot you with it. Right here in Carol's Café."

I got nothing from Troy for a moment, just the dark eyes and the inscrutable stare. Then he jabbed at Tiny with his arm. "Let's go, brother," he said. "Now."

"One more thing," I said, and the sound of my voice kept them in their seats. "Stormy's okay. In fact, she's fine."

Troy stared as hard as he could. "C'mon brother," he said and stood up suddenly, knocking his chair over backward. Tiny got up, too.

"Say hi to Wyndle," I said. "Barbour might be out there, too."

They left without paying.

The waitress came over with my tea, looked at the table and at me. She rooted around in her apron, took out a check, and put it on the table. "Left without payin', didn't they?" she said. The question seemed rhetorical.

I put some money over the check and got up to leave. She looked at the money.

"At least this way," she said, "I'll get a tip. That's a first with those guys."

39

This was a full-fury, window-rattling, tree-bending, street-flooding storm. Three inches of rain, a twenty-degree drop in temperature, and gone in an hour. But it's an hour that tells you what a Florida thunderstorm is capable of.

The wind blew sheets of rain across the parking lot as I ran for the Camaro. I saw the box truck just as it rounded a turn and disappeared.

I got in the Camaro and slammed the door. I was in no hurry now. I had a good idea where the Bledsoe brothers were heading. I'd check that out, then do what I wanted to do.

Through the shining rain and buffeting wind I drove out to the road to nowhere. I drove until the electric lines gave out, then I drove some more.

Until I came to a place I remembered, a nondescript turnoff to a place with no electricity, a place in the middle of the woods, a place near the shore of the gulf.

Wyndle's place.

The box truck was there, parked in the clearing near the cabin, right next to a Jeep Wagoneer and a Corvette convertible.

Exactly what I expected. Exactly what I wanted.

I left the Bledsoe family meeting and drove back along the road until the electric lines came into view.

A little farther there was a road on the coast side, but it didn't look right. I drove a little farther, and the rain seemed to slack off.

Another side road came into view. It was about the right distance. I slowed the Camaro until I'd gone just past the turnoff, then I pulled off the road and shut off engine and lights.

A quick, wet trip up the road confirmed what I'd guessed. There was the familiar road, the familiar clearing, the cabin. I trotted back to the Camaro and pulled up to the path where I'd parked the last time I was here. The rain was fierce and there was almost no light, a kind of false darkness.

I sat in the Camaro in the deep twilight, felt the wind and rain lash at the car. I waited until there was a lull in the storm, opened the car door, and jumped out into a morass of mud. I slammed the door and headed toward the cabin, feeling my way along in the darkness, back to the road, along the tree line, on to the dirt road, and back to the cabin.

There were no vehicles in the little clearing, and no lights showed in the cabin. I made my way through the mud and the underbrush until I was on the porch, under the dry overhang.

I listened. Only the sound of the storm. I slipped the small key-chain flashlight out of my pocket and trained it on the door. The lock was no more substantial than the one at V and L. Why stop at two felony B and E's? I thought as I extracted my credit card and pushed it inward on the lock. The lock gave, the knob turned, and the door opened inward, into the darkness of the cabin. I stood a minute on the porch, feeling the silence. I looked behind me, but there was only the deep and undefined blackness of night in the woods.

I stepped inside, and felt the musty warmth and dryness of the cabin's interior. The storm was dissipating, and the large windows provided some light. I switched off the flash, pulled the door closed behind me, and studied the room.

I'm not sure what I expected, but this was not it.

The cabin had been laid out hunting lodge style: a large public room, a kitchen off to one side, and a couple of doors leading to bedrooms. The ceilings were steeply pitched and beamed, the walls were knotty pine. The floor was rough pine planking.

House Beautiful it wasn't. But it wasn't the slovenly mess

you'd normally associate with a single man, especially a single man like Tiny.

The living room was spare of furniture—a couch with a floral print, a recliner, a couple of upholstered chairs, and a rocker. Not in bad shape at all. There were a couple of braid rugs thrown around, and a coffee table with a plant and a couple of comic books on it. There were no pictures on the walls, but there were a couple of houseplants. I had the odd sensation of being surprised they were alive.

It was as if, here, Tiny was trying hard to have some kind of life. I remembered the Wagoneer; it was clean, too.

The living room told me nothing else. I moved to the kitchen. This room looked more like a bachelor's domain, but I'd seen worse—in fact, an apartment I'd occupied in graduate school had been a lot worse.

There were the requisite dishes piled in the sink, and a dirty plate on the table. But there was nothing indistinguishable growing in the refrigerator, and it was even stocked with some condiments such as mustard, salad dressing, and sandwich spreads.

The drawers were a mix of tangled utensils and clutter, even a few food coupons. Just the stuff you find in a kitchen, nothing less, nothing more.

The bedroom looked more lived-in than the living room—some clothes hung over a chair, the top of the dresser littered with change, gum wrappers, a few toothpicks, a bottle of inexpensive cologne. The drawers held shirts and underwear and socks, not too neat, not just shoved in. There was a double-hung window left open, and I could hear the rain dripping outside.

I looked at the nightstand. A reading book, elementary school level, lay open. There was a colorful drawing and a few sentences in large type. There was another book, closed, titled *Help with Reading the Rinehart Way*.

Here he was trying to get a life, in his own sad way, huddled over a book trying to make out the words, trying to learn to read.

I shook off the sense of sadness. Tiny was a killer. He'd probably killed my hero. I wasn't here to worry about Tiny's life, I was here because of Redgrave's death.

There was a cheap pressboard desk against one wall. On the desk was a picture of an old woman in a cheap frame; another frame held a picture of Tiny and Troy, grinning and standing beside a shiny pickup truck.

Trying to get a life. I sat down at the desk. There was a top drawer in the middle and two drawers on the left. I opened the top drawer.

It was stuffed with comic books, mostly about war heroes. The books looked as if they'd been read a lot. There was nothing under the comic books, nothing lurking in the back corners. Just comic books.

The comic books made me think of the one Tiny was reading at the restaurant, which made me think about the Bledsoe family meeting going on. I wondered how long it would last. I wondered what they might decide to do about me. Try to kill me, probably. They'd found they couldn't scare me off, so they probably figured they had no other choice. I was becoming a real danger. Killing me would be highly suspicious; letting me live meant going to jail.

But for what? Wrecking the environment—yes. Killing Redgrave, if they in fact did kill Redgrave—only maybe. I still had no real proof of murder, just a ton of circumstances and my own stubborn intuition.

I sighed and turned my attention to the middle drawer. It held two boxes. One held receipts for work done on the Wagoneer. Oil at fifteen thousand miles, a warranty service from a couple of months ago, gasoline receipts—Tiny had a Shell credit card—and the warranty card for an expensive auto CD player.

The bottom box held more reading books. There was a piece of paper stuck in the top one, a thin volume titled *The Faraway Castle*. For some reason, the little book with its colorful cover made me feel sorry for the man who was trying to read it.

I took out the paper. It was a note that said, "Tiny, read the books. See you Friday for study. Sharon S."

Did he go for reading lessons with someone named Sharon? I couldn't tell much from the note; she'd obviously written it in words he could understand. Did he pay her, or was she a friend? No answers to any of that.

Trying to get a life. I put the lid on the box, shoved the drawer shut. The lower drawer held a jumble of baseball cards. Many were new, a number dated back several years. These were not collected systematically, just thrown in the pile.

I rooted through the cards. Behind them was a weathered baseball glove. Behind the glove was a shoebox. I took out the shoebox, placed it on the desk, and opened the lid.

It wasn't really a shoebox; it was a treasure chest, full of things that glittered and shone, a hodgepodge of trinkets and buttons and stubs of paper.

Right on top was a medal. A Bronze Star.

Mitch Smith carried his Bronze Star with him everywhere; it was his good luck charm.

Some luck. Mitch Smith is long gone and Tiny Bledsoe has his medal. Not good at all.

I rooted through the trinkets; there were bracelets and little plastic eggs, the kind of things you get out of vending machines. There were more baseball cards.

In the corner was a piece of paper folded neatly. I took out the paper and unfolded it.

It was a letter to Walker Redgrave, from an attorney in Atlanta. It was only a few sentences, and detailed what I'd already found out about Durel Barbour.

The letter I hadn't been able to find. In the same box with the Bronze Star. A sad memento, but my first real connection between Walker Redgrave and the Bledsoe brothers.

The letterhead was embossed in silver. Pretty. Tiny liked to collect pretty, shiny things. I slipped it back in the box, looked at the Bronze Star, picked it up, and put it in my pocket.

The sun had set during my search and it was very dim in

the room. Still enough light to see by, but that would only last a few minutes more.

I pushed the cards to the front of the drawer and started to put the box back. Then I noticed something, a piece of paper that had been under the box. I picked it up and unfolded it.

In the fading light I could make out a map, crudely drawn, rough pencil outlines, possibly a shoreline. One straight line might have been a road. A smaller line led to a small square. Dirt road and cabin?

And there were *X*'s, drawn here and there on the paper, seemingly randomly, a couple near the jagged line, one near the little square. A map to buried treasure? I wondered what kind of treasure might be hidden on the Bledsoe homestead.

I refolded the map and put it in my shirt pocket. Then I put the box back and closed the drawer.

Then the front door opened.

I sucked in my breath and held it. There were footsteps in the front room, but no voices. Probably one person, but I couldn't be sure.

I wanted a moment, still in the darkening room, and heard steps, then the sound of a door closing.

There was the sound of water running, then an enormous belch. Had to be Tiny.

I went out the window, as quietly as I could, and dropped to the wet ground below. There was a small window a few feet from the bedroom, and behind it a light glowed. I moved in the opposite direction, went around the corner of the cabin, and inched along until I was at the front corner.

The Wagoneer was parked in the clearing. That was fine with me. Might not be long before I found out what they decided at the Bledsoe family gathering.

I felt the small weight of the medal in my jeans. It made me feel a lot less sorry for Tiny Bledsoe.

▽

40

THE STORM WAS over. Now there was a moonless night, a brilliant canopy of stars. Much like a night I remembered in Captiva. But that was different. Then I was just beginning. I had no idea what lay ahead. Now the end was close. Had it only been a few days? It seemed to have taken an eternity for me to get to this place.

But now eternity was being prolonged a little longer; I had to crouch uncomfortably, squatting behind a thick oak tree on a soggy layer of pine needles. I had been crouching in the same spot for the better part of three hours. My leg muscles were beginning to cramp painfully.

A fat roach crawled up my leg and perched on my knee. I brushed him away with the back of my hand and he scurried off into the darkness. Mosquitoes buzzed around my head. Sweat covered my face; my clothes were soaked.

I watched the cabin. Still quiet, still the one light burning behind the shaded window.

Tiny, I thought, you've got to come out sometime. I knew they'd been spooked. And I knew Tiny, even slow dumb Tiny, could figure out I'd been rummaging through his things. I wondered how he'd react to that. Pout, probably.

I patted the pocket where I'd stashed my souvenirs. I felt good, even stooped uncomfortably in the dampness of this wilderness these boys called home. The waiting was about to be over. Let the Bledsoes hang themselves.

Tiny stepped out onto the porch.

He looked around for a minute, raised his head almost as if he were sniffing the air.

He stepped off the porch, walked past the Wagoneer, and headed toward a little shed. I could hear him muttering faintly, an almost hypnotic sound. He was carrying a Coleman lantern that threw a round pool of light, perfectly centering him as he walked. He reached the shed, opened the door, reached in, and took out a shovel. Then he walked toward the wood beyond the clearing, centered in the lantern's silver pool.

I left my hiding place and followed the spot of light into the woods, like a moth drawn to a candle. It was slow going in unfamiliar surroundings. The light grew dimmer but stayed in sight. I made my way as quickly as I could; my boots made squishing sounds as they sunk in the muck. A couple of times I almost lost my footing, and tree branches kept slapping my face. Still, I could see the light, wavering as Tiny moved.

Then the light became still. I took my time, very carefully picking my way a few more yards through the slippery underbrush. I came to the edge of a natural clearing perhaps thirty feet across, ringed with trees and underbrush. There was no surf noise here. The lantern stood on the ground in the middle of the cleared area, the edge of its circular beam almost reaching the foliage, circle within circle.

Tiny was digging methodically, without haste, slowly creating a pile of dirt beside a deepening hole. And still there was the hypnotic muttering.

Suddenly the lantern let out a harsh hiss and went out. Tiny didn't seem to notice, just kept digging steadily. The light from the vast starry night cast an eerie glow over the little clearing, a lurid luminescent twilight that clearly illuminated Tiny as he dug.

Finally he stopped, threw the shovel down, and peered into the hole. Then he got to his knees, reached in, and tugged at something in the hole. He began to grunt like a pig. Then he got in the hole and bent down. The grunting became louder, and I watched the top of a metal barrel come into view. Tiny bent down further, and with a sudden effort got the barrel out of the hole. It rolled a couple of feet, then was still.

Tiny stood up and crawled out of the hole, still grunting softly.

I stepped into the clearing. "Thanks, Tiny," I said. "I appreciate your efforts." I pointed the Colt at his fat belly.

Tiny stared at the gun, looking as stupid as he was.

41

I TOOK A couple of steps toward Tiny, keeping the Colt trained on his belly. He seemed to lean back almost imperceptibly. His stare never left me. His mouth hung open and I could hear him breathing, a soft bubbling sound.

I nodded at the mud-encrusted barrel. "Watcha got there?"

He looked at the barrel, then back at me. "Nothin'," he said.

A sudden thought struck me. "Is it Lonnie?"

"Lonnie? Naw, Lonnie's—" he caught himself, stopped.

I took my newfound train of thought one step further. I took the medal out of my pocket and dangled it in front of me, like an amulet. "Pretty, Tiny. Where'd you get it?"

"Hey," he said. He took a step forward. "Gimme that!"

I stepped forward too, closed the gap between us. I raised the gun a little, jerked the barrel once. He stopped, and I could hear the noisy breathing again.

"Doesn't matter," I said. "I think I know what's in the barrel. Anyway, the cops'll find out soon enough. I'm really here for another reason."

Tiny's eyes narrowed. He might have been thinking. He said, "Huh?"

"Walker Redgrave," I said.

One of Tiny's eyebrows went up slightly. His eyes shifted, looked toward the sides of the clearing. He clenched his fist and I sensed his body tensing.

"Move and I'll blow a hole in your fat stinking belly," I said.

That got through. Tiny relaxed his hands, still eyeing me warily.

"How?" I said.

"H-how what?"

I could feel the muscles in my shoulders and neck tightening. "How'd you kill him?" I said softly.

"Kill who?" he said.

"Walker Redgrave," I said calmly. "You remember him, tall fellow, silver hair, wrote books."

"Can't read," Tiny said, as if I'd mentioned something funny.

"But you can hear, Tiny," I said, trying to keep my voice patient. "What'd he do, find out something he shouldn't, walk into your nighttime activities? Catch you in bed with a cocker spaniel? That'd be about your style.

"Let me tell you how I think it happened. Redgrave pulled the trigger, that's not in dispute." I paused. "Sorry, that's a big word. What I mean is, we all agree." I glanced at the barrel and went on.

"So if he pulled the trigger someone made him do it. I figure that someone's you and your sweetheart brother Troy. I figure he found out something he had to die for, like these barrels you boys pick up and get rid of. And I figure you gave him no choice but to shoot himself."

I was breathing hard now, trying to follow along. "How did you threaten him, Tiny?" I said. "I'm trying to use little words so you'll understand." I kept the Colt pointed at his middle. "What kind of unspeakable things did you say you'd do to him?"

I pulled the map out of my pocket and held it up.

"It doesn't really matter, Tiny. I've got some interesting reading for the sheriff's people. I compliment you, this thing is easy to follow. I'll bet the cops'll find all sorts of interesting things when they start digging." I waved the map idly in the air. "Maybe we'll even find Lonnie."

Suddenly he bellowed and rushed me. I leveled the Colt at his legs and let go a round. The slug slammed into his right thigh.

The bellow turned into a yelp. He grabbed at the wound with both hands and dropped to his knees. Blood seeped from between his fingers.

I covered the distance between us in three steps. I kicked him in the chest, knocking him backward onto the ground. He landed near his newly dug hole in the ground. I got over him, lowered my knees hard against his upper arms, and leaned all of my two hundred and twenty pounds into the fat flesh.

I reached down with one hand, pushed his lower jaw open, and shoved the barrel of the .38 into his mouth.

Tiny thrashed and gagged as I pushed the barrel of the gun deep into his throat. Then he vomited; bile and yellowish chunks of half-digested food burbled out and ran down his chin and cheeks. The veins and muscles on his neck bulged.

I held the gun where it was and leaned my knees harder into his forearms.

"Why'd you do it Tiny?" I could barely contain my rage. My finger ached on the trigger. "Why'd you make Redgrave kill himself? Tell me or I'll blow the back of your head off—now!"

He tried to speak around the gun barrel and puke. "F-F-F-Fu—" His eyes rolled up in his head and he choked again.

I cocked the .38.

"Speak up, you fat creep!" I twitched the gun once, letting him feel it move. I twitched it again, hard this time. I heard a tooth crack.

His teeth chattered on the blued steel of the gun barrel.

"F-F-for f-fun," he gasped. "For fun."

I held the gun steady in his mouth while I looked down at him. For fun. A good man, a hero of mine, had been ruthlessly killed—for fun.

We were motionless in the clearing, caught in some macabre frozen point in time, me on top of Tiny, with my gun jammed down his throat, him moaning and blubbering softly, the only sound besides the night crickets.

A twig snapped, and I looked up. Troy Bledsoe stepped into the clearing. He was holding a double-barrel shotgun, butt at his shoulder, muzzle pointed at my head. It looked like two black evil eyes staring at me.

"Pull the gun out of his mouth, soldier," he said. His voice was muffled by the stock of the gun.

I pulled the Colt out slowly; the barrel came out slimy with spit and vomit.

"Uncock it and throw it away, over there." He motioned with a flick of the shotgun barrel toward the far side of the cleared space.

I gently eased the Colt's hammer down and tossed the gun away. It landed with a soft thud on the other side of the open grave.

"Now get up soldier," Troy said.

I eased my weight off Tiny. When I'd gotten to my feet, Tiny suddenly scuttled sideways like a crab through the dry dirt, ending up next to a small tree stump. He held on to the stump like a child holding a teddy bear. Tears ran down his face. His wounded leg glistened darkly in the moonlight.

"Let me shoot him, brother," Tiny said. His voice was raw and choked. "Give me the gun. I wanna shoot the—"

"Shut up," Troy said in a soft voice. He looked at the mud-covered barrel, looked for a long time. I tried to keep my breathing steady. Tiny sat and muttered.

Troy walked over to the barrel. I moved a step backward, reflexively. The shotgun swung toward me. "Unh, unh, soldier. You just behave till I figure out what I'm gonna do with you."

I looked at Troy, and held myself still. "Was it you who beat Stormy up?" My voice sounded cold and brittle.

"She got beat up?" He grinned. "I gotta hand it to you, ain't no way you scare easy. All this stuff happens and here you are." He gave me the ghost of a stark smile. "Don't matter much now, does it?"

He turned his attention back to Tiny.

"What's in the barrel?" Troy asked in the same soft, almost gentle voice. Tiny whimpered and tried to talk, but not much happened except that some spit bubbles formed on his lips.

Troy screamed suddenly, "What's in the barrel, brother?" He swung the shotgun toward Tiny.

I stood helpless, too far away from my gun, too far away from the trees outside the clearing, too near the menace of the shotgun.

Troy took a step toward Tiny. Even in the dim light I could see the eyes, clear and empty, those inhuman eyes I'd seen in the Florida Bar. The eyes of a killer.

Tiny found a voice. He looked up at his brother, like a kid who'd been caught being naughty, and said, "Mitch."

The clear eyes burned now, and Tiny squirmed under their gaze. Troy tilted his head, as if in wonderment, and said, "Mitch? Mitch Smith?"

"You know, the guy long time ago we hadda—"

"I know who Mitch Smith is, you idiot." There was the soft voice again, a voice to match the eyes. He shook his head, more wonderment. He glanced at me, then leveled his stare back on Tiny. "What's he doin' *here*?"

"I wanted to keep him," Tiny said.

That was it for Troy's self-control. He took another step toward Tiny, stopped, stamped his foot in the dirt, and flapped one arm in the air. "You can't keep him," he yelled.

Tiny started to get mad, too. "I can if I wanna."

"You can't do anything 'less I say. Look what you done, you let yourself get followed by this detective so he can see what we're doin', I come out here an' find you diggin' up Mitch Smith, who you was supposed to get rid of how I told you. Why ain't he out in the water? What's he doing *here*?" He acted like an irate father scolding his naughty child.

"He ain't hurtin' nothin' here," Tiny said. He tried to get to his feet, but the shot leg gave way and he fell back down.

"He ain't hurtin' nothin'? Figure it out, brother. First I hadda get rid of that writer 'cause you let him follow you here. Now I gotta get rid of mister detective—" he gave me a look at the gun muzzle again—"cause you let *him* follow you here. An' I gotta get rid of Mitch, like you shoulda done right the first time."

Troy stared at the barrel. "You can't keep him like he's a souvenir."

"You let me kill him," Tiny said petulantly.

Troy flapped his arm again. "You can't keep things. You done that your whole life, and all it's done is get you in trouble."

"He knows about Mitch," Tiny said.

Troy looked at me and he might have grinned. "That ain't gonna matter in a little while. He'll get to go in the water too."

Then Cecil Stubbs walked into the clearing. "Maybe so, maybe no," he said pleasantly. He was chewing on a toothpick, and he had his big .44 trained on Troy.

"Your turn, Troy. Drop it." Stubbs spat out the toothpick. He didn't take his eyes off Troy.

Troy looked at Stubbs, looked at me. He glanced at Tiny, who was looking up pleadingly by the stump. Then he looked back at Stubbs.

"Sure, whatever you say, soldier." He began to lower the barrel of the shotgun, then suddenly swung it up toward Stubbs.

The deputy fired off two rounds from the big Magnum. The shots shattered the night silence with an incredible roar. The fat slugs plowed into Troy's chest.

Troy made a dance out of dying. His head snapped up; he wobbled backward a couple of steps, knocking over the lantern. He stood wavering, looked down at the spreading blood on his shirt. Then he pitched forward, still holding the shotgun. When the gun pushed into the soft dirt it fired; the heavy recoil flung Troy off the ground and threw him backward. He spun in the air, an almost graceful gesture, and landed facedown, arms flung outward. The fingers of one hand twitched spasmodically. The exiting slugs had made mushy, doughnut-sized holes in his back.

Stubbs turned the .44 toward Tiny and cocked the hammer. Tiny tried to crawl behind the little stump. He made loud sucking noises.

I stepped toward Stubbs and put a hand out. "No, Stubbs," I said. "I need him. He's my witness. He's my link to Walker Redgrave."

Stubbs kept the gun pointed at Tiny. Tiny crawled toward me and wrapped his arms around my ankles. He buried his face between my boots and began to whimper.

Stubbs lowered the .44 and walked over to Troy. The twitching hand was still now. Stubbs lightly kicked at Troy's ribs.

"What a shame," Stubbs said. "Killed resisting arrest." He looked at Tiny, mewing at my feet. "One outta two ain't bad."

I looked at the dead man, and something occurred to me. I walked over to him and knelt down. His shirt wasn't tucked in, and I tugged it up on his sides and back. I looked up at Stubbs. "Do you mind?" I asked.

Stubbs said, "Unh-unh."

I hooked a finger under Troy's back belt loop and pulled up. His waist came off the ground a couple of inches and I was able to tug the shirt up farther, exposing his back and ribs. They were smooth and untouched. I got down low and pulled up on the belt loop again. Nothing on the stomach except dirt and a few leaves. No scratches, no cuts. Nothing that might have been made by a woman's fingernails. I let him back down.

I looked at the curve of the lower back, the thin hips, the well-defined muscles, the untanned skin.

"You know, Stubbs," I said. "He's not in bad shape for a dead man."

Stubbs grunted once, softly. "I always hated guys didn't have love handles," he said. Then, "You know, for a big-city detective, you sure are easy to follow around. And you were needin' it, for sure."

I didn't disagree with that.

42

A DETENTION DEPUTY led me down a starkly lit corridor that smelled of disinfectant and old body odors and unlocked a metal door. It was just after 9:00 A.M. "You're well dressed for a harness bull," I said. He gave me a blank stare. "It's a compliment," I said.

I didn't feel too bad for having gotten just enough sleep to need more sleep. Stubbs had let me go back to Stormy's. "We'll call when we need ya," he said as two ambulance attendants were bagging up Troy's body. He slipped into the plastic bag with a solid "thunk" and they flopped him onto the gurney. "You bowling Monday night?" one attendant asked the other. "Can't," said the other. "Wife's have a quilting party, I gotta hang around and entertain the guests, serve the punch."

Stubbs had kept his word. At eight Hirst called and said, "You-know-who needs you you-know-where."

I dressed, found my way to the Camaro, and let the Camaro find its way to the sheriff's office in Perry.

The deputy opened a door that led into a starkly lit room with a scarred table and three wood chairs. Sitting at the table was Tiny Bledsoe. He looked like he'd been rode hard and put away wet. His face was pallid in the sickly light from the unshaded ceiling bulb. He still wore the same clothes, which were caked with dried mud. He smelled awful.

Stubbs was there, standing near the table, looking dapper in his stone-washed jeans and crisp work shirt. If lack of sleep and killing a man had had any effect on him, it didn't show.

Deputy Hirst lounged in a corner, sitting on a chair turned backward. There was a third man I'd never seen before standing near one wall. He wore Duck Head khakis and a crisply starched plaid shirt.

I nodded toward the stranger.

"Advance contingent from the government," said Stubbs, "got here so fast he isn't even official yet. His name is Smith."

"I met a Mr. Smith, works for the Department of Environmental Regulation."

"No relation, I'm sure," the man said. That was the last thing he said during the whole interview.

I turned back to Stubbs.

"Seems like a small party. I'd have thought the sheriff would have been here, seeing as he's an elected official and all that."

"We can't find him," Stubbs said. "Seriously, his wife said he's gone on a three-day fishing trip. So I'm in charge." He grinned widely.

"That's what Alexander Haig said after Reagan was shot," I said.

"Yeah, but Haig was wrong," Stubbs said. "I'm right."

"No doubt," I said. "By the way, have you picked up Wyndle? I think you folks might want to talk to him, too."

"Already done," Stubbs said. He patted Tiny's shoulder. "We got the elder Mr. Bledsoe sittin' in another room right this minute. I even told Hirst to turn the lights up so he'd be real comfortable. You wanna talk to him too?"

I shrugged. "I'm not sure Wyndle will break as easy as this one. Besides, I can get what I want from our friend here. In fact, he's been kind enough to tell me part of it already."

Stubbs looked around the room, let his gaze linger on the state man for a moment. "So it's just our little party right now, we thought we'd get a head start before the circus comes to town."

During all this Tiny sat in his chair, looking from one

person to another, squinting his eyes. It was impossible to tell if anything at all was sinking in. He had not been the brains of the operation.

"Mr. Bledsoe here's been over to the hospital, doctor said he was lucky, the bullet just went clean through his leg—" He made a small whistling noise. "Didn't have to do nothin' but give him a shot and bandage him up. Heck, he can even walk on it—sorta."

Stubbs patted Tiny again. "He's been read his rights, we even let him look at the Miranda card. He don't appear to want an attorney at this time.

"We got this little problem though," Stubbs said. He gave Tiny another pat; the gesture was almost paternal. "He just ain't had a lot to say so far. But he seemed to light up when I mentioned you were coming over to ask him a few questions. I think he'll respond real well to you. You wanna chat with him a little bit, see what happens?"

"Do I get to use my props?" I said, patting at the armpit of my jacket.

Stubbs just grinned. I walked over to the chair on the opposite side of the table from Tiny. He eyed me like a cornered deer.

"How's your throat, Tiny, a little sore?" I said. "I bet that leg's bothering you, too."

Tiny stared back, expressionless.

Abruptly, I said, "Pull up your shirt."

Tiny stared at me for a moment, then reached his manacled hands down to the bottom of his shirt. He looked at me expectantly and held onto the fabric.

"Just pull it up, Tiny," I said.

He obediently pulled up the shirt until all of his fat belly and his lower chest were exposed. There was a lot of dark hair and an old ragged scar to the left of his navel. No scratches.

I told him he could pull the shirt back down. "Tiny, we're going to have a conversation. That means both of us talk, I ask questions, you answer them, you understand?"

He kept staring at me. I stared back at him for a moment, then brought my fist down hard on the table about an inch from Tiny's manacled hands. He yelped and started to whimper again.

"Do you understand?" I asked softly.

He nodded.

Stubbs broke in. "Believe me, Tiny, it's really best if you talk to Mr. Cole now. Or the rest of us'll have to go to the bathroom for a while."

Tiny seemed to sink inward. "Okay," he muttered, looking down at the table.

"Tell me about your little business, yours and Troy's."

"Troy dead?"

"You betcha, so you've got to do all the talking. Start."

He didn't say anything. Stubbs made a move toward the door and said, "Let's go, boys."

Tiny said, "No," and Stubbs stopped. We all looked at Tiny.

He kept his head down, but his eyes searched the room. Finally he said, "We jus' dumped the stuff, gave 'em a place out in the marsh to get rid of it or inna airboat."

"Do you know what 'it' was?" I asked.

"I dunno, oil an'—"

Stubbs cut in. "I can help some here. We've already found some fifty-five-gallon drums sunk in the muck out there. Some of the drums're marked with stickers say 'hazardous waste' and list lotsa fancy chemical names. A couple of the drums were sealed up tight, but one was oozin' some really smelly stuff out into the mud."

He grinned at the government man, almost as if the whole thing were slightly humorous. "Sounds like bad stuff to be dumpin' in our precious wetlands. I figure, find a few real fast, you're bound to find a whole lot more if you keep on lookin'. Once this thing becomes more official, if you know what I mean—" He gestured at Smith—"Lord knows what we'll turn up."

"Besides Lonnie Driggers," I said. Stubbs snapped his gaze

toward me, but I went on. "You might want to do most of your looking offshore. They used their airboat to haul the drums out to sea. Maybe they dropped some stuff in the muck on their property when it was too much trouble to dump it in the gulf. Either way, it's bad news for the water table."

I pulled the map out of my pocket and tossed it on the edge of the table. "This ought to help."

Stubbs narrowed his eyes. "Where'd you get that?"

"Why, Tiny gave it to me," I said. Tiny made a move to grab the map with his manacled hands, but I snatched it away. "Don't be an Indian giver," I said. I handed the map to Stubbs, who looked at it for a moment, said, "Oh boy, evidence," and handed it to Hirst.

I turned back to Tiny, and leaned forward in my chair until I'd risen off the seat a little way. I hovered over Tiny, only a few inches from his pasty, pockmarked face.

"Where'd the drums come from?"

"Truck brung 'em."

"No kidding, Tiny. Whose truck?"

"Vernon's."

I looked at the others in the room. "Try V and L Hauling right here in Perry."

Stubbs thought about that for a minute. "That's his cousin Vernon Gash all right. He and Lonnie Driggers've had that truck haulin' business for years. What's this about Lonnie? I heard he up and left his wife a while back, hit the road."

"I'll get to Lonnie," I said. I felt fine in spite of the night I'd been through. Everything was falling in place. I'd known a lot of the answers before I got to this room, knew about Vernon and Lonnie, knew why Walker Redgrave shot himself—was made to shoot himself. But I wanted it to come out this way, a little at a time, with Tiny participating. I didn't just want facts, I wanted a confession. And I was getting it. I cared about the wetlands, and the drinking water. But, right now, I cared about seeing Walker Redgrave's murderers brought to justice.

"Tiny, what kind of business is Vernon in?" I asked, still in the soft voice.

Tiny's responses were coming a little faster now. "He owns some kinda outfit picks up the drums from places all over."

"Very good. What kind of places, Tiny, all over where? Whoops, that's two questions, let's start with what kind."

Tiny gave me a blank stare. I repeated the question: "What kind of places?"

Tiny thought about that, screwed up his face, which made him look even worse. "I dunno, car garages, places they clean clothes, I think a place they put the chrome on bumpers, all kinda places. I just heard 'em talkin', they never told me nothin'. They'd leave in the truck, go to Gainesville, up to Perry, Jacksonville, all over. They was always comin' back late."

Stubbs looked at me. "I figure I know, but I'd like to hear you tell it."

"Hazardous waste," I said. "All kinds of nasty stuff generated by all kinds of businesses and factories. Things like solvents used in paint manufacturing, chemicals for electroplating processes, PERK, that's the cleaning solvent dry cleaners use, chlorinated solvents. And run-of-the-mill stuff like mineral spirits and contaminated oil."

I looked at Tiny, who clearly hadn't a clue. Stubbs said, "Where'd you find out all this?"

"Good solid detective work. Actually I talked to a couple of government people, including Smith at DER, and a nice guy who works at one of the utilities. They were most helpful. So bear with me. Some of this I know, some of this is conjecture. But it all holds together, and we can check it all out.

"This waste, it isn't some evil, glowing stuff. Most of it is pretty common. There are hundreds, maybe thousands of materials categorized as hazardous. And there are strict federal and state laws that regulate the disposal of these toxic materials."

I had their attention. The room was hot, humid. I didn't see an air-conditioning duct. I went on:

"Most of this stuff is picked up by licensed transporters and hauled out of state to designated facilities that incinerate it, purify it, recycle it, or bury it, depending on what it is and what the regulations say you can do with it.

"V and L Hauling is a fully licensed hazardous waste transporter, with a permit to take the drums to specific TSDs—that's treatment, storage, and disposal sites." That must have impressed Smith; he tilted his head about an eighth of an inch.

"And they did take it down the road," I said, "at least for a little ways. They just went a few miles and made a convenient detour into nowhere.

"That's where Tiny and Troy came in. They knew every inch of the wetlands, marshes, and woods around here. They owned some of it, they knew how to get in and out of some of the most impassable terrain in the county. And they had the means—airboats, four-by-fours, even ATVs. Troy was even trusted to make the pickup runs. Right, Tiny?" I said for effect.

"I got a airboat an' a four-wheel driver, paid good money for 'em." He was at least tagging along the edges of the conversation.

I turned to Stubbs. The government man, whom I figured for DER or EPA, didn't say anything, but he didn't look too comfortable, either.

"We all know Vernon's been in the business for years, him and Lonnie with their box truck. Here's how I think it developed:

"For a long time, V and L just did general hauling. They have connections with small businesses from here to Jacksonville. One thing they did was haul old oil and other flammables to Wyndle's sawmills to burn in the boilers."

Stubbs nodded his head a little. He seemed proud I'd done my homework, like I was his star pupil.

"Then came the late 1970s, and a whole slew of strict

environmental regulations on hazardous waste. These are honest businesses we're talking about, lots of mom-and-pop operations. All of a sudden these chemicals they're buying come with a complicated set of guidelines for mandatory disposal. And along comes Vernon and Lonnie telling them they'd get rid of it, handle it legally, take care of the paperwork.

"And they probably did—for a while. There's good money, legal money, to be made in this business. You can charge as much as six or seven hundred dollars, sometimes even more, to dispose of one drum of hazardous waste. So they began picking it up and driving it to Louisiana. For a while."

"Let me use my powers of analytical induction," said Stubbs. We all looked at him. "Correspondence course from the academy." He smiled. "Why make fifteen percent profit when you can pocket it all? Why drive all the way to Louisiana or wherever they take this crap, lose all that sleep when you don't have to? So Vernon or Lonnie come up with the bright idea: Just dump it in the swamp or drop it in the water. They had the customers. They had the truck. They understood the business. But Troy and Tiny and Wyndle, they had the swamp, they had the coastline, they had the airboats. And that was the key to the whole thing."

During all this discourse Tiny had been playing with the gouges and graffiti on the table. When he heard his name he looked up, as interested as he ever got. "Me and Troy, we know the swamps."

"Sure you do, Tiny," Stubbs said. "We got lotsa questions about the swamps. You just be patient." Then, to me:

"So, mister detective, how'd they keep from gettin' caught?"

"Here's the kicker," I said. "Correct me if I'm wrong." I looked at the government man. I might as well have been addressing a cigar store Indian.

"The government requires the paperwork, but the government doesn't collect the paperwork." I reached inside my jacket and brought out the muddy manifest. "Here's your paperwork."

Stubbs said, "Hey, that's evidence."

"Sorry, I forgot," I said. "The hauler fills out this manifest form, puts in the license number of the disposal facility, maybe even forges a signature and sends a copy back to the place he picked up the drums. Who's going to check? The business owner is happy; he has a piece of signed paper to put in his file cabinet. Of course the disposal site never gets a copy since the waste never made it that far. There's a copy for the transporter. But nothing—not one thing—goes to the government. I'm sure Smith here can verify that."

No one looked at Smith. I was on a roll now, and I had everyone's attention but Tiny's, who seemed to have become fascinated with his hands. "The manifests are easy to get, they're available from form printers, and they're easy to forge by anyone who knows what to write in the blanks," I said. "And I hate to say this, Stubbs, but you and I know that enforcement of such regulations might be, how shall we say, spotty.

"You think you're undermanned, Stubbs," I said. "Call the DER, find out how many people they got around here. There's an office in Live Oak, it has one person. The next nearest office is Gainesville, they got maybe three. And these aren't enforcement people, that's just one little part of their job. You think they're going to spend their time running all over the countryside checking to see if all the dry cleaners and garages have the proper paperwork? That's a rhetorical question, by the way. And if by some strange chance they do happen onto some paperwork, what do they see? An official, signed document that looks just fine as far as they're concerned."

I turned to Smith. "How am I doing? I'll take silence as an affirmative gesture."

Smith said nothing. "See there," I said to the others in the room. "I have an ally."

Stubbs said, "I'm gettin' hungry, Cole. Can we wrap this up?"

"There's not much more. They had literally hundreds of

small and medium-sized customers. They'd make their runs, pick up one drum here, two there, maybe a few times a month hit a mother lode and get ten drums. Let's say, for the sake of argument, they collected three hundred drums a month. That's not out of the question at all. Multiply it. A conservative estimate would be a hundred and fifty thousand dollars. The money is pure profit, it goes right into their pockets. And the stuff goes right in the water table.

"Tiny and Troy would load the drums off the truck onto a four-by-four or an airboat and sink the stuff in the muck, or take it offshore and drop it in twenty feet of water. Who'd ever know? And the stuff wouldn't seep into the environment for a long time, not until the drums rusted through. But they do that, after a while."

I stopped talking. There was silence in the room.

"I think that'll play," Stubbs said after a moment. "What about Lonnie?"

"Have you opened the barrel Tiny dug up?"

"Not yet," Stubbs said. Then his eyes got wide. He said, "Is Lonnie in the barrel?"

"No, Mitch Smith is in the barrel."

"Whoa, wait a minute, stop," Stubbs said. "You mean Smitty's boy, the marine. Didn't he up and hightail it outta here a few years ago?"

"In a manner of speaking. Let me tell you about Mitch Smith. That'll get us to Lonnie, which'll bring us to Durel Barbour—" that got everyone's attention—"and finally we'll get to what I'm really interested in."

"And that is?" Stubbs said.

"Just one thing," I said. "Walker Redgrave."

43

I TOLD THEM about a young marine, a boy who went to Vietnam and returned a man, a very troubled young man. But who finally started to get the best of his problems, who began to embrace life, who enrolled in college and got a job with a hauling company—a company his sister's husband worked for—to make money for his tuition. And who found out too much.

"They killed Smith," I said. "The only problem was, Troy told Tiny to put the body in a barrel and dump it offshore. But Tiny, who likes to keep souvenirs of his little deeds, decided to put him in the swamp, kind of keep him close by. Boys like Tiny do that.

"When Tiny got spooked, he tried to get rid of the evidence. If I hadn't interrupted, Mitch Smith would be in forty feet of water now. Where Lonnie is. I figure Lonnie wanted out, maybe he was scared, who knows? And Vernon and the Bledsoes obliged, in their own way."

Then I told them about Durel Barbour. "He followed Stormy and me the night my tires were slashed, probably on orders from Wyndle. That was right after I'd gone to see the old man. By the way, he's listed on state documents as being a director and legal counsel for V and L Hauling. And he's listed with the bar as a specialist in environmental law. What a coincidence."

"Wyndle hopped up and down yellin' for Barbour, so we're tryin' to get in touch with Durel. He's hooked up with V and L, huh? Always did strike me as the shady type. We'll take it up with him when he gets here, but that won't be for a while." Stubbs ran his hand through his hair. He was beginning to look fatigued. "This thing keeps gettin' more complicated all the time," he said. "And now we get to Walker Redgrave."

"Why don't you bring in a steno? It's about time we got some of this down on paper. And I'd like Tiny to tell us about Redgrave, so it's all nice and legal."

They brought in a man who took down some of what Tiny said, and a lot of stuff Stubbs suggested that Tiny had said. From time to time, they'd read it to him.

They got it all down. He seemed to warm up to the idea of confessing after he got started, liked being the center of attention, and didn't need much prompting at all.

Finally, he told about Walker Redgrave, who'd had the rotten luck to stumble on the brothers as they were dumping barrels in the muck. "We hadda kill him 'cause he maybe saw us stuffin' Lonnie in the barrel," Tiny said.

And I heard how Tiny and Troy had put the pressure on.

"He knowed he was gonna get kilt," Tiny said. "Troy told him over an' over how we was gonna kill him he didn't shoot hisself. Troy's real good at scarin' people that way, tellin' all the things he's gonna do to 'em."

Stubbs cut in: "I still don't see how you made him do it. Why couldn't he have just shot the gun into the mattress, waited for the cops, and told what had happened?"

Suddenly it was clear, something that had been bothering me, so faint and subtle I didn't even know it was bothering me; not even worth mentioning to Lisa. The little meaningless detail that ultimately means everything. Facts colliding and becoming truth.

"I think I can answer that, Stubbs," I said. He nodded, waiting. The room was still, hotter now. Hirst cleared his throat.

I walked over to Tiny, sat in the chair across from him, and gave him a gentle smile.

"Was it fun, Tiny, watching him pull the trigger?"

Tiny looked at me, letting it sink in. Then he said, "I didn't watch."

That stopped me for a moment. Was my whole theory about to go up in smoke? "Who watched?" I asked a little wildly.

Tiny stared up at me. "Don't hold out on me, Tiny," I said harshly. "You're looking at taking a seat in Old Sparky. Answer me."

"What's Old Sparky?" Tiny asked.

I slammed my fist on the table. "It's the electric chair, you fool. We're going to fry you for the murder of Walker Redgrave."

Finally there was a glimmer of fear in Tiny's eyes. He shook his head slowly. "Hey man," he said. "I didn't watch nothin'."

With a huge effort of will I brought myself under control. I looked at Stubbs and said, "You boys mind leaving the room?"

Stubbs said, "Bathroom break." Hirst got up out of his chair.

Tiny said, "Wait."

Hirst sat back down. Tiny looked at Stubbs, then at me. He held my stare for a moment, then he seemed to cave in. His shoulders dropped, and I could hear the exhalation of breath. There were tears in his eyes.

"It was Troy, an'—and Durel."

"Durel Barbour," Stubbs said under his breath, as if he weren't entirely surprised.

I turned to the room. "The police report said that the light was on and the shade on the rear window was pulled open. Isn't that odd, a man turning on a light and leaving the curtain open while he commits suicide?"

Stubbs was nodding, his head bobbing up and down, knowing now how it happened.

"That's why Redgrave couldn't fake it, why he had no way out," I said. "Nothing was left to chance. Troy and Barbour were no doubt armed. They told Redgrave exactly what to do, then they went around to the back window and *watched him do it*. He's got one bullet, two guys with guns watching, and no way out."

The telling of it made me sick at heart. I had what I wanted, and I couldn't stand it there any longer. "You can have it, Stubbs. You don't need me anymore." I left the room.

I walked out of the building into the hot Florida night. A car pulled up to the curve, a late-model Corvette, and stopped in a loading zone. Durel Barbour got out and headed toward me. When he got close he stopped.

"My oh my," he said. "Have you stirred up quite the mess. I was located eating some of Buster's excellent barbecue. Have you talked to the prisoners already and now you are leaving?"

"I did get to chat with Tiny for a moment. Very enlightening conversation."

His stare glinted hard. "So it would seem. I'm not surprised. It does, though, give me some excellent tactics to use in court, such things as coercion and—"

I grabbed Barbour by the lapels of his jacket, hard. His head snapped back and he sputtered. I got close.

"You think you got trouble? You don't have any idea what real trouble is."

I tightened my grip on his coat and looked around. I saw Stubbs watching from the doorway. I eased off in my grip, let him lean back for a moment, then jerked him back toward me. He was starting to turn red.

"You know all about the barrels. I'm betting you know all about Mitch Smith and Lonnie." I could feel it coming on now, that same feeling I had in the woods. I reached down with one hand and ripped his shirt open. On his stomach was a long scratch, still fresh, just starting to scab.

"But I know a couple of things, too," I said, my voice rising. "I know about Redgrave. I know how he died. I know it was murder. And I know *you watched*."

I pulled Barbour so close our noses touched. "Stubbs wants to talk to you," I whispered. "You might be in there a while, maybe they'll tow your car." Then I let him go.

He staggered for a moment, trying to keep his balance, breathing deeply. He backpedaled a couple of steps and looked toward the door of the sheriff's office. Stubbs stood under a floodlight and said, "Come on down, Durel."

I walked away. Away from Durel Barbour, and from Tiny Bledsoe, and Wyndle and Deputy Stubbs, and from the swamp and the madness and the stink of death.

44

THE DOOR TO Smitty's storefront was wide open when I drove up. Smitty was behind his counter, looking slightly lost, when I came in.

"I need to see Mickey," I said.

He looked at me, but the slightly lost expression didn't go away.

"You need to see Mickey?" He looked oddly stunned. "She's not here. We had a fight."

I had a feeling the tension in the family was escalating.

I waited a moment, and when Smitty didn't say anything else, I pressed on.

"What was the fight about?"

He looked at me like I was a dog trying to get in a garbage can.

"You," he said. "Among other things."

I nodded, waiting to see where he was going to take this.

He stood up, an old tired man, leaned his weathered hands on the scarred counter.

"I don't know, Mr. Cole. I don't know." He looked at me, and his eyes seemed a distant pale blue. "You show up here, and nothin's the same. You're diggin' up the past."

He turned from me and looked at the picture of the young marine. Then he said, "I don't see where it's going to do any good diggin' things up. Any good at all."

The floor fan in the corner oscillated, barely stirring the air in the hot room. The piles of receipts and papers on the counter fluttered feebly in the draft. Everything in the room looked old, the shelves, the groceries and supplies, the auto parts, everything seemed old and unwanted. Even Smitty. Maybe even me.

"I promised your daughter I'd tell her some things I found out. I'm going to keep that promise, whether you help me or not."

For just a moment his eyes flared; if he'd been twenty years younger he might have come across the counter at me. As it was, he raised a fist and slammed it down on the counter, sending papers scattering. But that was all; then he went back to being old and tired.

"Nothin' you do is gonna bring him back," he said.

"Mickey needs to know. Maybe it'll put some things to rest for her. Maybe you need to know, too." I knew they'd hear soon enough, and it would be easier from me, or from Mickey.

He stood behind his counter, trying to keep himself erect. Then he seemed to slump, seemed to give up.

"Out by the water," he said and shuffled out of the room.

I went outside. It was early afternoon now, and clouds were gathering in the west, out over the gulf. At the end of the dock Mickey stood looking out at the clouds. She wore a faded denim sleeveless jumper over a plain blouse, but her strawberry hair cascaded down her back.

I walked to the edge of the dock and said, "Mickey?"

She stood motionless for a time, still looking at whatever it was she could see, and then she turned around. The little dock was only about ten feet long and I could see from that distance that she'd been crying. Her pale, freckled face glistened in the hard sunlight.

"Mr. Cole," she said.

We sat on the dock and swung our legs over to the side, above the water. I'd done that so much as a kid, but those times were carefree, these times seemed full of woe.

"Some things have happened," I said.

She looked at the clouds.

"There's only a little time before the newspapers are here, and a lot is going to come out. You need to know."

Again, a nod.

"Your brother is dead."

She said nothing, but her whole body tensed and gave way to a shudder. She turned to me, an inquiring, fearful look.

"He was killed by Tiny and Troy. Tiny and Wyndle are in jail. Tiny's confessed to killing Walker Redgrave. They forced him to shoot himself."

"Troy?"

"Troy's dead, he was shot by Stubbs. I'm sorry to have to tell you that."

"Don't matter. I'm a long way past carin' for Troy Bledsoe."

She didn't ask about the details of that. She said, "Why'd they kill my brother?"

I filled her in on the background. "He may have stumbled onto something like Redgrave did. They probably killed him because he wouldn't go along with the illegal stuff." I had no idea if that were true, but there was no harm in letting her hear it that way. As if I could soften this kind of blow.

"Never knew nothing 'bout no dumpin'. Maybe I thought somethin' was up. Maybe I just didn't want to know." She shook her head.

"It's not your fault. If you'd have found out, they'd have killed you, too."

She looked at me, as if I'd redeemed her. I took her hand in mine, and pressed the medal into her palm.

She closed her hand around it, then looked down and opened her hand. She looked at the Bronze Star and began to cry again. Big tears and gentle sobs. I put my arm around her and after a little while she stopped. She wiped a sleeve across her face and sniffled. She kept holding the medal.

"I knew he musta been dead," she said. "But now I know. That doesn't make sense, but—"

I told her I understood.

She sat quietly, looking again at the clouds. Then she said, "Do you know how he died?"

I told her what I knew, about how I'd found Mitch. It wasn't easy, but she needed to know.

She didn't move during the telling, but her hand squeezed hard on the medal as she listened.

At the end she stood up. "I gotta go tell daddy. He needs to hear it from me."

She took a couple of steps and half-turned to face me. "He ain't never let got a that kid, he was so proud. Not knowin' like to killed him. Knowin' might, but if he can stand it, he might can go on again."

I said, "I hope so, Mickey."

She gave me a thin smile, and glanced one more time at the clouds. She said, "Goodbye, Mr. Cole," and turned to walk back to her father.

I got up to go call Alexandra Redgrave.

45

THE PRESS JUMPED on the story like ticks on a cur dog. I ducked all the interviews. Stubbs, however, made the *New York Times, Washington Post,* all the major networks, and CNN. I watched him at a press conference along with the national president of the Sierra Club, who fervently patted him on the back and called him "a point of light and a guardian of the environment." If Stubbs would have grinned any wider, he'd have ripped his lips.

I waited a couple of days, until the ruckus died down.

It was late in the evening when I picked up the phone. The house was quiet; only the light in my study burned. I sat at the old banker's desk, dialed the number, and waited.

After a couple of rings she came on the line.

"Is Linda Loring there?" I asked.

"I'm sorry," she said. "There's nobody here by that name."

"Never mind. Here's another question. Which one did you decide to read first?"

"Pardon me?" She sounded confused.

"Chandler, like I suggested, or did you run out and get *The Glass Key* because I said it was the best hard-boiled novel ever written?"

"Cole," her voice jumped about an octave. "I read all about what happened. I can't believe it, those awful men made Mr. Redgrave shoot himself."

"They weren't men, they were animals."

"I tried to call you. I tried more than once. There wasn't any answer."

"I was taking a low profile. Telling all of it to Mrs. Redgrave about did me in."

She didn't answer right away. I was beginning to get used to her pauses, get comfortable with them.

"Was it bad? Besides having to tell his wife?" she asked.

There was nothing to say to that. I could feel her presence over the long-distance silence. I listened to the faint ghostly voices that spilled over onto our line. After a little while I said, "I'm not sure why I called. I don't even really know you. This is a little awkward now that I think about it."

Another pause. She said, "Would you like to come down to Sanibel?"

"It would be nice to have someone to talk to."

"*Someone*? And I'm the most convenient person. Boy, you must be hard up in Atlanta."

"Whoops. Let me rephrase that. It sure would be nice to have *you* to talk to. By the way, would you let me drive?"

"If you could handle the Bledsoes, you can handle my driving. By the way, who's this Linda Loring person?"

"A good friend of a buddy of mine," I said. "I'll explain when I get there."

I told her I'd check the flight schedules for the next day. She said to let her know when I'd be coming in and she'd pick me up at the Fort Myers airport.

Before I hung up I said, "You still haven't answered my question—about the books."

"I didn't do either," she said. "I didn't read Chandler and I didn't read *The Glass Key*."

"I finished Mr. Redgrave's book."